OTHER BOOKS by KASSANDRA LAMB

The Kate Huntington Mysteries

Psychotherapist Kate Huntington helps others cope with trauma, but she has led a charmed life...until a killer rips it apart. (10 novels)

The Kate on Vacation Mysteries

Even on vacation, Kate Huntington can't stay out of trouble. (4 novellas)

The Marcia Banks and Buddy Cozy Mysteries

Marcia Banks trains service dogs for veterans, and solves crimes on the side, with the help of her Black Lab, Buddy. (13 novels/novellas)

The C.o.P. on the Scene Mysteries

Eight days into her new job as Chief of Police in a small Florida city, Judith Anderson finds herself one step behind a serial killer. (spinoff from the Kate Huntington series; 2 novels–more to come)

Romantic Suspense

written under the pen name of Jessica Dale

POLICE PROTECTION

A Kate Huntington Mystery

Kassandra Lamb

Published by *misterio press LLC*

Edited by Marcy Kennedy

Cover design by Melinda VanLone, Book Cover Corner

Police Protection is a work of fiction. All names, characters, events and most places are products of the author's imagination. Any resemblance to actual events or people, living or dead, is entirely coincidental. Some real places may be used fictitiously. Dulaney Valley Hospital is a fictitious institution.

The publisher does not have control over and does not assume any responsibility for author or third-party websites and their content.

ISBN: 978-1-947287-50-1

I dedicate this final book of the series to
my wonderful Kate Huntington readers.
I so appreciate your loyalty and support
through the years!

(Pssst, Kate isn't going away completely.
She makes appearances in my new spinoff series
about Lieutenant Judith Anderson.)

PROLOGUE

The dreary spring day did nothing to improve his mood.

Turning his jacket collar up against the misting rain, Detective Andrew Russell exited the Towson precinct, wondering yet again if the transfer to narcotics had been a mistake.

His new partner slapped his shoulder. "See ya Monday."

Andy stifled a wince. The guy meant well. "Sure, see ya." He turned to the right.

Crawley paused to open an umbrella.

Andy walked a bit faster. Pete Crawley might mean well, but his constant cheerfulness was exhausting. And those expensive suits... Andy figured he was insecure, trying to impress, but with his red hair and freckles, he looked like a kid dressed up in his big brother's clothes.

Two blocks away, the odor hit him first. The acrid, sweaty smell of pure fear. If he hadn't been so damned tired, he might have caught on sooner.

Before the kid plowed into him.

Andy staggered to the side, and the kid kept going.

"Stop! Police!" A uniform a block and a half back, coming hard. "Stop," he yelled again, his voice huffing.

Should be saving his breath for running. Andy could tell in an instant that the kid was going to get away. He pivoted and gave chase.

"Stop. Police," he echoed, pulling his detective's badge off his belt and holding it up in the air, more for the uniform's benefit than the perp's.

The kid was short, skinny, medium brown skin—Andy's cop brain ticked off the details. Maybe ten or eleven. He was pretty quick, but he was tiring.

Andy's chest swelled. His mouth tugged up in a small smile. *I still got it.*

He was gaining on the kid, despite the extra pounds he'd put on around the middle lately, while the huffing of the officer behind him was getting fainter.

The kid veered to the right into a side street.

Andy rounded the corner in time to see him dart into an alley. He poured on more speed and followed.

He assumed the puddle was water. His foot hit the slick surface, his mistake registering a nanosecond too late.

Arms flailing, he landed hard, his head smacking painfully against the oily asphalt.

A moment of numbness, then throbbing agony exploded in his skull.

Misty rain wet his face. Andy fought the darkness.

He lost.

CHAPTER ONE

Kate Huntington listened to the voicemail message on her office line for a second time. "Um, this is Andy Russell, BCPD. You know, from the Strategic Electronics case. I'm, uh, a little jammed up, and I was hopin'..." A pause. "Never mind."

Andrew Russell, the detective who'd tried his damnedest to put her client in prison for industrial sabotage and murder. And who'd tried to sabotage *her* with the governor's task force on PTSD among the police in Maryland.

But he'd come through in the end.

"I probably owe him," Kate grumbled under her breath.

She called him back and, against her better judgment, agreed to meet him for lunch the next day—at Mac's Place, the restaurant where she and Rob met for lunch almost every Wednesday.

Kate didn't bother to mention that her best friend, who also happened to be her lawyer, would be present as well.

———— ◆ ————

Andrew Russell was already there when Kate arrived at Mac's Place. He sat alone on one of the low, padded benches provided for people waiting to be seated. The lunch crowd was just beginning to fill the restaurant.

His off-the-rack suit jacket didn't fit all that well. He'd gained weight since the last time she'd seen him. He was clean-shaven, his complexion pasty.

She greeted him with a brief handshake. "Follow me." Without giving him time to respond, she turned and headed to a booth in the back, where Rob was already seated, his silver mane of hair sticking up some above the crowd.

Kate stepped up beside the booth. "Detective Russell, you remember my friend, Rob Franklin?"

Rob knew Russell was coming. He stood and offered his hand. "Detective." At six-two, he had a couple of inches on Russell. But his much more expensive suit hung loosely on him.

He'd had a heart attack last year, which had scared the crap out of all of them. Liz had put him on a strict diet, and it seemed to be working. His color was good too. He had a slight tan from the daily walks he and Liz were now taking.

Russell raised his eyebrows at Kate as he shook Rob's hand. "Call me Andy, please."

Rob resumed his seat, and Kate and Andy Russell slid onto the bench across from him. It would have been a tight fit but the detective left one knee dangling over the end of the bench, his foot sticking out in the aisle as if he might take off running at any moment.

Maybe he's thinking he might need to do just that. Kate hoped the busy waitstaff didn't trip over his leg on their way to and from the nearby kitchen.

She and Rob sat by the kitchen out of habit. Back when Mac's Place was smaller and her friend since childhood, Mac Reilly, was still running it himself, they'd taken this booth to save the more desirable ones for other customers. And also so Mac could readily stop by and visit if he wasn't too busy back in the kitchen.

Now the redecorated restaurant was run by a manager, who came by to exchange pleasantries with them once their drink orders had been taken.

Some instinct told Kate not to introduce Andy Russell, even though Jack, the manager, was giving him curious looks as they chatted.

Once the manager had walked away, Andy squirmed a little next to her. Then he leaned toward her and said in a low voice, "Um, what I was going to talk to you about is confidential."

"Rob's a lawyer, remember? He's used to keeping confidences." That came out sounding snarkier than Kate had intended, but she was already getting tired of the cloak-and-dagger mood.

She rethought that when she heard what he had to say.

"I'm on paid leave, pending an investigation into a bad shoot last week."

Rob sat up straighter. "The kid all over the news, that was you?"

Andy glanced around nervously, but no one could overhear them in the noisy restaurant. "Yeah, they've managed to keep my name under wraps so far, but that won't last."

"What's the boy's status?" Rob asked.

Andy swallowed hard, his Adam's apple a small bobbing lump in his thick neck. "He's still in a coma. They..."

He trailed off when a waitress approached with their iced teas. "You ready to order?"

Kate shook her head and pointed to the menu lying untouched in front of Andy.

The waitress smiled. "I'll give you a few minutes."

Andy dutifully picked up the menu.

Kate tucked a too-long, salt-and-pepper curl behind her ear. *I need a haircut*, she thought as she watched the detective in her peripheral vision. She always seemed to need a haircut these days. There was never enough time, between her clients, her classes at Towson U, and trying to be home more when the kids were off from school.

Andy's demeanor next to her—big shoulders sagging as he read the menu, corners of his mouth pulled down in his broad face—suggested he was eating because he should, not because he actually wanted to. There was a lot more gray mixed in with his short brown hair these days.

Finally, he dropped the laminated menu onto the table.

Rob motioned the waitress over. She took their regular orders of crab cakes and salads, then looked expectantly at Andy.

"I'll have the same as her." He pointed to Kate. The waitress nodded and walked away.

Andy glanced around again, then leaned forward some. "The problem is I got no memory of the whole thing. I was chasing the kid when I hit a puddle of motor oil and went down, hit my head. Next thing I know I'm standing over him, and he's lying on the ground, bleeding from a head wound. And I've got my backup piece in my hand."

He stopped, pulled the straw out of his iced tea and took a big swig. He set the glass down carefully and stared at it. "It only half registered that the muzzle was hot. It had been fired. I guess my head was still a little muddled. Then the uniform, who'd been chasing the kid in the first place, caught up..."

He turned his head toward Kate. "Isn't there a way to jog my memory? With hypnosis or something?"

Her chest tightened. She felt for the guy, but she didn't know him well enough to judge if he would shoot a kid, especially if he thought the boy was armed. She did know he wasn't going to like the answer to his question. "If you were knocked unconscious, then you suffered at least a moderate concussion–"

"Yeah, that's what the doc said—a concussion."

"A concussion essentially bruises the brain. The cells in the area are damaged and have to repair themselves. It knocks them offline, if you will, for a while."

"Yeah, okay. Can you help me remember?"

Kate chose her words carefully. "It's unlikely that all of what happened even registered in your brain. Some bits and pieces may come back over time, but there's really no reliable way to speed up that process. And probably a lot of it will never come back, because it didn't get recorded in the first place."

She watched the hope die in his eyes. "Wait, you said you slipped in motor oil and went down. How far was the boy from the puddle of oil?"

"About forty feet."

One part that might come back later was how he got to the child, but she didn't want to tell him that and give him false hope.

"Okay," she said, "concentrate and walk me through it. But only tell me what you actually remember. Not anything that you are assuming or someone else told you."

Andy Russell closed his eyes. "The kid ran into me on the sidewalk, and then I heard the uniform behind me, yelling for him to stop. I realized he was too far back, wasn't gonna catch the kid. So I took off after him." He paused, his face scrunched up. "I don't remember falling. Last thing I remember was seeing the kid dart into that alley."

His eyes popped open and his face relaxed some. "But I know I landed in that puddle 'cause I had oil all over me. Ruined my suit. And there were oily footsteps from the puddle to the kid."

"Okay, falling in the puddle is likely accurate," Kate said, "but be careful as you try to remember. The human mind automatically fills in gaps in our memories. What it comes up with—assumes, that is—may or may not be true. Now you said you had your backup piece in your hand. Where was your regular gun?"

"Still in its holster." Andy rubbed a big hand over his face. "I.A.'s saying I must have been operating on auto pilot. I'd been chasing the kid. He probably made some menacing gesture. I was all woozy and thought he must be armed, so I shot him."

"Who's I.A.?" Kate asked.

"Internal Affairs," Rob translated. He'd been quiet for the last few minutes, his gaze moving back and forth from Kate's face to the detective's.

Now he leaned forward. "You got any history of questionable shoots?"

Andy reared back, his eyes wide. "No." His tone sounded offended.

"They check for gunpowder residue on your hands?" Rob asked, his tone that of a cross-examining attorney.

Kate winced. "Rob—"

"Yeah," Andy said, his face now sagging. "And they found some." He briefly waved his right hand in the air.

Rob sat back and crossed his arms, his expression closed. Kate thought of it as his court face.

Then another thought struck her, something one of the law enforcement officers had said in a task force meeting awhile ago, about how one could identify police officers with anger issues. "How often do you charge people with resisting arrest?"

Andy jerked away from her and turned halfway on the booth's bench. "Almost never, even if the shmuck deserves it. Just more paperwork. Why are you asking me that?"

The waitress chose that moment to appear next to their table. She leaned a large tray against its edge and offloaded their plates of food, emptying half the tray.

Once she'd left, Andy turned straight ahead again, leaving a bit more of a gap between them. Kate wondered if it was intentional.

He picked up his fork with his left hand, which gave Kate her answer. He was left-handed. That's why he'd needed more room between them.

He was staring down at his food. "Police work isn't like what you see on TV." His voice was low and tense. "Detectives almost never even draw their guns, except at the firing range. I don't think I would've pulled it and shot somebody on 'auto-pilot.'" He made air quotes with his free hand.

"And the kid was truly a kid, no older than ten or eleven. I figured he'd shoplifted something. I wasn't thinking I was chasing a hardened criminal."

His fork upside down, Andy jabbed a cherry tomato in his salad, but he didn't put it in his mouth.

"Which side of your suit was oily?" Kate asked.

"The left." He dropped the fork and skewered tomato back onto the salad plate.

"You raised your right hand, when Rob asked about residue."

Andy shrugged. "I'm fairly ambidextrous. I practice shooting with both hands at the range."

Motion in the corner of Kate's eye. The waitress was headed for the kitchen doors, her tray now empty, balanced on the fingertips of one hand.

One of the doors swung open, a busboy surging through it. The door clipped the edge of her tray and it hit the floor with a sharp clang.

Andy jumped a good two inches off the booth's bench and jabbed Kate with his elbow as he reached for a holster that wasn't there.

Rob's head swiveled from where he'd been watching the apologetic busboy retrieve the tray. He stared at the detective across the table from him, his eyes narrowed.

Andy abruptly heaved his bulk up from the bench and reached into his pocket for his wallet. "Look, thanks for your help." He dropped some bills on the table and pushed past the waitress and busboy, headed for the restaurant's door.

All this before Kate could even open her mouth to respond.

Rob arched his bushy eyebrows. "His auto response *isn't* to reach for his gun?"

Kate shrugged. Several other things didn't add up. "When I dealt with him before, he didn't strike me as the impulsive type. I'm having trouble imagining him shooting first and asking questions later."

"I don't know. He seemed pretty hard-boiled to me. He was determined to hang a murder rap on Skip or your client, or both."

"Oh, he definitely pushes suspects hard in interrogation, and he's cynical as he can be."

She flashed to one of the things Andy Russell had said to her, in a candid moment the last time she'd seen him. *After a while in this job, there is no light left in the world, only shades of gray.*

At the time, she'd thought that poetic, profound and incredibly sad.

She still didn't know if the man was capable of shooting an unarmed kid, and if he was, she wanted nothing to do with him. But...

"Two things I know for sure," she said out loud. "One, auto-pilot for him is to reach for his belt, where his service revolver would be, like he did just now. *Not* for his backup piece—and with his left hand, not his right. Where would he keep that gun?"

"What, the backup piece?" Rob had turned his attention to his plate. He swiped the pickle slices off of hers and added them to his own on top of the broiled crab cake he'd ordered without a bun. "Maybe his pants pocket, or an ankle holster? I don't know. Skip would be the one to ask about that."

Kate nodded. Her husband had been a Maryland State trooper for over a decade, before going private.

"What's the other thing?" Rob asked, his fork full of crabmeat and pickle poised halfway to his mouth.

Kate's chest suddenly felt heavy. She stifled a sigh. She was cutting back on her private practice, easing herself out of the role of psychotherapist, because she was burned out on dealing with other people's misery. And yet, it was still all around her some days.

She shook her head and picked up her knife to slather tartar sauce on her crab cake's bun. "Detective Andrew Russell has PTSD."

The house was quiet, too quiet. Even after all these months, Kate's ears perked out of habit, expecting bustling sounds from the kitchen or footsteps above as Maria cleaned the kids' rooms in their absence.

But Maria hadn't bustled around the Huntington-Canfield kitchen since her wedding a year ago last fall, and she now had her own house to clean. Kate took a deep breath. When would she stop missing the plump woman's daily presence?

She kicked off her shoes and dropped her briefcase on the sofa. It was full of student papers instead of the insurance forms she had once brought home from work. Kate's vague plan was to grade those papers some time before tomorrow.

Vowing she would tackle them soon, she sat down at the computer in the study to research the shooting the previous week. But first she checked her email.

She was deleting the junk mail—discount offers from online stores and such—when her hand froze on the mouse.

Edith in the "from" column, followed by *no subject* in parentheses.

Edith Huntington? What the H does she want?

Mystified by an email from the woman who had once been her mother-in-law, she clicked on it.

Dear Kate,

I hope you and Edie and the rest of your family are well. I was wondering if we could set up a time to chat, either by phone or in person.

In person would be my preference. I have some concerns I wish to discuss.

Best wishes, Edith

Kate imagined it had taken Edith Huntington at least an hour to hone that missive to its most formal and least informative state.

She shook her head to clear it of that unkind thought, then considered how to word a response. After a few moments of mental blank, she gave up. She'd deal with Edith later.

Opening a new tab in the browser, she typed in *Towson boy shot* and skimmed down Google's offerings.

There were multiple articles, and a GoFundMe page someone had organized for the family, for funeral expenses.

She went back to the first offering, a *Baltimore Sun* article, and opened it. A grinning child stared at her—probably a school picture—the epitome of innocence. His skin was medium brown, his eyes shining with intelligence.

Wait, I know that child!

The image blurred. She blinked and swallowed hard.

She skimmed the article and finally found a reference to the boy's school at the very end. She'd gone there for a career day, back in September, held for the fifth graders. This boy—she quickly checked his name—Tyrell Brown had asked a bunch of questions about becoming a psychologist.

And he'd come up to her after her presentation, told her his big brother was studying psychology. He'd ducked his head shyly, then admitted that he might become a psychotherapist too someday.

She'd given him an encouraging smile and told him to study hard. He'd flashed that grin at her and then scurried off to join a couple of friends who were hanging back, waiting for him.

She forced her mind back to the article. Pressure behind her eyes made it difficult to read the headline—*Eleven Year Old Shot by Unidentified Towson Cop.*

She blinked again, trying to rein in her emotions.

Her chest and throat still tight, she went back over the article, reading it more thoroughly.

Following some sketchy details about the shooting itself—not even as much as Andy had told them—was a statement from a representative of the Baltimore County State Attorney's office. *We are not at liberty to disclose the name of the officer at this time, but I can assure you that a full investigation is underway. And if the shooting is determined to be unjustified, the perpetrator will be prosecuted to the full extent of the law.*

Kate let out a low groan.

Oh Andy, you are so screwed.

CHAPTER TWO

Rob's wife called a half hour before the kids were due home from school.

Kate grabbed up her phone when she saw who it was, glad for the excuse to take a break from grading papers. "Hey Liz, how's it going?"

"Going fine on my end. How are you doing?"

"Okay, I guess, all things considered. Aren't you still at work?"

"Yes, but there's a lull in the action at the moment."

Kate wondered how much action could be involved in an actuary's job. "Well, it's good to hear from you. What's up?"

"Nothing much. Just wanted to check on you." Liz's voice sounded serious.

A lightbulb went off in Kate's brain. Liz was concerned because the anniversary of Eddie's death was coming up fast. For years, despite her happiness with Skip, Kate had gotten depressed around this time of the year. But this April, she hadn't even thought about the events of fourteen years ago, until now...

"You sure you're okay?" Liz said.

Oops, her friend had apparently taken her earlier "all things considered" comment to mean she was down about the anniversary. She'd actually been thinking of her former mother-in-law. Talking about her seemed preferable to dwelling on Eddie. And Liz might have some sage advice for her, having raised two girls to adulthood.

"Yes. It gets a bit easier each year," she said. "I heard from his mother today."

"Oh, about what?"

"I don't know yet, but usually it means she wants to see Edie. They pop up in their granddaughter's life about once or twice a year."

"And you're not crazy about that, judging from your tone."

"No, especially now. Edie's gotten so rebellious, and I can just imagine Edith Huntington becoming her eager ally against us." Well, mostly against her. No matter what happened, Edie seemed to continue to adore Skip. But her mother, not so much these days.

"Any advice?" she asked Liz.

A low chuckle. "Afraid not. My mother-in-law was a gem."

Kate paused for a moment, remembering how devastated Rob and Liz had been six months ago, when the elder Mrs. Franklin passed away.

"Hey, how's Aunt Betty?" Kate was always a little afraid to ask, since the woman was now in her nineties. She was Rob's great aunt, the widow of his grandfather's youngest brother. And twelve years ago, Kate had helped Rob and Liz clear her of a murder charge, also with some help from Skip, in his newly-established role at the time of private investigator.

Indeed, she and Skip had first fallen for each other during that case.

A burst of Liz's signature laugh pulled her out of her reverie. She envisioned her petite friend on the other end of the line, her creamy complexion still relatively smooth for a woman in her late fifties, and her hair still strawberry blonde, thanks to her hairdresser. Her deep, booming laughter was always so startling coming from her tiny body.

"She's doing fine," Liz said. "Still pumping out a couple of romance novels a year."

"Wow."

"Hey, back to your mother-in-law problems–"

"*Former* mother-in-law. My current one is also a gem."

"You know she has no standing legally, right?"

That wasn't totally true. Grandparents had been known to sue for visitation rights. Even one of Kate's clients had faced that, despite the client's memories of being abused by her father and the parents' continued verbal and emotional battering even after she was an adult.

Kate wouldn't put it past Edith to try such a lawsuit. Besides...

"That seems kind of cruel, since they've lost their only child."

"I agree, but it's something to keep in mind, if they really get out of line."

"Okay. I should probably keep it as an option." Or a possible threat. But she knew she'd never actually do it, no matter how annoying Edith Huntington could be.

She and Liz chatted for a few more minutes and then signed off with a "let's have lunch soon."

Kate sighed and went back to her students' papers.

⊷◈⊶

She still hadn't decided what to do about her former mother-in-law's email by the time she and Skip settled on the sofa for their evening chat after the kids were in bed.

Unfortunately, their chat time was shorter these days. The kids had later bedtimes, while the demands of their jobs and parenting hadn't changed all that much. If anything, evenings were more hectic without Maria to fix dinner, and Billy still needed close supervision regarding homework. His ADHD meant that assignments had to be checked and rechecked.

By the time they got to "sofa time," as Kate thought of it, they were close to exhaustion. Their own bedtime was all too often moved up. They'd even been known to both fall asleep on the sofa, sitting upright.

Resting her head against Skip's broad chest—he was enough taller that she could tuck right under his shoulder—Kate opted to go straight to the discussion of Andy Russell's situation.

"Wait a minute," Skip said when she was only halfway through her explanation of that day's meeting at Mac's Place. "This guy we're talking about, he's the one who accused me of murder?"

"Yeah, but he came through in the end."

His arm still around her shoulders, he leaned a bit away to look down at her. His hazel eyes were wide with exaggerated disbelief. "That's not how I remember it. I had the situation completely under control when he arrived."

Kate stifled the urge to argue that point and plastered on a smile. "Look, he's jammed up, and I'm not sure he deserves to be. Can you–"

"No. We can't keep doing this, Kate. It seems like every few months we're dealing with one of your clients' calamities." He pulled his arm from behind her shoulders to count off on his fingers. "First there were the false-memory crazies when we were dating. Then your former client dragged us into an international assassination plot." He ticked off another finger. "Then there was the firefighter, accused of murdering his drug dealer–"

Pressure was building in her chest. "*Former* drug dealer."

Skip's face, usually just a shade or two darker than her own fair Irish skin, was now flushed. He tapped another finger. "And then that client committed suicide–"

Bristling, Kate pulled away. "Which turned out to be murder, and no one would've known that if I hadn't investigated."

Skip ignored the interruption, waved his thumb back and forth. "And then last year, yet another client gets accused of industrial espionage and murder."

Kate sprang to her feet. "I seem to recall that case was as much about clearing *your* agency's reputation as it was about saving my client from jail." She stood in front of him, hands on hips, chest tight. "And you're conveniently forgetting *your* crazy client who tried to kill *me*!"

Skip sighed, his broad chest deflating some. He reached out a hand and grabbed hers, tried to pull her back down beside him.

She resisted.

"It's just that we seem to constantly be tripping over other people's problems." He let go of her hand and skimmed unruly brown hair out of his eyes. "And this time, I don't even like the guy."

"Okay, you don't have to like him. But I still think he might be getting a raw deal. Can't you at least ask Dolph to see if he can get a copy of the police report on the case? I'm curious if there's any more evidence, other than what he knows about."

"Your curiosity is like that of the proverbial cat, and you've already used up your nine lives." He sighed again. "Okay, I can ask, but it's been a while now since Dolph retired. His influence is waning."

Kate resisted the urge to argue that point as well. As long as Skip's friend and employee, "Dolph" Randolph had a former partner who was a lieutenant in the homicide division, Dolph would have an in with the Baltimore County Police Department.

Skip patted the sofa beside him.

She relented and sank back down beside her husband. "Ask him, please."

"I will." Skip's arm slid around her shoulders again, and she snuggled against him, letting the short flare of anger dissipate.

He tilted her chin up and looked down into her eyes. He had a small smirk on his face.

"Skip Canfield, if you say I'm cute when I'm mad, I will have to slug you."

The smirk expanded into a grin. "That wasn't what I was going to say at all. I was going to say that your eyes are like sunlight glinting off the ocean when you're pissed."

She shoved her fist into his ribs. "That's the same thing."

"Ow! What, I can't compliment your pretty blue eyes anymore?"

"Oh, shut up and kiss me."

———— ◆◦◆ ————

Skip had forgotten that Dolph wasn't coming in on Thursday. He was taking his wife to Ocean City for a long weekend. Skip couldn't recall the occasion—Sue's birthday?

He had appointments with potential new clients tomorrow, but today's schedule was light. So he decided to test how much juice he had with BCPD in his own right.

Judith Anderson, sitting behind a wood-veneer desk, let out a mock groan when he walked into her office. "What do you want, Canfield?"

He looked pointedly at the uniformed officer who'd escorted him to the homicide division. She was still hovering in the doorway, her eyes wide with anxiety that maybe she'd screwed up.

Judith waved a hand in the air. "Close the door on your way out, Officer."

The young woman scurried backward, pulling the door closed as she went.

Skip studied Judith for a second. She had a few lines in her pale forehead and on either side of her grimly set lips. But otherwise she hadn't changed much in the decade that Skip had known her. Same short cap of dark hair, slender figure and tailored clothes—a black pantsuit and crisply ironed white shirt.

She quirked a thin dark eyebrow in the air. "You just sightseeing or you got some reason for coming by to bother me?"

Skip flashed her a grin. "Good to see you too, Lieutenant."

She gave a slight shake of her head but there was a playful glint in her brown eyes.

"Kate and I got to know one of your detectives last winter, during the Strategic Electronics case. Andrew Russell."

The light went out in her eyes, the lids drooping slightly. Otherwise her body language didn't shift.

She was damned good at hiding her reactions, but he was equally good at reading them. He'd struck a nerve.

"Yes. What about him?" Her tone was clipped.

Skip opted for honesty. "I understand he's jammed up over a questionable shoot."

She said nothing, still and silent, waiting for him to go on.

"He approached Kate, wanted her to help him remember what happened. She's..." He trailed off. Maybe he should've waited until next week and let Dolph handle this.

Judith leaned back in her chair. One corner of her mouth turned up. "And Kate has shifted into her mother bird mode and has taken Andy Russell under her wing."

Skip nodded. "I was wondering if I could get a peek at the report."

She shook her head at the same time as she gestured for him to take a seat in front of her desk. She stared at him for a long moment, then tapped a few keys on the laptop sitting on the desk. Turning it so he could see the screen, she said in a low voice, "For your eyes only."

A jerky image appeared on the screen, a street scene, bobbing up and down slightly as the cop wearing the body cam walked. The only audio was slightly heavy breathing. Then a sharp crack, and the cop sped up. Blurry buildings moved past. The thud of shoe soles on pavement, more heavy breathing.

Another loud crack.

A blur blocked the camera as the cop reached for his radio. "Adam Two. Shots fired! Repeat. Shots fired." The intersection he gave wasn't far from the Towson precinct, in an area heavy with cheaper housing. Which meant students, which meant drugs.

The cop had his gun out in front of him now. He was veering into alleys, scanning the buildings on each side, jogging up to dumpsters and checking behind them, nudging discarded boxes to make sure they were empty.

Skip knew the routine, from when he was a state trooper. The officer was looking for the source of the shots.

Or the victim.

The cop turned another corner. A blurry image of a figure, maybe a hundred feet down an alley, turned slightly away and swaying a bit.

"Sir, drop the gun."

No visible response.

The cop slowed, approaching with caution. The sound of air being sucked in.

"Sir? Detective, can you hear me? Please drop the gun."

The swaying figure was clearly a man, in a business suit with a dark stain down one sleeve and pants leg. He held a small pistol in his right hand.

The cop was closer now. The man was looking down. From what little Skip could see of his expression, he seemed dazed.

"Detective, can you hear me?"

No reaction from the man.

Damn good thing the uniform recognized Russell or he might have shot him. And it would have been a solid shoot.

The public didn't realize how fast someone could raise a gun and fire. Failure to drop a weapon when told to by the police was grounds for the officer to shoot.

In the video, the cop stepped closer and relieved the man of the snub-nosed pistol.

Shuffling of shoe soles as the cop maneuvered around to keep an eye on the man while he stooped down. The camera focused for a quick moment on a black kid lying face down on the pavement. Thick fingers reached for his neck, feeling for a pulse.

Then the camera panned upward to the shell-shocked face of Andrew Russell.

The video froze. Judith swiveled the laptop back toward herself.

"Why did you show me that?" Skip asked.

Judith shrugged.

"Are you going to let me see the report?"

She shook her head. "I really can't involve civilians in such a delicate police matter."

"So, I repeat, why'd you show me the video?"

She shook her head a little harder. "I didn't *show* you anything. I had it on my computer when you came into the office uninvited and looked over my shoulder."

Skip worked to keep his expression neutral, even though he wanted to frown and glare at her. "Come on, Judith. What are you saying? The door's closed. Just spit it out."

She leaned forward over the desk. In a low voice, she said, "Andy Russell technically isn't mine anymore. He transferred to narcotics a few weeks ago. He's a good cop." She paused, visibly swallowed hard. "And he was my first training officer, when I was a rookie."

Skip kept his voice low as well. "So you owe him, and you think he's getting a raw deal."

"I don't know what to think. I'm not privy to I.A.'s investigation." She stood up. "And now I need to go to the rest room. Make yourself comfortable until I get back." She leaned over, punched a few keys on her laptop, then left the room.

Skip scooted around to her side of the desk and perched on the edge of her chair. A police report—*the* police report—was on the screen. He scanned the uniformed officer's report, a succinct summary of what Skip had surmised from the video. He grabbed the mouse and scrolled down.

Not much else in the way of evidence, except ballistics had confirmed Russell's pistol as the source of the lethal bullet. Two shots had been fired. The crime scene techs hadn't found the second bullet, which the detective on the case was assuming had gone wild.

Skip's gaze ran down the crime scene log. Judith's name was toward the bottom. His eyes went back up, searching for the note he'd seen—next to the sixth name down. The keeper of the log, probably the uniform first on the scene, had indicated that Peter Crawley was Russell's partner.

He scrolled back up to that responding officer's report and read more carefully.

He spotted a detail that he'd skimmed over before. His stomach tightened. The uniform had been chasing the boy because a BOLO had been put out on him, as a material witness in a drug case.

The issuer of the BOLO was Andrew Russell.

Judith came back into the office.

Skip vacated her chair, and once she'd sat in it, he stood beside her and pointed to that part of the report on the screen.

She shook her head. "He swears he never issued that BOLO." Again, her voice was low. "And that he has no idea who the kid is."

"Log says Russell's partner was on the scene."

She nodded. "I took his statement myself. He and Andy had just finished their shift. He was almost to his car when he heard the shots. By the time he found the alley, other back-up had arrived. So he hung out with Andy, offering moral support. He said he told Andy to wait until his union rep was there, before giving a statement. Since Crawley didn't have anything helpful to contribute, I sent him home. He seemed kind of shaken, had trouble looking at the boy." She stopped, then added under her breath, "We all did."

"I didn't see Russell's statement in there."

"His lawyer wouldn't let him make one. He, the lawyer, said Andy remembered nothing from hitting his head to when he was standing next to the boy and the uniform was talking to him."

"Good lawyer," Skip said. "That's pretty much what Russell told Kate."

"I'm not sure that's a good move at all," Judith said, her voice terse. "It makes Andy look guilty, that he won't talk to I.A."

Skip walked around to the front of the desk. He studied Judith's impassive face. Her eyes were red-rimmed, but otherwise she gave nothing away.

He sighed. "Lemme guess. You'd be happy if Canfield and Hernandez discreetly looked into this case."

Judith flashed him a small smile. "Thanks for stopping by, Skip," she said, no longer keeping her voice down. "Always a pleasure."

CHAPTER THREE

A few minutes before noon on Thursday, Kate arrived at the swank Towson restaurant that Edith had insisted on and found her former mother-in-law already seated. The *maitre'd* led the way to the table.

Knowing it was expected, Kate leaned down and gave Edith a peck on the cheek. The woman responded with an air kiss and a pat on Kate's arm. That constituted more affection than she had ever received from Edith Huntington in the past.

Her curiosity piqued, Kate sat down and told the waiter she would start with iced tea. She surreptitiously studied Edith as she pretended to peruse the menu.

The woman was past seventy now, but the Huntington money had provided the resources to keep age at bay, for the most part. Her wavy, silver hair shone in the soft lighting of the restaurant, and her face was relatively wrinkle free. Even the crepey neck that usually gave away an older woman's age was missing, until Edith lowered her chin to look at her own menu. Then the skin of her chest and neck crinkled.

She was still slender, almost too thin. Her hands reminded Kate of a bird's claws as they clutched the menu. She lowered it to the table and pointed a well-manicured nail at one of the selections. "Broiled, no potatoes. Sauce on the side, please," she said to the waiter hovering behind her.

"Of course, madam," he replied and turned to Kate. "And you, ma'am?"

Kate noted that being called *ma'am* no longer bothered her, although she would hate becoming a *madam*. But Edith seemed to take it as her due.

"I'll have a chef's salad, with the house dressing." She hadn't really looked at the menu, but every restaurant had some rendition of chef's salad.

He gave them a slight bow and deftly removed their menus.

"So, how are the children?" Edith asked.

Kate groaned inside while slapping on a smile. She hated small talk with people she didn't like.

"They're fine." She hoped her smile didn't look as forced as it felt.

"And that young Texan you married?"

Her smile a bit more natural, Kate said, "He's fine too, and he would be flattered that you called him young." *And Texan*, she added mentally. She'd yet to meet a Texan who wasn't fiercely loyal to their home state.

Edith Huntington took a sip of water and then looked Kate in the eye. "I'll get straight to the point."

Please, please do!

"Your father-in-law may be dying."

Kate's mouth fell open. If Edith's goal had been to shock, she'd accomplished it. "What's wrong?" she stammered.

Edith waved a hand in the air. "Oh, he's not going to go in the immediate future, but he's been diagnosed..." She trailed off, leaned forward. "With prostate cancer," she said in a whisper.

Kate's twisted gut relaxed a little. "Doesn't that progress fairly slowly?"

Edith had shrunk some in her chair. Her eyes were shiny. "He seems to have a more virulent strain. He's going in for surgery in a few weeks. The doctor is unwilling to say if that will completely stop..." she choked a little, "...things."

Edith straightened her spine and took another sip of water. "He'd like to see Edie before he goes into the hospital."

"Of course," Kate said quickly. "I'm sure we can make that happen."

"And once he's better, we'd like to see more of her. This has brought home to Ed—and to me, of course—that we aren't getting any younger and we should enjoy our granddaughter while we can."

Kate's sympathy morphed into annoyance. She bit the inside of her lower lip to keep from blurting out something rude. The Huntingtons had been content with little more than a yearly birthday lunch for the last twelve years, even though they lived less than an hour from Kate's house.

Edith was now looking down, rearranging her silverware. "Edie has called us a couple of times in the last few months."

Alarm bells clanged in Kate's mind. Her chest tightened.

But before she could find words to formulate a response, Edith went on, "She only chattered about inconsequential things, but we take her calls to mean she would like to have more of a relationship with us as well."

Kate's mind was madly creating a list of ground rules, but a somewhat less panicked part of her prevailed. She needed to buy some time. Choosing her words carefully, she said, "I'm sure she would. Let me give this some thought, check the calendar and see how we can fit more visits into the family's schedule."

Edith bristled.

Apparently my choice of words wasn't careful enough.

The arrival of their food saved Kate from the urge to say more, which would probably make matters worse.

"Can I get you ladies anything else?" the waiter asked.

They both shook their heads.

Probably the only thing we'll agree on anytime soon.

Edith pounced as soon as the man was gone. "Do you object to our seeing Edie more often?"

"Not at all. I think that would be good for everyone." She made herself stop there and picked up her fork.

Darn! This restaurant's rendition of chef's salad included anchovies and black olives. She didn't care for either. That's what she got for not reading the menu.

"Your expression belies your words," Edith said.

Who the heck says belies *out loud these days?*

"No, my expression says I don't like anchovies." She picked up her bread plate and flicked a few of the offending morsels onto it.

Edith was still staring at her.

Kate took a bite of salad.

Edith got the hint and used her fork to break off a corner of her sole fillet. Stabbing it more strenuously than it deserved, she lifted the fish to her mouth and chewed it slowly. "It's a bit dry."

Which is why there's a sauce. Edith hadn't touched it.

"Would you like to send it back?" Kate asked.

"No. Now tell me what objection you have to us seeing our granddaughter more often."

"I don't have any objection. I'm just trying to sort out how to do it, the logistics and such."

"It's not that complicated, Kate. We make a plan, pick her up, take her somewhere, bring her back."

Kate stifled a sigh. "Okay, not logistics so much as the dynamics of it all."

Edith lifted a thin eyebrow as she carefully chewed another bite of fish.

Why can't the kitchen catch on fire or something? Anything to give her some time. How could she explain her concerns when she'd had less than five minutes to sort them out for herself?

"The family dynamics are a little delicate right now."

Edith switched eyebrows and ate a green bean.

"Edie's at a tricky age," Kate tried again.

Edith picked up her water glass. "Psychobabble poppycock," she muttered against its rim.

Kate went rigid. She'd wondered when Edith's good behavior would go by the wayside—or what passed for good behavior with her mother-in-law.

Kate slowly drew in air through her nose and counted to ten. Then she said, "Right now, Edie is thirteen going on twenty-three. Her world view is that her parents are the most stupid people around."

And last year, Edie's rebellious actions had almost gotten her killed. But Edith didn't know about those events, and Kate wasn't about to tell her.

Now mother and daughter had a delicate truce going on, with Kate making a concerted effort to spend more quality time with the kids, especially Edie. Kate wasn't going to jeopardize that because the Huntingtons suddenly saw mortality staring them in the face.

She took a sip of iced tea to lubricate her suddenly dry mouth. "I need to give some thought to how to bring other adults into her life in a way that is positive."

"We're already in her life. We just want to see more of her."

Lord, give me strength!

"No, seeing her once a year is not 'being in her life.'"

Edith put down her fork. "Kate, I have no intention of taking your place, nor does Ed wish to supplant... your husband as a father figure."

Bet she doesn't even remember Skip's name.

"I'm not worried about that." And she wasn't. This cold fish of a woman would never replace her in Edie's heart, but having a sympathetic adult to complain to might tip the delicate balance back to Edie keeping secrets and sneaking behind her parents' backs.

And who knew how Edith Huntington would twist whatever Edie told her and try to use it against Kate?

"Look," she said, "let's set something up for some time in the next week or so, before Ed's surgery. We'll sort out the rest after that."

After a moment, Edith nodded slightly, then applied herself with concentration to the rest of her fish.

The sauce on the side remained untouched. *No wonder she's so skinny.*

As she finished her salad, picking out the stray anchovy or olive, Kate prayed fervently that Ed, Sr.'s surgery would be a huge success, and the Huntingtons would go back to being relatively disinterested grandparents.

——◆——

Kate had a few errands to run. She got home a few minutes after the kids had been dropped off by their respective school buses. In the living room, she passed Billy playing a handheld video game, and the vague rumblings from Edie's room over her head were most likely the girl chatting on her phone with a friend.

They'd given that cell phone to Edie when she'd turned twelve, after years of the girl complaining that all her friends had their own phones. It had been both a blessing and a curse. Kate was grateful that she had a ready way to communicate with her daughter to make sure she was okay. But the phone had given Edie a little too much freedom at times.

Kate went into the study and sat down at the computer, intending to make a list of her concerns regarding her former mother-in-law's request, and some possible strategies for addressing those concerns. It was such a complicated situation that she was afraid she'd forget something when it was time to discuss the whole mess with Skip later this evening.

When she hit a key to wake up the monitor, she discovered that she'd never closed out the Baltimore Sun site from the day before. Tyrell Brown was grinning at her.

"Yahoo!" came from the living room. Apparently Billy had just won the game, advancing to a new level of Super Mario Brothers.

A fist squeezed Kate's heart. This boy on the screen was the same age as her son. How must the boy's mother be feeling? How did mothers of color cope, day in and day out, worrying about their kids being attacked, verbally or physically, by racists, or even being shot by the very police who were supposed to be protecting them?

She felt an urge to visit this mother and offer her support, tell her about meeting Tyrell at his school.

And maybe find out more about what happened? a little voice said in the back of her head.

Skip's frowning face flashed into her mind's eye. She shook her head to dispel the image.

Would her story of meeting Tyrell bring comfort, or would it bring pain, reminding his mother that the boy might not live to fulfill his dreams?

She'd have to give that some thought. The last thing she wanted to do was cause the woman more suffering.

Okay, first things first. She returned her focus to the list of concerns regarding her former in-laws.

———◦———

The next day, Kate was looking forward to her session with Carol Foster with a sense of bittersweet anticipation. After fourteen years as her client, Carol was finally "graduating" from therapy.

The younger woman had a particularly stubborn version of major depressive disorder and had continuously struggled with her moods, waxing suicidal off and on for years. Finally a new-to-the-market antidepressant had turned out to be a life-saver, literally. And with the brain chemistry part of the depression better controlled, Carol was now able to apply the techniques for coping with life that she and Kate had worked on through the years.

The session went as expected, a case of mixed emotions for both client and therapist.

"It's going to be weird not seeing you," Carol said. "All week, I catch myself thinking, I need to remember to tell Kate about this or that. Now..." She gave her head a slight shake. "But I know you're here if I need you."

Until I retire completely, Kate thought, but didn't say out loud. When that day came, she would call or write Carol to let her know that she was available to give a referral should she need it, but she wouldn't be able to see her again. For now, the woman needed the safety net of knowing her therapist was still available.

And Kate was, for now.

"So how are things going with your husband?" He and Carol had separated for a while, but had recently started seeing each other again.

Carol broke into a big grin. "Pretty good. Now that he sees how I can be when my brain chemistry isn't out of whack, he's getting it that I had no control before." She ducked her head. "He moved back in last weekend."

"That's great news." Kate glanced at her watch. "We're almost out of time. Do you have any other concerns?"

Carol shook her head. "Not about me, but there is something else I wanted to ask you about. You know I've been working at the new hospital for the last year?"

Kate nodded.

"I've, um, noticed a possible pattern. One of my duties is to file the death certificates with the state, for the patients that don't make it." She paused, looked down at her hands in her lap.

"Yes..." Kate prompted, afraid they would run out of time before she even found out what the issue was.

"There's been a sharp uptick in the last two and a half months."

Kate was tempted to dismiss it as a random variation. After all, people died in hospitals sometimes.

She resisted the temptation. "And that concerns you," she reflected back instead.

"Yes, but I'm not sure who to talk to about it. I'm only a lowly clerical worker."

"What do you know about those cases?"

"Not much other than cause of death. But an unusual number of the cases list heart attack as COD."

"How is that unusual?" Kate asked.

"Because some of them are younger, in their twenties or thirties."

"I happen to know one of the social workers at the hospital. Would you like me to mention it to her?"

"Yes, but I'd rather you not give her my name. If it's nothing..." She trailed off, shrugging her shoulders.

"Okay." Kate rose and smiled. "And now, as my Dad would say, 'Get on with ya, lass.'"

Carol stood and hugged Kate. "I'm going to miss you," she whispered.

Kate stepped back, her hands on the young woman's forearms. "And I'm going to miss you, but you're more than ready to fly solo. Go forth and have a good life."

Carol smiled. "I plan to."

Once she had left, Kate quickly called her colleague, Theresa Barlow, at Dulaney Valley Hospital, afraid she would forget if she left it for later in the day.

As she suspected she would, she got voicemail. "Hey Theresa, I hope all is well with you and yours. I happen to know someone who works there at the hospital, and they have some concerns that I told them I would pass on to you. Seems there have been an unusual number of deaths in the hospital lately, especially due to heart attacks, even in some younger people. I told this person that I'd ask you to look into it. Give me a call if you need more info." She rattled off her office number, even though she really didn't know any more information than she'd just given.

She disconnected and breathed out a sigh of relief. That task was done, and her responsibility for Carol was behind her. Although she would indeed miss the woman, she was glad to have one less obstacle in her way to full retirement from doing therapy.

"Burnout is a bitch," she mumbled as she grabbed her coat and purse to leave for the day.

In the car, the lead story on the radio's afternoon news was about the shooting of the unarmed black child. In an appropriately mournful voice, the news anchor reported that the boy had died the previous night, without having regained consciousness.

CHAPTER FOUR

Skip leaned against the doorjamb of his partner's open doorway. "Hey, do you have any contacts in BCPD's Internal Affairs division?"

Rose Hernandez swiveled away from her computer and stared up at him. Her compact body was dwarfed by the big black leather desk chair, the twin of the one down the hall in his own office. It suited his six-five frame much better than her five-foot-even one.

"You've gotta be kidding. The rank and file stay as far away from I.A. as we can get."

Skip bit back a chuckle. Even after a decade of being a P.I., Rose still identified with her old comrades in blue.

"I get it, but I figured it didn't hurt to ask."

"Why *are* you asking?" Rose said.

"Remember the homicide detective on the Strategic Electronics case, Andrew Russell?"

She nodded.

"He's gotten himself jammed up with what might be a bad shoot. And he came to Kate asking for help to better remember what happened. Seems he fell and got knocked out for few minutes."

Rose narrowed her eyes at him. "You're not gonna let Kate drag you into one of her cases again, are you?"

"No, and he's not her client. But she did ask me to try to get a look at the police report–"

"Wait!" Her eyes had gone wide. "Are we talking about the black boy who just died last night?"

"Yeah. They were trying to keep Russell's name out of the press, but that's not gonna last now."

"Skip, we are not getting involved in that case." Rose leaned forward in her chair. "There are protests all around Baltimore City and the county, and the chances are good that some of them will turn into riots before the day is done."

He held up a hand. "I know, I know. And I'm not about to become officially involved, but I talked to Judith Anderson..."

"And?"

"And I got the distinct impression that she would like us to look into it, unofficially. Seems Russell was her training officer when she was a rookie."

Rose flopped back in her chair. "Ho boy."

"She's helped us out a lot through the years. We owe her. She didn't say anything directly, but I think she's calling in some of those chits."

Rose ran a hand over the side of her head, as if smoothing back her thick black hair, but, as usual, it was neatly tucked into a tight bun.

"She also showed me, on the QT, the police report and the video from the responding officer's body cam. It shows Russell standing over the body, looking dazed, with a gun in his hand."

"That's pretty damning."

"Yeah," Skip said, "but the gun was his backup piece, and it was in his right hand."

"So?"

"His service weapon was still in its holster, on his *left* side."

Rose rubbed her hands up and down her arms, clad in a crisp white shirt. "I don't like this."

"Me neither, but I think we need to unofficially check it out, if we want to stay in Judith's good graces."

Rose flashed him a quick smile. "Not to mention Kate's."

He gave her a lopsided grin back. "Yeah, not to mention. You wanna come with me to check out the crime scene?"

"Lemme call Mac and have him meet us there."

Skip nodded. Mac Reilly, Rose's husband and Kate's lifelong friend, was also one of their best operatives. He had a good eye for detail.

Stomach tied in knots, Kate took a deep breath and punched the number she'd researched into her phone. She hoped it was the right number, for the correct Wanda Brown.

It went straight to voicemail and a mechanical voice instructed her to leave a message.

"Hi, my name is Kate Huntington-Canfield. I, um, wanted to stop by and offer my condolences, but I don't want to intrude..." She trailed off, unsure what else to say. Now the idea of telling Mrs. Brown her little story about meeting Tyrell seemed silly.

A screeching sound in her ear. Kate winced.

Then, "Hello, hello." A woman's voice, on the deeper end of the spectrum, a mature woman most likely.

"Um, hi, I–"

"You a reporter?" the voice demanded.

"Huh? Oh no! Of course not." Kate cleared her throat. "Um, I met Tyrell, at his school on career day. I was one of the presenters. And I also have a semi-official reason for wanting to speak to Mrs. Brown. I'm on a governor's task force. But if she isn't feeling up to it–"

"Clarrie, where's your mama?"

"Don't call me that baby name." A teenager's voice in the background.

"Cla-ris-sa," the woman pronounced each syllable in a stern tone, "where is your mother?"

"In Jared's room."

"Hold on," the woman said to Kate. The clatter of the phone being set down on a hard surface.

Kate wondered what part of her inane babbling the woman would repeat to Wanda Brown. A couple of minutes ticked by.

A clunk as the phone was picked up again. "She says she'll talk to you. You wanna come over now?"

"Yes, if it's not an intrusion."

"Not an intrusion as long as you ain't one of them damned reporters. You turn out to be a reporter, we gonna kick you out on your ear." The woman hung up.

Kate's GPS helped her find the apartment complex where the Browns lived, but what she found there gave her pause.

The streets and parking lots were full of people milling around. Mostly young—college students probably. Mostly black. But a number of older people and white and tan faces mixed in too. Also a wide array of attire, from casual to dressy.

And a smattering of *Black Lives Matter* signs.

Kate's chest constricted as the image flashed in her mind again of that young boy, Billy's age. But Tyrell would never see another birthday.

Can I do this? Face the mother of that child? Her throat closed.

The people huddled in clumps on the sidewalk in front of Mrs. Brown's first floor apartment were mostly dressed in funereal black. Kate assumed these were friends and family, come to pay their respects.

She had to circle through the 1960s-vintage complex several times, looking for a parking space. The buildings were brick, three-story rectangles. Every other unit had a stucco veneer, perhaps the original developer's optimistic attempt to lend some class to the place.

But Kate knew working-class housing when she saw it. She'd grown up in a bungalow in a neighborhood similar to this one, with two adults and four kids sharing three small bedrooms and one and a half baths. The half bath had been carved out of a corner of her parents' bedroom by her plumber father.

She finally found a parking space and pulled in. The afternoon had warmed up, so she left her coat in the car. But even her navy suit jacket was a bit too much as she made her way through the crowd. A trickle of sweat ran down her spine.

Kate approached the sidewalk leading to the front door of the Browns' apartment.

A young woman with tawny skin and dark corn rows, dressed in a little black dress and low-heeled shoes, stepped out of the nearby group of people and into Kate's path. "Can I help you?" Her tone was clipped.

Half a dozen young people drifted over to block the sidewalk.

"I'm here to see Mrs. Brown," Kate said, "if she's up to visitors."

"Depends. Who are you?"

"I called a while ago. My name's Kate–"

"Clarissa! Mind your manners." A woman's voice, coming from an open window next to the apartment's door.

"Let the lady come in." A slightly different disembodied voice, the alto one from the phone.

The young woman—Clarissa apparently—froze for a second, then she stepped aside.

The other young people blocking her way slowly shifted to the sides, creating a narrow tunnel between them.

Fortunately as a therapist, Kate knew how to hide her emotions. She gave the people she passed—kids really—a nod and a slight smile.

A few snickers followed her.

A throat cleared. The snickers abruptly stopped.

Kate glanced over her shoulder.

A middle-aged black man, dressed in a dark suit, stood near the curb. He stepped on a cigarette butt he'd apparently just dropped, grinding it back and forth with the toe of his shiny black dress shoe. "I'm Mrs. Brown's brother, Jake Johnson. Go on in, ma'am." He gestured toward the door.

Kate nodded and stepped inside the apartment.

A medium-sized living room was filled almost to capacity with a half-dozen women, mostly middle-aged or older, all African-American.

One gray-haired woman, sitting at the end of a large sofa, gestured to Kate. "You the young lady I talked to?"

"Yes, ma'am."

The other women weren't paying much attention to her. They hovered around the heavyset woman at the other end of the sofa. Kate assumed she was Mrs. Brown. Her black curls were about the same length as Kate's—neither super short nor long—but there was no gray in them. They created a soft frame around her russet-toned, round face.

Between her and the older woman sat a pencil-thin teenage boy in sweats. Mrs. Brown held his hand. His skin was a couple of shades lighter than hers, and his face had a glazed expression.

Two of the hovering women stepped back.

Mrs. Brown gestured to an empty armchair. "Please, have a seat," she said in a louder than necessary voice. "How can I help you?"

Kate suspected her exaggerated manners were for her daughter's benefit.

As she turned to sit in the chair, she spotted Clarissa, now hanging at the back of the small crowd of women. Kate lowered her estimate of the girl's age. She couldn't be more than sixteen or seventeen.

Mrs. Brown was looking at her expectantly. The whites around her brown pupils were slightly bloodshot and her cheeks were puffy from crying, but her expression was neutral.

"Ma'am, my name is Kate Huntington-Canfield. I, um, do have a semi-official reason for being concerned about your son's case. But mostly I'm here as a mother, to offer my condolences. I have a boy about your son's age."

"Which son?" Mrs. Brown said, her voice sharp and strained, her face now pinched. Then she shook her head slightly. "I'm sorry. That was rude. I have three sons. Jimmy, my oldest, is twenty. Clarissa," she tilted her head at the young woman, "is next, and then Jared here." She gave the boy's hand a squeeze. "Tyrell is..." her voice thickened, "...*was* my youngest."

Tears pricked Kate's eyes. "I am so sorry for your loss."

Mrs. Brown nodded, her posture stiff, her eyes shiny.

"You said somethin' on the phone," the gray-haired woman said, "about knowin' my grandbaby."

Kate nodded. "I met him at his school's career day. I was there, talking to the kids about being a psychotherapist. He asked a lot of good questions."

The two women, Tyrell's mother and grandmother, were watching her, leaning forward their expressions intent.

And Kate knew, in that moment, that this was the right thing to do. Despite the fact that the boy had only died last night, their grief was not fresh. He'd been in a coma for almost a week, with a slim chance of recovery.

Perhaps her story would bring them some small comfort.

"Afterwards, he came up to me. I was impressed by his enthusiasm and intelligence. He said his older brother was studying psychology and he wanted to as well."

Tears pooled in Mrs. Brown's eyes but she had a slight smile on her face. The grandmother brushed a hand over her cheek.

The woman in the armchair across from Kate, a slightly younger version of Mrs. Brown—her sister, most likely—leaned forward and offered a box of tissues to the grandmother.

Kate was thinking she might need one too, when Clarissa said, in a sing-song voice, "Well, thank you so much, nice white lady, for coming all this way to tell us my brother was a bright boy." She paused. "For a black kid," she added in a snide tone.

"Clarissa!" Her grandmother said. "Mind your manners!"

"Mind your manners," Clarissa mimicked.

Kate started to rise. "I should probably go." She didn't know what kind of family dynamics she'd stepped into, but obviously her presence was making things worse.

Mrs. Brown held out an imperious hand in her direction. Kate sank back down onto the edge of her chair.

"Clarissa," Mrs. Brown said, "please tell me that my ears have malfunctioned. I did *not* just hear you sass your grandma, did I?"

The girl's face darkened and she ducked her head. "Sorry, Grandma."

"And?" her mother said.

Clarissa crossed her arms over her chest. She glanced Kate's way, then looked away again. "Sorry," she mumbled.

Kate's brain scrambled for something to say, her gut telling her that anything she came up with would probably be wrong. But no awkward silence ensued as she'd expected.

Mrs. Brown turned to her. "You said you also had a *semi*-official reason for coming, and on the phone, something about a governor's task force?"

Kate took a deep breath, no longer sure that this part of her reason for coming was such a good idea.

One of her mother's favorite sayings echoed in her head. *The road to hell is paved with good intentions.*

"Yes, I'm a member of a task force, set up by the governor awhile ago, to study PTSD in police personnel around the state. How common it is, what are the impacts, what can be done about it, et cetera. During the course of our efforts, we got into the whole area of potential 'bad shoots.'" She made air quotes.

She heard a loud snort and figured it came from Clarissa. Mrs. Brown's glare in the girl's direction confirmed that suspicion.

"We're not looking for ways to excuse police behavior when they use excessive force," Kate quickly said. "We're looking for explanations so we can find solutions. One of the symptoms of PTSD is anger, so police officers suffering from the disorder may be more inclined to escalate situations, instead of de-escalating them, and they may end up making bad judgment calls."

"Sure sounds like excuses to me," Clarissa said. "My brother's dead because of a 'bad judgment call.'" Her air quotes were exaggerated. "And now you're here to tell us it might be because the bastard who shot him had PTSD?"

"Language, girl!" Mrs. Brown's sister said.

Clarissa narrowed her eyes at her.

"Listen to your auntie," another woman said. "Your mama's got enough going on without having to deal with your bad manners."

Mrs. Brown raised her hand. "I'd like to hear this lady out, if you all don't mind." She nodded at Kate.

Kate sucked in extra air again, felt heat rising in her cheeks. "I'm...*we're* looking for explanations, because they lead to answers, ways to stop these tragedies. And I'm not saying PTSD had anything to do with this case. But my role on the task force has made me more sensitive to these bad-shoot situations. I... I want to find a way to keep these horrible losses from happening."

"Why don't you stop pussyfooting around, lady?" Clarissa said in a hard voice. "They be killings, not just 'losses,'" more exaggerated air quotes, "or 'tragedies.' My little brother didn't die of leukemia or get hit by a car. He was murdered! By the police!"

Mrs. Brown's lips pinched together, and her eyes bore into the side of her daughter's head.

"You come here, white lady," Clarissa spat the words in Kate's direction, "offering your condolences you say, but the only reason you even notice that black kids be gettin' shot is 'cause you're on this lame task force that's all about helping the pooor, siiick po-lice who can't handle their jobs no more."

Kate managed to squash the desire to become defensive, another skill learned as a therapist, but one she wasn't always able to apply in the rest of her life. Keeping her voice even, she said, "That's actually a fairly accurate assessment."

Clarissa had opened her mouth to say more. Instead, she stared at Kate, some confusion but mostly anger in her eyes.

Kate's chest constricted again. She couldn't blame the girl, and in that moment she wished she had something other than lily-white skin.

A whimper from the sofa. The boy, Jared, was looking up at his mother, his face screwed up as if he were about to cry. He moaned out a word that sounded like, "Bear." And he was flapping his hands toward a doorway across the living room.

Kate turned her head in that direction. She could make out a wooden table and chairs against one wall and assumed the room was an eat-in kitchen.

She returned her attention to Mrs. Brown. But the boy opened his mouth and let out a high-pitched scream.

Kate jumped. The others didn't seem surprised by the outburst.

He flapped his hands harder, and it definitely looked to her like he was pointing toward the kitchen.

Mrs. Brown smoothly rose to her feet, bringing the boy up with her as she gestured to his sister. "Clarrie's gonna take you to your room now, son," she said in a calm voice that was almost drowned out by the screaming.

Clarissa's expression had shifted to chagrin.

She isn't objecting to the "baby name" this time, Kate thought.

Clarissa stepped over to the sofa and wrapped both arms loosely around her brother. She began to maneuver him toward a hallway that no doubt led to bedrooms. The boy was still screaming but he went with her.

"Let him take a shower if you can't get him to calm down," Mrs. Brown called softly after them.

Autism? Kate's chest was so tight, she could hardly breathe.

She considered again getting up and leaving. But Mrs. Brown might see that as rude, and the woman seemed to put a lot of stock in manners.

Kate twisted her hands in her lap. "I'm so sorry I've upset your children."

Mrs. Brown heaved a sigh and resumed her seat on the sofa. "Not hard to do, with either one of 'em these days." The words seemed spontaneous, not as carefully chosen as her earlier statements. Again, tears pooled in her eyes. Then under her breath, "'Fraid she's gonna come to a bad end too."

Kate wanted to say that she understood—that black kids growing up in a prejudiced world would of course be prone to bitterness and anger, and that those angry kids were more at risk of getting into trouble, or worse yet, getting into an argument with a cop that led to their death.

But she said nothing. How could she claim to understand what this woman and her children, her family and friends were dealing with?

As a distraction, she said, "Your oldest son. Tyrell seemed so proud of him. Is he here? I'd love to meet him."

And see if he knows anything about what happened in that alley, commented the curious part of her internally.

The pooling tears spilled down Mrs. Brown's face. She took a deep breath. "I haven't seen Jimmy since the day his brother was shot."

.

CHAPTER FIVE

"I'm so sorry," Kate said for the third time in less than twenty minutes. She rose from her chair, the curious part of her now subdued by the part that just wanted to get the heck out of there. "I should be going."

Mrs. Brown shook her head as she stood up. She straightened herself to her full height, which couldn't be more than five-four. "Mrs..."

"Huntington-Canfield, but please, call me Kate."

"Kate, would you help me in the kitchen for a moment?"

Startled, she nodded.

Mrs. Brown's sister rose from her chair. "We can get whatever you want, Wanda."

Mrs. Brown shook her head again and moved to the open doorway to the kitchen.

Kate followed her. She stood in the middle of the room, while her hostess prepped a white and red plastic appliance, pouring in water, adding tea bags and sugar to a small basket, and filling the pitcher with ice.

There was a back door, a small window in it, with sheer curtains pushed to the sides. Beyond, more brick and stucco walls maybe forty feet away, across a narrow alley.

The table and chairs were oak, the appliances recently updated. But the ceramic tiles halfway up the walls were avocado green, dating the room in the sixties or seventies.

Mrs. Brown pushed a button on the iced tea maker and turned around. She seemed to have regained her composure.

"Please, don't mind Clarissa—"

Kate held up a hand. "I have a thirteen-year-old daughter."

Her hostess rolled her eyes toward the ceiling. "Lord Jesus, watch over this woman. She's gonna need your help for a few years yet."

Kate snickered.

Mrs. Brown gave her a half smile and gestured toward the table. Kate took a seat.

The woman reached above the sink, to a set of shelves that held three-by-five photos in thin frames. She took down two of the pictures. Then she sat down opposite Kate and handed over one of them.

The iced tea maker gurgled on the counter as Kate studied the photo. A much younger and somewhat thinner version of Wanda Brown stood next to a tall, thin, older white man. They were dressed up in good clothes, his suit dark blue, her dress a creamy color that made her skin glow. She held a bouquet of pink roses and was grinning from ear to ear. The man, his dark hair and beard sprinkled with gray, was also smiling, but it was a more subtle, cat-ate-the-canary type smile.

"Your wedding?" Kate said.

Mrs. Brown nodded. "To James Whitmore, my first husband, twenty-two years ago next month." Her face took on a vaguely nostalgic look. "He was a good man. I was a secretary in the philosophy department at Towson University. He was a professor, twenty years older and divorced. He had two grown children by his first wife, but he was happy to start another family, until Jared came along. James tried, he really did. But he couldn't cope with the idea of a child with autism. He was brilliant, you see..." She trailed off, turned her face away.

Then she rose and fussed with the iced tea maker, which had ended its cycle. She pulled two tall glasses from a cabinet and poured the tea.

She placed the glasses on the table. "He was very generous, let me stay in the house with the kids. Paid alimony and child support and then some."

Kate took a small sip of the iced tea. It was sweeter than she cared for, but she took another sip, to be polite.

Wanda Brown handed her the other photo, of a handsome black man in a marine uniform. "I married Tyrell Brown two years later, but still James insisted we live in his house." She sat down again at the table. "How lucky can one woman get that two good men loved her?"

Kate's stomach clenched. A soft groan escaped her lips.

Wanda Brown raised her eyebrows at her.

"I was widowed young," Kate said, and surprised herself by adding, "The anniversary of my Eddie's death is next week." Her throat tightened. She cleared it. "And I also remarried."

"Your second husband, he's a good man?"

Kate smiled. "Yes, very much so. He's a private investigator."

Mrs. Brown's eyes lit up, then her face sobered. "It all fell apart when Tyrell Jr. was seven. His daddy was deployed in Afghanistan, when James died. He'd left the house to me, but his grown kids sued to get his will overturned. I didn't have the money to fight them. And then," she looked away, "we got the word that Tyrell had been killed."

Why was this woman telling her all this, her life story? But Kate's heart softened toward Clarissa, who would have been three or four when her parents split. A bad age for that to happen—old enough to know that Daddy had left her, but not old enough to understand why. And then she'd lost her stepfather as well. No wonder the girl was angry.

Wanda Brown leaned forward, her eyes flashing. "I lived in your world for ten years. Most of James and my friends were white, all were professionals, not rich, but financially comfortable. I know how things work. If you're on this task force and know the governor, than you've got some clout in that world."

She stopped, took a deep breath. "I want you to find me some answers." Her voice turned fierce. "Your task force, they want answers, well so do I. Why is my little boy dead?"

Kate blinked. Her stomach had hollowed out. "I don't know what I..." she stammered and trailed off.

Wanda Brown was watching her with the same intent expression she'd worn earlier.

Kate shook her head. "I don't really have any clout. I don't know the governor."

Narrowed eyes gazed at her. "What about your husband? You said he's an investigator."

"Um, yes."

"I want to hire him."

Kate's jaw dropped.

"I've got the money. My sister, she set up a GoFundMe thing. It's raised thirty-thousand so far."

"Holy crap," Kate blurted out.

The small smile again. "That was my reaction. I was trying to figure out how to return the money, beyond what we need for the funeral. But finding out what really happened to my boy, that seems like a worthy use of it. So how do I go about hiring your husband?"

"Uh, I'll ask him."

———◆◆◆———

A crowd of people milled the streets near the crime scene. Skip parked his SUV several blocks over, and the three of them walked to the alley.

There were white faces in the predominantly darker-skinned clusters of people around them, but they were young, probably residents and probably students at the university, less than a mile away.

He and Mac stood out like a sore thumb, especially him, towering above others' heads.

Rose shot him a wary glance. Her beige skin, straight dark hair and youthful appearance—she never seemed to age—helped her blend in. But she was probably wondering if she'd have to defend her husband and her business partner from the crowd.

They got some stares, a few curious, most hostile, but they made it to the entrance of the alley without incident.

A remnant of crime scene tape, wrapped around a telephone pole, fluttered in the breeze. Stuffed animals, candles and flowers, in varying degrees of freshness, were piled nearby. The sight of a little pink bear—similar to one Edie had once treasured—made Skip's chest hurt.

Sounds from the crowd out front filtered between the apartment buildings, but the alley itself was deserted, the air stale and quiet.

"Eerie," Mac growled under his breath.

"Yeah," Rose said.

"The police report said that two shots were fired." Skip grimaced. "One hit the boy, but the other wasn't found."

Mac groaned and pointed to some kind of covered crosswalk, connecting the second floors of the buildings on either side of the alley. It looked industrial, which didn't surprise Skip. He'd checked into the background of the complex. One never knew where a useful tidbit of information might come from.

It had been a manufacturing plant in the 1950s, converted to apartments in 1968.

In more recent times, some industrious soul had painted the crosswalk with bright blue paint. And even more recently, another industrious soul had somehow climbed up there to spray paint *Black Lives Matter* across it.

"Gonna be a bitch searching that thing," Mac said.

"Let's start down here." Skip pointed to the brick walls. "We each take a third of the alley."

Rose and Mac nodded and moved away.

Skip braced himself and headed for the far end, where the shooting had occurred. Trying to block out the sight of the child-sized chalk outline still barely visible on the cement, his mind pulled up an image of the police report. He wished he'd had more time to take notes.

The boy had been sprawled forward on his stomach, but he had been shot in the front, in the forehead. Had the impact spun him around?

They had the bullet that had struck the boy, so how extensively had the police and crime scene techs searched for the stray bullet?

Skip began to search, squinting at every rough spot or crack in the buildings' walls. He rooted through a pile of empty boxes that might or might not have been there on Monday when the shooting occurred.

Then he walked his section, back and forth, his gaze focused on the pavement, looking for signs of the bullet but also anything relevant that the crime scene techs might have missed.

A shout from the other end of the alley. Mac stood beside the building there, gesturing for Rose and Skip to join him.

Skip jogged over and looked where Mac was pointing—at a hole in the mortar between the bricks of the wall. There were scratch marks around its edges and a few cracks radiating outward in the mortar.

Mac ducked his head down. Rose and Skip both followed his line of vision.

All Skip saw was sidewalk, but Rose crouched down and touched its surface. She stood and held her hand out. Tiny grains of something rested on her fingertips. "Could be cement dust." She sniffed her fingers and nodded.

Skip let out a low chuckle. "How the heck do you even know what cement dust smells like, partner?"

"We've been building a block wall on one side of our property," Rose said.

Mac frowned and grumbled, "Took us the last two weekends, and we still ain't done. Neighbors on that side tend to think old appliances and broken-down cars make good lawn ornaments."

Skip hid a grin. The neighbors were probably glad to not have to see Mac as well. He was a wiry man, on the short side, usually a bit disheveled and prone to wearing old tee-shirts and baggy jeans.

He and Rose—who was always impeccably groomed—were the odd couple on the surface, but they'd been together for as long as Skip had known Kate, over a decade now. And still going strong.

"So, what have we got here?" Rose tilted her head toward the hole. "Assuming that's a bullet hole, when was the bullet removed and by whom?"

"Not by the crime scene guys," Mac said, "or it would've made it into the report."

"And I doubt they would have missed it, if the bullet had still been in there," Rose added.

"But if it was removed before they got here..." Skip trailed off. That didn't make any sense. Did Detective Russell remove it? In the video, it had only been a few minutes from the time the shots were fired until the uniform entered the alley. The scene would have been secured after that and only police, the medical examiner, and crime scene techs allowed in.

"Maybe they didn't look so hard down this end of the alley," Mac said, "'cause they were thinkin' the second shot was also fired at the boy."

Skip turned and scanned the area nearby. A dark oily stain in the middle of the alley was parallel to where they were standing.

"I think Mac's right. They didn't focus that much attention on this end." He pointed to the stain. "That's where Russell fell and hit his head. But," he pivoted and pointed down the alley, "by the time the uniform arrived, he was down there, standing over the boy."

Rose looked toward the oil stain. "He might've had the gun in his hand when he fell, and it went off accidentally."

Mac nodded at the hole. "Bullet went straight in. It'd probably be on an angle if it was a wild shot."

"I'll ask him if he remembers drawing it beforehand." Skip shook his head. "But why his backup piece from its ankle holster instead of his duty weapon?"

"Yeah," Mac said. "That makes even less sense if he drew it before he hit his head. Afterwards, maybe. People do all kinds of screwy stuff when their concussed." He ran a hand over his buzz cut. "You gonna call Judith so she can get the crime scene guys out here again?"

"Nope," Skip said. "I'll tell her, but she can't send the techs out. She can't get anywhere near this case."

Rose nodded, then tilted her head toward the hole again. "Okay, so we know where the second bullet went…"

"But now we have more questions than answers," Skip finished for her.

CHAPTER SIX

On the way to her office on Saturday morning, Kate was still processing what had happened at the Browns' apartment the previous day.

She hadn't told Skip yet about Wanda Brown's desire to hire him.

Friday nights were family movie nights, so they hadn't had much alone time. And she still wasn't sure how to broach the subject.

Would it be a conflict of interest, since Skip and his agency were already unofficially working the case *pro bono* on Judith Anderson's behalf, trying to clear Andy Russell? But did it really matter who was doing what for whom, as long as they ultimately found the truth?

Kate snorted. *How naive!* Of course, it mattered, especially in a case like this, which would be under the media microscope.

Yesterday, Mrs. Brown had recruited her brother to escort Kate back to her car.

Kate had appreciated it, even though the man said very little during the walk. He gently held her elbow to steer her through the crowd, which parted somewhat reluctantly in front of them.

At her car, he'd waited for her to retrieve her keys from her purse and start the engine, before nodding and turning away.

What was the man really thinking and feeling behind that cordial exterior? She had nieces and nephews. Although the wound wouldn't cut as deep as losing her own child, she would be devastated if anything happened to them.

What must it be like to have to hold your emotions in around white people, lest one of them turn out to be a bigot who might use your feelings against you?

Kate had attended a conference a few years ago on counseling diverse clients. She'd gone into it smugly believing that she already had a good handle on the subject. After all, she had African-American and Hispanic friends.

Three days later, she'd come out of that conference humbled, and excruciatingly aware of how little she understood about what it was like to be an other-than-white person in American society.

And a question she'd often wondered about had been answered. In the twenty-plus years she'd been a psychotherapist, she could count on the fingers of one hand the number of African-American clients she'd had. Now she knew why. Because it was hard enough to get up the nerve to seek counseling and to open up once there, without having to worry if your counselor might be prejudiced, or might subscribe to a multitude of subtle stereotypes and misconceptions.

Kate turned into the parking lot across from her office building and forced her mind back to the present and her own life. She had two clients this Saturday morning, both of whom she would need to refer to new therapists. She was anxious to start that process, since finding a good match for them could take several weeks or longer. She needed to close her practice soon. The fees from her few remaining clients barely covered the office rent.

And now that she was no longer all that enthralled with doing therapy, she particularly hated having to spend Saturday or evening hours away from her family, in order to accommodate clients who couldn't get off from work for their sessions.

Up in her office, she found a message on her voicemail from Theresa Barlow, asking if she was free for lunch soon, today if possible.

Hmm, that's odd. She and Theresa had crossed paths at a few professional events and they had a cordial collegial relationship, but they weren't really friends.

She shrugged. Skip had plans with the kids today, dropping Edie at the stable so she could ride her pony, and then he and Billy were going to the movies. Having lunch with Theresa beat sitting around ruminating about the Tyrell Brown case, or grading papers. Definitely better than grading papers.

Kate called Theresa back, got her voicemail and agreed to the restaurant near the hospital that the other woman had suggested. Then she pulled up her personal email on her office computer and dashed off a quick note to her former mother-in-law, suggesting a couple of times when she and Ed could get together with Edie.

She still wasn't comfortable with the situation, but she couldn't bring herself to deprive Ed, Sr. of a chance to see his only grandchild before going under the knife.

———— ◄O► ————

Kate arrived first and grabbed a table in the small Italian bistro. She ordered an iced tea and people-watched while pretending to peruse the menu. The place was filling up fast, with most of the lunchtime crowd sporting scrubs.

She spotted Theresa coming her way. She was an unimposing woman, fortyish, straight-up-and-down slender, maybe an inch taller than Kate's five-seven, with fair skin and a sprinkling of faint freckles. Her short hair was curly, borderline frizzy, and light auburn, the color of a penny that has been in circulation long enough to wear some of the brightness off its coppery glow.

She settled into the chair across from Kate, smoothing the skirt of her beige suit and tugging on the cuffs of her pink blouse. It clashed a little with her hair color. "Thanks for coming over this way, and for grabbing a table. I'm on a tight schedule today, I'm afraid."

On a Saturday? "Not a problem. I didn't have plans for today, except for grading papers."

"So how are you liking teaching?" Theresa asked.

"Some aspects, more than I expected to. Others, like grading, not so much."

They looked over their menus and placed their orders.

Then Theresa glanced around the restaurant. "Maybe not the best choice." She leaned forward and said in a low voice, "I wanted to bring you up to speed on the issue you called me about, um, your patient's concerns. How long ago did he notice this trend?"

Hmm, she'd never mentioned in her message to Theresa what exactly her relationship was with the concerned party. But the assumption that it was a client was a logical one.

"A couple of months ago," she said. "And we call them *clients.*"

Theresa nodded. "This client, where does he work in the hospital?"

Kate was tempted to correct the *he,* but confidentiality constraints stopped her. Saying anything that might give away a client's identity was *verboten,* so maybe it was best that Theresa was assuming it was a man.

"I don't know." Which was the honest truth. All she knew was that it was some kind of clerical position.

Theresa sat back, shrugged, but she still kept her voice low. "Okay, I was just curious. Only a few departments have information on the in-house deaths."

Kate had some trouble hearing her as the noise in the restaurant grew.

Theresa unwrapped her silverware and placed the cloth napkin on her lap. "Anyway, I wanted to let you know that he might be onto something. I'm looking into it, discreetly of course."

"Okay, I'll pass that along. I'm sure it will be reassuring."

"And tell him that if he notices anything else that looks suspicious, he can call me directly."

"Thanks, Theresa, I'll do that," Kate said.

The woman across from her smiled. "I use Theresa professionally, but my friends call me Terry."

"Okay, *Terry*." Kate returned her smile. "I'm sure my client will be glad to hear you're on top of it. I think...they were worried about whether or not to report it."

"Well, no need for that now. If I find anything that looks fishy, I'll take care of it."

The waitress arrived with their food, minestrone and a salad for Kate and a turkey sandwich and salad for Terry.

A turkey sandwich struck Kate as an odd selection in an Italian restaurant. They ate in silence for a few minutes. "Do you eat here often?" she asked to make conversation.

"Sometimes, but Italian's not my favorite. It's handy to the hospital though, when I'm short on time." She glanced at her watch. "I have a meeting with a patient's family in forty-five minutes."

Kate was tempted to make an all-work-and-no-play comment, but she really didn't know Theresa...Terry quite well enough. The woman might take it as actual criticism instead of teasing.

And who am I to talk, seeing clients on a Saturday and then going home to grade papers.

They made small talk as they ate. Kate asked if Terry had a family.

The woman shook her head. "No, I tend to be a workaholic. I don't have much of a social life."

Kate waited for the woman to ask about her family, but it didn't happen.

Instead, Terry checked her watch again. "I hate to cut this short, but I have some prep to do before this meeting." She waved down a busboy and pointed to the quarter of her sandwich left on her plate and her untouched salad.

"So you like your job at the new hospital?" Kate asked, again mostly to make conversation.

Terry grimaced. "Most days, but not when I have to have a meeting like today's. The patient is terminally ill, and I need to get the family to begin to focus on final arrangements, and to start their grief process."

They probably already have, if their loved one is terminally ill.

The waitress arrived with a plastic box. "Is everything okay?"

"Yes." Terry flashed her a smile and took the box. "I just have to get back to work."

"I'll get your check."

Terry didn't wait. She dumped her sandwich and salad into the box and then dropped a twenty-dollar bill on the table. "That should cover mine. Let's do this again soon."

She stood up. "Don't forget to tell your client to come to me if he sees anything else that seems off."

She turned and hurried toward the restaurant door, passing the confused waitress who was bringing the check.

————◄O►————

After dinner, when the kids were in their rooms—ostensibly working on their weekend homework, although video games and texting with friends was more likely what was going on upstairs—Kate and Skip settled into their usual spot on the living room sofa.

Kate's butt sank down into the cushions.

"Is it me," Skip said, "or are the springs starting to sag here?"

"Definitely sagging. We should probably replace the sofa."

"Can't we just get it fixed?" Skip slid an arm around her shoulders. "It would feel weird to have a new one, like..." He trailed off and gave a small shrug.

She smiled up at him. "I get it. This sofa seems like it's part of our relationship."

"I kissed you for the first time here."

"Second time," she corrected him.

"Yeah, but I'm not sure the first time counted, since you made me wait forever before I could do it again."

Kate sighed. "That was so long ago."

"Twelve years, but somehow it seems longer." He gave her a mock frown. "Maybe 'cause life with you has been a bit more excitin' than it oughta be." He'd let a little of his native Texas creep into his voice.

"It sure hasn't been dull."

"So how was your day, Mrs. Huntington-Canfield?"

"Kind of odd actually." She told him about her lunch with the social worker from the new hospital on Dulaney Valley Road. "I can't figure out if she was making an overture to become friends, or if it was only about–" She stopped abruptly, realizing that trying to explain further would lead into Carol Foster's concerns.

Skip gave her shoulders a slight squeeze. "Or what?"

She turned slightly to face him. "Okay, this is confidential."

"Ack!" Skip threw his hand up in the air. "I hate when you say that."

Kate shook her head. "No, it's nothing we need to get involved in. One of my clients works for the new hospital, and she's gotten concerned that more deaths are happening there than normal."

Skip gave her a skeptical look. "People sometimes die in hospitals."

"That was my thought when she brought it up, but she files the death certificates, so she would know what a normal number of deaths would be. So I passed her concerns, without naming names, on to Theresa who works at the hospital." Kate paused for breath. "Supposedly her reason for asking me out to lunch was to tell me she was discreetly looking into it, but our conversation was kind of stilted. And then she dashed off after about forty minutes, with part of her lunch in a box."

She paused again, wondering if the next part was purely her imagination. "And I think she was trying to pump me for information about who my client is."

Skip rubbed his chin with his free hand, then skimmed hair back off his forehead. "So what part exactly am I supposed to keep confidential?"

"That the client is a female, and she files the death certificates."

Skip gave her a baffled look.

"I think if I'd given any information to Theresa about who it was... I don't know. Maybe I'm being paranoid." Kate shoved some of her own curls out of her face.

"In this kind of situation," he said, "I'm not sure you can be too cautious. If your client is right and something bad is going on, she might not fare too well as the whistle-blower."

"That's exactly my concern, and she doesn't need any more drama in her life."

"Nor do we," Skip muttered.

"So what's happening with Andy Russell's case?" she asked, figuring this was the best segue she might get.

"Judith texted me today, from her private phone." He paused, and she felt his chest expand as he took a breath. "She said she'd pay for our time if we can clear Russell."

Kate's stomach dropped.

"And *that's* confidential," Skip said, "the fact that she's hiring us. Judith could lose her shield if any of this got back to the powers-that-be."

Kate took a deep breath and turned slightly in the circle of his arm to face him. "Well, we've got a dilemma then. Because Tyrell Brown's mother asked if she can hire you, to find out why her son was shot."

Skip grimaced. "That would be a conflict of interest."

Kate nodded. "I suspected it would be, even when you were just poking around *pro bono*. But I need to figure out what to tell Wanda."

"Tell her I am looking into it, but wouldn't take her money."

She cringed inside, then shook her head. "Have you ever heard of the white savior syndrome?"

"No, but I can guess at what it is."

"That's what it would look like, that the white folks are sweeping in to save the helpless black woman." Kate waved a hand in the air. "I'll figure it out tomorrow, when my brain isn't so tired."

She took another deep breath, actively letting the tension go. Then she poked Skip's knee with her index finger. "So let's get this straight here. You are looking into this for Judith's benefit, not mine."

He gave her a small grin. "Yeah, but you set the ball rolling."

"So, what did you find yesterday at the crime scene?"

"A hole in the brick wall, where we think the second stray bullet was dug out, by someone other than the CSI techs."

"Who dug it out?"

Skip shrugged. "No clue."

"Could Andy have fired a warning shot while he was chasing the boy?"

"Hell no. Police are trained never to do that. Way too risky that the bullet will go somewhere you didn't intend, especially in a congested residential area like that."

Kate shuddered, realizing it could have gone through a window instead of into the wall, and maybe hurt or killed yet another innocent.

Skip was shaking his head. "And it totally doesn't make sense that he pulled out his backup piece from its ankle holster instead of his duty weapon from his waist. His instinct would always be to go for that gun first."

"Wait, he landed on his left side. Maybe that arm and his waist holster were pinned under him. Then it might have been easier to reach down with his right hand and..." Kate leaned forward on the sofa and demonstrated pulling a phantom gun from an imaginary ankle holster with her opposite hand.

"That would make sense. Can you ask if he remembers drawing his gun *before* he fell? If he did, it might have discharged accidentally when he went down."

Kate settled back next to him. "Hmm, I'll have to think of a way to phrase it so it isn't leading him to answer a certain way, but my guess is he won't remember when he drew the gun. It probably happened right before he was concussed or right after he began to come to, in which case it most likely didn't get recorded in his memory at all."

Skip nodded, then frowned, his hazel eyes shifting toward a muddy brown. "The kid was only about twenty feet from his own back door. If he'd been a little quicker, he'd be alive today."

Kate's heart raced. She jerked around to face him more fully. "What? The shooting was right there, behind the Browns' apartment?"

"Yeah, in the alley."

"I didn't know that was where it happened." She flopped back against the sofa, processing. Did Jared's hands flapping toward the kitchen, toward the *back* of the apartment, have another possible meaning?

She definitely needed to visit Wanda Brown again.

Kate swallowed hard. Would she have the nerve to probe yet another painful wound for the woman—the capabilities of her autistic son?

———— ◆ ————

Rose had kept a close eye on the news reports over the weekend, even though they made her stomach churn. Similar to three years ago—after Freddie Gray's death while in police custody—protests had turned violent in parts of the city.

Sunday evening, Rose's throat hurt as she watched the late news. The smoke from tear gas canisters, the people running, the police in full battle gear. It was too easy for her to imagine living in one of those rowhouses she glimpsed occasionally through the haze.

She was keenly aware of how lucky she was.

She'd been a baby when her family emigrated from Guatemala to escape a brutal civil war. But she had heard the stories from her parents, and from her cousin Maria who had emigrated thirty years later, when the homicide rate there was one of the highest in the world.

Rose wasn't afraid of violence. As a cop and then as a P.I., she had taken down more than one man who was twice her size. But whenever she witnessed this kind of violence—the fabric of a city, a community being ripped apart—it tore at something deep inside of her, as if the memories of her native country's troubles were embedded in her genes.

Why can't we humans get it right? Why can't we figure out how to live and work in harmony? And why do the children end up in the crossfire?

They weren't new questions. And to Rose's way of thinking, they were questions that were getting quite old. *We need some answers!*

A hand dropped on her shoulder, making her jump a little.

"Come on, honey bun," Mac said, without the usual growl in his voice. "Turn that off and let's go to bed."

She gave him a small smile. "I'll be along in a few minutes."

He nodded and headed for the bedroom.

Rose turned off the TV and went into the bathroom. Squinting in the mirror, she stared at the crow's feet around her eyes and the tiny frown lines at the corners of her mouth.

She forced herself to smile. It wasn't her best effort, but the frown lines temporarily disappeared.

Her genuine smiles, few and far between, could still stop men in their tracks, mouths hanging open. But she'd been even slower to smile these last few months than usual.

There hadn't been much to smile about. First, her beloved *madre* had passed away, and now her adopted city was once again turning on itself. Not to mention her birthday coming up.

Turning forty hadn't particularly fazed her, so why was the thought of forty-two giving her the heebie-jeebies?

She pulled her bun loose and fanned long black hair across the shoulders of her white shirt. No gray yet, but then her family was slow to gray.

Her chest aching, she mentally voiced the question she'd asked herself a thousand times in recent months. *Should we have had children?*

They'd talked about it off and on through the years, each time concluding that neither their temperaments nor their vocation lent themselves to dealing with rug rats.

Billy and Edie were as close as they'd come. Yes, she had nieces and nephews, and she loved them. But she and Mac had helped raise the Canfield kids.

And now they were growing up. And in the last few months, she'd somehow become Edie's confidante. She felt both surprised and honored by that, and also a little anxious that she'd somehow blow it and say the wrong thing.

"I guess I shouldn't be so surprised," she murmured to herself. She'd had a favorite aunt when she was a teenager, with whom she'd discussed things she couldn't possibly talk about with her parents, or so she'd believed at the time.

A flash of movement in the mirror. She whirled around.

Mac stood there in a white tee and his boxers, his rugged face and muscular arms tanned a darker tone than her own beige skin. But his sinewy legs, that never saw the sun, announced his Irish heritage.

For a moment, she imagined him in a kilt. It was a sexy look.

She kept the thought to herself, knowing he would be horrified that she'd mixed the Scottish and Irish cultures that way, just as she hated it when people assumed she was Mexican.

But the fantasy lifted her mood.

"It's gettin' late," he said gently.

Rose flashed him a smile. "Be right there."

He nodded and turned away.

A ping from the pocket of her khaki slacks. She pulled out her phone.

You still up, Aunt Rose? I need to talk. I'm so mad at Mom.

Rose let out a low groan. Not tonight. She could pretend she hadn't gotten the text until morning.

But she hated to leave Edie hanging. The girl might do something stupid.

Headed for bed, she texted back. *Can it wait until morning?*

Yeah, I guess.

Can you give me the quick version?

She won't let me see my grandparents.

The image in the mirror wrinkled her brow. *The O'Donnells in Florida?* Why wouldn't Kate let Edie visit her own parents?

Understanding dawned. Ed Huntington's parents. She'd never met them, but she'd heard stories from Kate. Her description of her late husband's mother always reminded Rose of Lorelei's mother on *Gilmore Girls*.

Definitely not a place she wanted to go tonight, and definitely not via text messaging.

I'll call while you're on the school bus tomorrow, okay? That would roughly correspond with Rose's commute to the office.

Better to talk about this when my brain isn't tired, she added.

Nothing for a moment, then, *Okay. Night.* The words were followed by a smiley face with zzz over its head.

Phew. Teenage angst diverted, for tonight at least.

Rose glanced up at the mirror again. The woman looking back now seemed worried.

Teenage girls will always fight with their mothers, Rose reminded herself, as she had with her *madre*. And they'd both survived it.

To cheer herself up, she revisited the mental image of Mac in a kilt. The woman in the mirror grinned at her.

CHAPTER SEVEN

After her morning classes on Monday, Kate called Andy Russell while she drove to the Browns' apartment complex.

"Hello." His voice sounded rusty, unused.

"Andy? It's Kate Huntington."

"Yeah."

Kate scowled at her car's Bluetooth screen. She'd intended to ask how he was doing. It would be the polite and caring thing to do, but suddenly she wasn't sure she wanted to deal with his obvious bad mood.

Not that she could blame him.

"Got a question for you. Do you remember drawing your gun at all?"

Only a brief pause. "No. But I do recall now the sensation of my feet going out from under me."

Kate quickly assessed how best to couch a follow-up question. "And where were your hands when that was happening?"

"Whadaya mean, where were they? Flailin' all around, trying to catch my balance."

Was he slurring his words slightly? Had he been drinking already? It wasn't even quite noon yet.

She tried one more time. "Can you think of any reason why you would draw your backup gun?"

A slightly longer pause. "I've wracked my brain." His voice was more civil now. "Can't think of one."

"Okay, just double checking. Hang in there..." She caught herself. She'd been about to tell him that Skip and the agency were looking into the case.

But if he was hitting the booze now, he might blurt that out to the wrong people, like the I.A. investigators.

"A lot of people are rooting for you," she said instead.

"Yea, team." He disconnected.

Kate shook her head. If all this were only about clearing Andy, she might not be all that motivated to help. But now it was also about finding Wanda Brown some answers.

She wasn't sure that arriving unannounced at the Browns was a great idea, but her attempts to phone had failed. The mechanical voice had answered when she'd called the home number. She'd left a message, talking slowly to give someone who might be listening a chance to pick up. But no one had. Perhaps the reporters had gotten so annoying, the Browns weren't even bothering to screen calls anymore.

Then Kate had called Towson University's math department, where Wanda was now the office manager, on the off chance she'd returned to work already. The young woman who'd answered told her Mrs. Brown had gone home for a long lunch.

Apparently, single mothers didn't always have the luxury of taking time off to grieve. Or perhaps, staying busy was helping Wanda Brown cope.

Kate pulled into the apartment complex's main entrance. She was surprised to find that the parking lots and side streets of the complex were virtually empty, with only the occasional resident walking to or from their car or strolling along with a dog. Apparently the uproar over Tyrell's death had been transferred to BCPD's headquarters and to downtown Baltimore. The reports of demonstrations and some rioting still dominated the news.

With some trepidation, Kate rang the doorbell of the Browns' unit. Seconds ticked by with no one answering. She was about to turn away when the door swung open.

Mrs. Brown stood there, in a long-sleeved cream blouse and black dress slacks. "I got your message. Come on in, but stay in the living room."

The woman closed the door behind Kate, throwing the deadlock as well, then walked past her into the kitchen.

Okay, that was a strange greeting.

A low rumble of voices from the kitchen and Mrs. Brown reappeared, pulling two swinging doors closed behind her. "Sorry. I came home to give Jared's aide a break, but she's willing to sit with him for a few minutes."

She gestured toward an armchair and settled herself on the sofa. "What can I do for you, Mrs. Huntington-Canfield?"

"Kate, please." She sat down in the chair.

Mrs. Brown gave her a small smile that didn't reach her eyes. "Then call me Wanda."

"Jared doesn't go to school?" Kate asked, carefully keeping her voice neutral. She didn't want Wanda thinking she was judging her arrangements for her son.

"He's in a special school." Her lips thinned into a tight line for a moment. "I had to fight long and hard with the county for that placement." She waved a hand in the air, as if shooing away the aggravation of having to advocate for her son's needs.

No doubt it's a constant battle, or at least a frequently recurring one.

"They're off for a few days every six to eight weeks, supposedly to give the kids a break from the intensity of school, but mostly it just messes up the schedules of us working parents."

Kate nodded, stifling the urge to say that she could relate to the upheaval that school closings create in a working family's routine. Her own situation was hardly comparable to all that Wanda Brown was dealing with. Kate could only begin to imagine how the woman coped.

"I'll get straight to the point then, so your aide can take her break." She looked down at her lap, not sure how to broach this. "I, um, wasn't totally forthcoming the other day. I happen to know the policeman who is accused of the shooting, although I don't know him well."

Wanda scowled at her. "Then you know a hell of a lot more than I do."

"They haven't told you who it is?" Kate asked.

"Nope. They didn't tell me nothing." She crossed her arms over her ample chest.

Kate sighed. "Lemme guess, they gave you the they're-still-investigating line." It was one she'd heard way too many times during the investigation into Eddie's murder.

Wanda let out a small snort. "It's been almost two weeks. My guess is they're really waiting for the community's anger to settle down. And then they'll announce that my boy somehow did something to cause it."

Kate wasn't sure how to respond to that, especially since she could be right. It was quite possible that the BCPD brass would look for a way to spin things, so they could say their officer believed the boy was armed.

"So what did your husband say?" Wanda asked.

Kate hated the lie she was about to tell, but she didn't know this woman well enough to trust her with sensitive information. If she told the press, or anyone for that matter, that Skip was poking around in an official I.A. investigation, that would backfire big time on him and Judith Anderson.

"I'm afraid he's swamped right now. But..." She leaned forward. "Look, I'll tell you as much as I can, if you'll agree to something in return."

Wanda's eyes narrowed. "What?"

"You let me talk to Jared."

"Jared?" Her eyebrows flew up. "Why would you want to talk to him?"

"Does he communicate at all?"

The woman's nod seemed a bit reluctant. "We have a system, and he draws a lot to express himself."

Kate smiled. "That's great."

The woman scowled. "Be better if he talked."

Heat flooded Kate's cheeks. "Of course it would. I'm sorry, Wanda. That was insensitive."

Suddenly, the woman's stiff shoulders sank. She unfolded her arms and rubbed her palms against the thighs of her black slacks. "No, you're right. It is good progress. He's come a long way since he's been in this school." She sat back. "What can you tell me?"

Kate took a deep breath. "One, they haven't found any eyewitnesses. Two, it wasn't a uniformed officer. He's a detective, experienced. I don't think he'd harm an unarmed boy."

Wanda Brown stiffened again.

"No, I'm not saying that Tyrell did anything to deserve getting shot. I'm just saying that the man I know isn't impulsive or careless." She stopped, realizing she really didn't know Andrew Russell all that well. It was more that she had a gut sense of who he was, based on her dealings with him.

But she could be wrong.

"The man is an acquaintance, not a friend," she added. "I'm really not invested in the outcome of this. But like you, I want to know the truth. You see, the detective fell as he came into the alley." She'd decided to leave out Andy Russell's name, for now. "He hit his head and doesn't remember what happened. There's definite evidence that supports his claim that he fell though. But other things don't add up."

"Such as?" Wanda Brown had crossed her arms again.

"For one thing, the detective wasn't chasing Tyrell for his own sake. He jumped into the chase when a uniform was going after the boy. He had no reason to believe Tyrell was dangerous, no reason to even draw his weapon."

"But he did, and my boy's dead."

Kate nodded. "There are a lot of missing pieces, and I think maybe Jared may have some of them. Was he home that afternoon?"

Wanda stared at her for a few seconds. She finally said, "Yes, and so was Clarissa. She said Jared was in his room chillin' when the shots were fired. He usually needs some alone time after school."

"What did she do?"

"Nothing. She thought it was firecrackers or a car backfiring. This isn't the ritziest neighborhood, but we don't have drive-bys, that's for damned sure."

"So Clarissa didn't react," Kate said. "Understandable. But Jared may have looked out his window?" She phrased it as a question.

Another few-seconds stare, then Wanda nodded slightly and pushed her large body to a stand. "Let's see if we can find out anything from the boy." She led the way through the swinging doors into the kitchen.

Jared sat at the table, shoveling yogurt from a plastic container into his mouth with a small plastic spoon. An empty container, with a picture of strawberries on the side of it, already sat on the table.

"He wanted another one." A blue-eyed, blonde young woman in a green flannel shirt stood up, revealing fashionably torn jeans.

"That's fine. That new medicine makes him hungry. You can take your break now, Lisa. Thanks for hanging around."

Jared pushed the second, now-empty container away. He looked toward the refrigerator, his eyes wide. "Gurt?"

The teen was tall and thin, but his face was broad. When he filled out, he would be a big man. Kate fleetingly wondered how Wanda would manage then.

"That's enough yogurt for now. You want some fish?" His mother reached into a cabinet.

"Fish!" he said expectantly, a small smile playing on his lips.

The "fish" weren't the scaly kind that swam in the sea. Wanda pulled out a big bag of fish-shaped crackers. She poured some directly onto the red plastic tablecloth covering the kitchen table.

Jared picked up several and stuffed them in his mouth.

"Son, did you look out the window, that day when Bear was out back?" In an aside, Wanda said to Kate, "He calls his brother Bear."

Wanda pointed to the kitchen window. "Did you look outside, that last day we saw Bear?"

Jared stared at her, then grabbed up more crackers and stuffed them in. He struggled to chew, his mouth now too full.

His eyes grew shiny, and he looked toward the window.

"Can we try going to his room?" Kate said in a low voice.

"Good idea." Wanda picked up the bag of crackers. "Let's have some more fish in your room, okay, Jared?"

He got up and followed his mother, Kate trailing behind.

She stopped in the boy's doorway, trying to be unobtrusive.

Jared sat on his bed, and his mother poured some crackers on the bed-spread next to him. Then she stepped to the window and opened the mini-blinds. "Did you see Bear that day?"

Jared flapped an arm in the general direction of the window, while stuffing crackers in his mouth with the other hand.

Wanda sat down beside him and rested a hand on her thigh. Kate realized this was intentional when Jared poked her hand twice.

"Two is for yes, one is for no," Wanda said softly.

"How reliable is that?" Kate matched her low, gentle tone.

Wanda shrugged. "Did you see someone with Bear?"

Again, Jared tapped her hand twice, while cramming more crackers in and chewing.

Wanda winced slightly at the cracker crumbs floating to the floor.

"Sorry," Kate whispered. She gathered that Jared was not normally al-lowed to eat in his room.

Wanda shook her head slightly. "It's okay," she whispered back, "if we get at the truth."

She turned again to her son. "This is a tough one, son. Can you tell Mama if the person was black like you and me, or white like this lady?" She gestured for Kate to step forward.

Jared didn't seem to even hear her, but then he tapped his mother's hand twice. "Black like you and me?"

One tap this time. He flapped his hands in the air, scattering more cracker crumbs.

"I'm not sure, but I think he might want you to come closer," Wanda said.

Kate took another step and stooped down to Jared's eye level. "Hey, Jared," she said softly.

He didn't meet her gaze, but he reached out and poked her cheek twice.

Kate gave Wanda a questioning look.

"It's my fault," Wanda said. "I should have stuck to yes/no questions. Jared, honey, was the person black like us?"

He looked away, toward the other end of his room, but tapped her hand twice.

"So they weren't white like me?" Kate said softly.

Jared turned his head toward her, his eyes dull and not making contact with hers. Then he poked her cheek twice again.

But she wasn't sure what exactly that meant. The negative in her question had further confused the issue.

Jared became more agitated, flapping his arms.

"He's getting frustrated," Wanda said. "We'd better stop."

"I don't blame him." Kate wished she'd thought through her question better. She pulled back some before pushing herself to a stand.

Jared grabbed a big artist pad from the end of his bed, making screeching noises as he flapped it in the air.

"Okay, okay," his mother said, shoving herself to her feet. She took two steps toward a small desk and picked up a colored pencil. "Purple okay?" she said to her son.

He made no response, which Wanda seemed to take as yes, that was okay. She carried the pencil to him.

He flipped the pad open to a blank page and made slashing marks on it. Still standing, Wanda watched the pencil's movements, a smile slowly spreading across her face. "You are such a smart boy."

When the pencil stopped moving, she tugged a little on the edge of the pad. "Can I show her?"

Jared looked away toward the end of his bed again, but he relinquished his hold on the pad.

There were two stick figures side by side. Jared had made purple slashes through the round head of one. The other was white inside the circle, not even any eyes or mouth.

"Two people," Kate said. "One black, one white."

Jared tapped the bed twice. "Fish?"

"I shouldn't. You've already had enough..." Wanda leaned down. "Hug?"

The boy seemed to hesitate, then he opened his arms. His mother gave him a quick hug. "I've always gotta ask first," she said to Kate. "Sometimes he's not up for it."

She poured more crackers on the bedspread and turned to shoo Kate out of the room.

Once they were back in the living room, Wanda asked, "What does that really tell us though?"

Kate felt her shoulders droop. "Not much, I guess. He probably saw the detective and the uniformed officer who followed him into the alley a few minutes later."

"I'm assuming this detective is white or they wouldn't be so hush-hush about it."

"He is, but come to think of it," Kate said, "I'm not sure about the other officer. I'll have to ask."

"Please don't tell anybody that Jared saw them. I don't want the cops trying to interrogate him. They'll scare the crap out of him."

"And he would probably shut down forever on the subject after that." Another horrible thought sent ice through Kate's bloodstream. "And if the detective they *think* fired the shot actually did *not*, then whoever did might come after Jared."

Wanda's face turned an ashen brown. Her eyes went wide.

Kate held out her hand, offering to shake. "Neither of us says anything just yet. Um, I may be able to get some answers in other ways. I'll get back to you."

Wanda shook her hand. "I'm gonna ask the art therapist at Jared's school to work with him. I'll say it's 'cause he's traumatized about his brother being gone."

"How is he processing his brother's death?" Kate gently asked.

"I don't know if he really understands the concept, but I think he knows Bear isn't coming back." Tears pooled in the woman's eyes.

Kate really wanted to hug her, but she wasn't sure how that would be received. She grabbed her hand again and gave it a quick squeeze instead, then let go and started to turn toward the door. "Wait, your older boy, have you heard from him?"

The tears broke loose as Wanda shook her head. "He goes to Towson U, has his own place. Well, with roommates." She brushed at her cheeks with the back of her hand. "They haven't seen or heard from him either."

Kate tried to fathom what that meant. Was it just a coincidence? She knew what Skip would say—the line he'd picked up from Dolph—that he's allergic to coincidences.

Kate patted the other woman's shoulder. "I'll be in touch."

She reached for the deadbolt to open it.

"Wait, there's a button on the side." Wanda stepped around her and showed her the button one had to push in before turning the deadbolt's knob. "It's to keep Jared from being able to open it and wander off when we're not looking."

So the deadbolt being engaged wasn't to protect those inside from the outside world. Kate had wondered why Wanda had engaged it during broad daylight, since she'd made a big deal about the neighborhood being safe.

That is unless you're a black kid running from the cops.

Kate had parked around the corner, in a stretch of spaces marked for visitors. She rummaged in her purse for her keys as she walked, only half looking where she was going. As she rounded the corner, something bumped her shoulder.

She jumped back, her head jerking up.

A quick impression of a ski mask and then she was bent over someone's arm, her purse being yanked from her hands.

She stared at the ground, heart pounding. The man's polished shoes reflected back her distorted image.

Then hot breath against her ear, and she was back in a dark parking lot, on hands and knees, being attacked and threatened by a child molester.

Only she wasn't. It was daylight and she was still on her feet.

The source of the hot breath growled, "Learn to stay out of places you don't belong, white bitch."

CHAPTER EIGHT

Gloved hands roughly shoved Kate down. She fell forward, her hands hitting the sidewalk.

Footsteps slapped as the man ran away.

She shook her head to rid her brain of the remnants of the flashback. That attack had happened over two years ago.

"That was then, and this is now," she said out loud, a grounding technique she taught her clients.

And I've just been mugged.

Heart still ricocheting in her chest, she staggered to her feet and stumbled in the same direction the mugger had gone. Not out of any sense of bravery—she intentionally slowed to give him time to get away. But without her purse, she had no car keys and no phone to call for help.

She headed for Wanda's door, hoping she didn't freak Jared out. Her suit jacket was all twisted around her. She pulled it straight and ran her hands over her hair.

Her palms stung. She stopped and stared at them. They were skinned up, oozing blood.

She moved forward again, rounded the corner. And stopped.

Something black and boxy lay on the sidewalk. Her purse!

She grabbed it up and rifled through the contents. Everything was there, including her wallet. She pulled it out.

She'd had about forty dollars in cash. It was gone.

She shook her head again and staggered back to her car. Getting in and locking the doors, she sat there trembling for a good five minutes, her mind racing.

She should call the police. But she really didn't want to.

She took a deep breath. How would she explain even being here without involving Wanda Brown? She could say she was here paying her respects, but...

Suddenly exhausted, all she wanted to do was go home. Would the police even expend all that much effort trying to find a mugger who only got away with forty bucks?

She knew she was rationalizing, but she put the key in the ignition and started the engine.

With more than a little trepidation, Rose made the call she'd been putting off all morning. There was no way she would win completely in this situation, or rather no way that she wouldn't lose something important to her—either Edie's trust or Kate's friendship.

Her fear for Edie tipped the scales. She hadn't liked the hints the girl had dropped that she was considering running away. The thought of the thirteen-year-old out on the streets sent a chill down Rose's spine.

"Hello." Kate's voice seemed shaky, with that echoing quality that meant she was in the car and on Bluetooth.

"You okay?"

"Yeah, just driving and traffic's kind of heavy."

"Where you headed?"

"Home. Um, I'll be there in ten minutes. Can I call you back?"

"Sure."

Rose lolled away the time clearing up some paperwork on her desk. She checked her watch. It had been twelve minutes. She waited another five.

Praying nothing had happened to her friend in that heavy traffic, she called Kate again.

"Hey, sorry. Um, that took longer than I thought, to get home." The echoing sound was gone but not the shakiness.

"What's wrong?" Rose said.

"Nothing, I'm fine."

She sounded better, but somehow Rose didn't believe her.

"You got clients this afternoon?"

"No."

"Good. I'm on my way over. I've got something important to talk to you about." Rose intentionally hung up before Kate could respond.

As she suspected, Towson midday traffic was no worse than usual.

"Okay, what's going on?" Rose demanded as soon as she walked through the door. She stopped abruptly at the sight of Kate's face, smudged a bit with dirt, and her hands wrapped in white gauze.

Her stomach twisted and her chest tightened. She should've realized that if Kate was shaken... "What happened?" she asked in a gentler voice.

Kate sucked in air. "I was mugged."

"You okay?" Rose gestured toward one of her hands.

"Yes. They're skinned up, that's all." She turned away, toward the kitchen. "You want some tea or something?"

"I'll get it," Rose said. "You sit." She grabbed the tea kettle off the stove and went to the sink. "What'd they take?"

"Just the cash in my wallet, then he dropped my purse. So I'm only out forty bucks." She lowered herself into a chair at the table. "And my dignity. It all happened so fast. I didn't even try to fight back."

Rose put the kettle on to heat and pulled mugs out of a cabinet. "You should get back to Aikido classes." It came out harsher than she'd intended.

But Kate didn't take offense. "I should. I've been letting that slide lately. Not enough time or energy anymore, it seems."

Rose turned and leaned back against the kitchen counter, studying her friend. Kate had always been quite energetic. What was going on?

Kate returned her stare and answered the unasked question. "It's called perimenopause. Happens to the best of us eventually."

Rose stuck her fingers in her ears and yelled, "Na, na, na, na," imitating Rob's response any time someone wandered into too-much-information land.

Kate laughed.

The desired effect.

"So where were you when you got mugged?"

"About to get into my car." Kate looked away, staring intently at the kettle that was beginning to make tiny warbling sounds. "And before you ask, no, I didn't call the police."

The kettle went into full-blown whistling mode. Rose grabbed it and moved it to another burner. "Why the hell not?"

"Because I was just outside Wanda Brown's apartment, and I didn't want to draw attention to the fact that I was there."

Rose poured hot water over tea bags in the mugs, giving herself time to muster a little more patience than she was currently feeling. "And why was that?" she asked as she carried the mugs to the table and sat down.

Kate took a deep breath. "One of the dead boy's brothers—not Jimmy, the one who's missing—his other brother, Jared. He's on the autism spectrum, nonverbal but able to communicate in other ways, to some degree."

Kate told her about her interaction with the boy. By the time, she'd finished, their tea had cooled. Kate lifted her mug and took a sip.

Rose sat back in her chair, processing. "If this boy saw what happened, he could be in danger."

"Exactly. That's why I didn't want to draw attention to the Browns."

Rose blew out air. "Can you come to our staff meeting tomorrow morning?"

Kate gave her a curious look. "I've got a client at nine, but I could be there by ten-thirty."

"Good. I'll delay the meeting until then. That'll give Dolph time to do some digging."

"What are you thinking?" Kate asked.

"That this is now about more than Judith's training officer getting a bad rap." Rose scrubbed a hand over her face. "Look, I've got something to tell you that is not going to improve your day."

She filled Kate in on her phone conversation with Edie that morning, trying not to violate the girl's confidentiality any more than necessary.

"That... Grrr!" Kate started to clench her fists, then winced. "I knew I couldn't trust her."

"Edie?"

"No, my former mother-in-law. I told her we'd work something out, and I emailed her yesterday with some times for them to get together. But that woman just couldn't wait to say something to Edie, making it sound like I'm resistant to her seeing them."

"Which you are," Rose pointed out.

"Yes, because I knew Edith Huntington would try to undermine me. I'm tempted now to tell them forget it, they're not seeing her. But it's not Ed's fault that his wife is that way."

"He married her."

"Yeah, but no doubt she was sweet as molasses until the ring was on her finger."

"You need to tread softly with Edie. She was making noises that sounded like she considered running away as an option."

Kate face blanched.

"You'd think she would've learned better after last winter," Rose quickly added. "But she saw some dumb movie about a teenager who ran away and was taken in by a family that treated her better than her abusive parents. Now she thinks that's what happens to most runaways."

Kate propped her elbows on the table and dropped her face into her hands. "Oh no. What am I going to do?"

A thought popped into Rose's head. "Hey, I've got an idea."

Kate looked up.

"Wait, let me think it through."

"No, just spit it out. Your instincts are usually pretty good where kids are concerned."

Rose laughed a little. "Not really, since I've never had any."

"But I think you remember what it's like to be a kid better than most adults do."

Rose shrugged, but the words warmed her heart, which took her a bit by surprise. "Okay, here's my idea. The kids' spring break is coming up soon, isn't it? Is that before or after Ed, Sr.'s surgery?"

"Before. He isn't going into the hospital until the following week."

"Good, so suggest to your mother-in-law that Edie stay with them that whole week. Longer would be better. Of course, it could backfire."

"Maybe, but I think you're onto something. My former mother-in-law is not good at bending and flexing to accommodate others, and she's a clean freak."

"While Edie is a slob," Rose said with a small smile.

Kate nodded "My guess is they'll get on each other's nerves big-time. But I will also have a little chat with Edith about not undermining my relationship with my daughter, if she wants to continue to see her."

"Sounds like a plan." Rose flashed her a full-blown grin.

"You know it's kind of a shame that you and Mac never had kids."

Rose felt her grin fade. "Maybe, but we're really not suited to that parenting stuff. Can you see us with a two-year-old running around the house. Mac would want to put it in a cage."

Kate grinned. "And you just called your potential offspring 'it.'"

They both laughed, but Rose's chest felt hollow as they said their good-byes.

━━━◄O►━━━

Kate felt somewhat better after Rose left. But holding a pen was making paper-grading an even more torturous task than usual. She unwound the bandage from her right hand and dropped it on the kitchen table.

The bleeding had stopped. She picked up the pen again—less awkward but still a bit painful.

The landline phone rang in its charger on the counter.

Kate jumped, and the pen went flying.

She got up and grabbed the phone, then bent down to retrieve the pen. Her attempts to do so with the bandage still on her left hand distracted her for a moment from the caller's words.

"Mrs. Huntington, this is Amanda, Benjamin Horowitz's assistant. I got a call from–"

"Yes, Amanda. How's Ben doing?" Kate finally managed to get the pen in a pincer grip and stood up.

"He's coming along, still recuperating."

Ben Horowitz was one of the movers and shakers in Baltimore County and the State of Maryland. He had a behind-the-scenes finger in many of the political pies of the region, and he was the head of the PTSD task force.

But his demanding schedule had finally taken its toll on his elderly body. He'd had a heart attack several months ago, and was still under doctor's orders to stay home and take it easy for another month.

The task force had filed a preliminary report with the governor's office, but the meetings to finalize things had been put on hold.

"I just got off the phone with the governor's chief of staff," Amanda was saying. "The governor wants the task force to reconvene asap, and, um, he wants you to be the temporary chair, until Ben's back on his feet."

Kate covered the mouthpiece of the portable phone and groaned. Could her life get any more complicated?

"Mrs. Huntington, are you there?"

"Yes, I'm here."

"Would you be available to meet one night this week?"

"Maybe, probably. I'll have to check with my husband. Why the rush?"

A beat of silence, except for the whir and soft thunk, thunk of a copy machine in the background.

Kate propped the phone against her shoulder and unwound the other bandage. The scratches there had also stopped bleeding.

"Um, I'm not sure, so don't quote me on this," Amanda finally said. "But I think the governor is getting some... pressure regarding the Tyrell Brown case. His chief of staff said his understanding was that you all were going to propose some specific actions to be taken that would relate to unwarranted police shootings, as well as to PTSD in our police forces."

"Yes, that was the tentative plan, but we hadn't come to a consensus on it yet."

"I think he wants that proposal sooner instead of later."

This time Kate managed to swallow the groan. "Have you talked to any of the other members yet?"

"No, I called you first."

"Okay, can you call the others and see how many of them can make it on short notice? And we're going to need to work up an agenda."

"I've taken the liberty of doing that for you, ma'am."

Ah, thus the thunking of the copy machine.

"I'll get started on those calls right now."

"Thanks, Amanda. You're a gem."

"Thank *you*." The woman disconnected, and Kate threw her pen across the kitchen.

While thrilled that the governor seemed open to the task force's ideas, she did *not* want to be its chair, not with everything else that was going on.

She stared at the stack of student papers in front of her, then got up to retrieve her pen.

CHAPTER NINE

Skip sat at the conference room table with a brick-sized lump in his gut.

Kate had acted strange last night. When he'd called around five, to let her know he had an unexpected dinner meeting with a potential client, her voice had sounded a bit off.

But when he'd asked her what was wrong, she'd said she was fine and then changed the subject to the newly resurrected task force. She'd gone on and on about having mixed feelings, since she'd been named the temporary chair. He hadn't wanted to seem like an insensitive husband so he'd listened, but the whole thing had smacked of smoke screen.

When he got home around eight, the kids were still up, but Kate was in bed, curled up on her side with her light out. He'd leaned down and whispered near her ear, "Are you okay?"

She'd ignored him, pretending she was asleep, but he knew she wasn't.

She must be mad at him, he'd concluded. But even then it wasn't like her to just go to bed, without telling him what was going on.

Then this morning, she'd gotten up early and left him a note in the kitchen that she was taking the dog for a long walk. She still wasn't back when he'd left for work, after making sure the kids were fed and headed for their bus stops.

When he'd arrived at the agency, Rose had informed him that Kate would be attending the second part of their staff meeting, but *she* wouldn't tell him what was going on either, saying he should wait for the meeting.

He glared across the table at his partner, who was studiously avoiding eye contact while she wrote on the white board on that side of the room.

Dolph Randolph sashayed in and gave Skip a cheery smile. "Mornin', bossman."

Normally that would set off some good-natured ribbing back and forth. Today, Skip wasn't in the mood.

Instead he distracted himself by trying to remember Dolph's real first name. Had he ever known it? Rose had to know, since she handled the personnel records.

Dolph's slightly rumpled suit jacket would no longer close over a recently acquired paunch, but otherwise he was still fairly lanky. His gray hair and mustache only had a few rusty streaks left in them, indicating his original coloring. Even his bushy eyebrows were completely gray now.

Skip glanced across the table at Mac Reilly. He'd known the man for over a dozen years now, but Mac really hadn't changed much. Then again, he'd looked old at forty—a rugged, weathered, lived-life-hard old.

The man wore his usual uniform of baggy jeans, faded Army-green tee-shirt and, in deference to the cooler weather today, a dark plaid flannel shirt, unbuttoned and hanging open. His feet, in old Army boots, were propped up on the chair next to him.

Kate entered the room. Dolph clambered to his feet. Skip was halfway up when she waved them both back down into their seats.

What's that on her hand?

Mac had not attempted to extract himself from his comfy set-up. Instead he waved. "Hey, sweetpea."

Today, the childhood nickname grated on Skip's already frayed nerves.

"How ya doin'?" Mac asked.

"Not bad, all things considered." Her voice sounded tired.

Some of Skip's annoyance at her melted away. She had been pretty restless last night. Had she gotten any sleep at all?

She looked around the room, as she sank into a chair. "Thanks for delaying the meeting so I could be here."

"Not a problem," Rose said. "Skip and I met with our other operatives first, regarding their assignments. And it gave Dolph time to do some research. Now we'll address Detective Russell's situation." She pointed toward the title she'd written on the white board—*Russell Investigation.*

Dolph leaned forward, shaking his shaggy head. "Judith told me she was gonna pay for our time. However, I think we should do this one *pro bono.* We owe her." He sat back again. "Course it's not my agency. I know you have bills to pay."

Skip flashed back for a moment to a few years ago, when Kate's former boss, Sally Ford, had been kidnapped by a serial killer. Judith had not only let them be part of the investigation, but she'd convinced the FBI agents involved to go along with it. And then there was the time she'd shown up in the nick of time, out in the middle of the Chesapeake Bay at night, along with the Coast Guard and the Baltimore City port police...

Rose cleared her throat, yanking him out of his reverie. "Don't know that we can afford *pro bono.* But we'll give her a decent discount."

Skip nodded. "I'm okay with that."

Rose gestured for Kate to speak. The room was silent as his wife described going to the Browns' apartment again, convincing Wanda Brown to let her talk to the autistic brother of the dead boy, and what the brother had communicated, through tapping and stick figures.

Skip had only known the first part, that she'd gone to the dead boy's home and talked to the mother again.

"I'm convinced that Jared witnessed what happened," Kate concluded, "and that there was someone else in that alley besides the boy and Andy, when the shooting occurred."

"He was the white stick figure," Dolph said, half under his breath, "but there was a black man there too?"

"Not the uniformed officer," Skip said. "He's white."

Kate shook her head. "We can't assume it was a man, or even an adult. It could have been another kid. Jared was getting agitated, so we had to stop asking him questions. Wanda's going to see if he can tell her anything else, and she's going to ask the boy's art teacher to keep an eye out for anything in his artwork. He often draws things to process feelings and such."

Kate turned to Rose. "I'm worried that the boy might be in danger. If the real killer figures out he saw what happened—"

Skip suspected where she was going and put up his hand to cut her off at the pass. "That's a bit of a stretch. There's no reason to believe the 'real killer,'" he made air quotes, since he wasn't totally convinced yet that Andy Russell was innocent, "has a clue about that. Even the police didn't think to try to talk to the boy."

Kate looked at him, her eyes pleading.

What the...?

"Someone may be watching their house," she said. "I, um, was mugged leaving there yesterday."

Something exploded in his chest. He was on his feet with no recollection of having stood up. "Damn it, Kate," he yelled, "you are just now telling me this?"

She was shaking her head. "I'm sorry. I'd already gone through it all with Rose, and I wasn't up for talking about it again. And then having to go through it, yet again, here today..."

Skip turned his glare on his partner.

"Sit down, Skip." Rose's voice was low but firm.

He ignored her.

"I wasn't hurt." Kate quickly turned her hands palm down on the table. "And all he got was the cash from my wallet. But it was what he said—"

"Show me your hands," Skip demanded.

She turned her hands over. The palms were crisscrossed with red lines, a few with scabs.

"That's all. I fell forward on my hands. He grabbed my purse and ran, and I found it and my empty wallet around the corner."

Skip threw his hands up in the air. "You went after him?"

"No." Her tone was now angry. She narrowed her eyes at him. "My phone was in my purse, and my car keys. I was going back to Wanda's to call for help, when I found the purse."

"Why didn't you tell me last night?" he yelled.

She glared at him. "Because I wasn't up for dealing with this," she yelled back. She waved a hand at him. "For you exploding like you do."

Skip froze. Heat flooded from his chest up into his face.

"Settle down, son," Dolph said in a low voice from beside him.

Skip forced himself to unclench his fists. He took a deep breath and sat down.

Kate continued, "At first I assumed the mugging was random, but he told me I should stay away from places where 'I didn't belong.'" She made air quotes.

"And something else was off..." She trailed off, staring down at her hands.

Skip was only half listening, trying to sort out his feelings. How did she always manage to get into messes like this? And what the hell happened to his usual easy-going personality whenever there was a threat to her or the kids?

Kate was avoiding looking his way. He'd blown it. She hadn't been angry before, but now she was.

Vowing he would work on his short fuse where his family's safety was concerned, he turned his attention back to the conversation at the table.

"There's another piece to this," Rose was saying. She gestured toward Dolph.

The older man gathered some papers in front of him, but he didn't look at any of them. Even in his late sixties, Dolph's memory was better than most.

"Tyrell Brown's oldest brother, James Whitmore, Jr. went missing the same day that Tyrell was shot." Dolph tapped the top of the stack of paper for emphasis. "His mom filed a missing person's report, but nobody seems to be paying much attention to what connection there might be between the two events. Seems like way too big a coincidence."

Mac grinned. "And I'm allergic to coincidences," he and Dolph said in unison.

The ripple of laughter around the table eased the earlier tension.

Skip glanced at his wife. The corners of her mouth were quirking upward.

Their eyes met across the table. Hers were still hard with anger.

He gave her a lopsided smile, a nonverbal, temporary apology for losing it.

She pursed her lips, blew air out through her nose. Then she rolled her eyes at him.

He clamped his lips together to keep from grinning. She was getting over her anger. Best not push his luck.

Dolph had actually picked up one of the sheets of paper. "I looked into young Whitmore's background."

Mac held up a hand. "Why the different last name?"

Dolph gave a small nod. "Wanda Brown married James Whitmore, Sr. when she was twenty-five and he was forty-five." He glanced up. "He was white." His eyes returned to the page. "They split shortly after Jared was diagnosed as a toddler. Mom remarried, a Marine, Sergeant Tyrell Brown. He was killed in Afghanistan four years ago."

Skip looked across the table again, caught Kate's pained expression. His own chest ached.

That was a lot of tragedy for one woman to endure.

"All the other kids in the family are squeaky clean," Dolph was saying, "But James Jr. had some scrapes with the law as a juvenile, including a shoplifting charge, for which he got probation and community service, and a grand theft auto charge that was later dropped."

"I thought juvenile records were sealed once the person reached eighteen," Kate said.

Dolph gave her a mock scowl, pretending to be offended that she would question his hacking skills.

"Sorry," Kate said with a slight chuckle in her voice, "I forgot who I was talking to."

Dolph grinned at her, then his face turned serious again. "Jimmy's a student at Towson and has his own place near campus, but his roommates are claiming they haven't heard from him in days. I think we need to find this kid and see what he has to say."

"I agree." Rose pushed up from her chair. She grabbed a marker and started writing on the board again, adding things to the *What We Know* column. "Can you check in with Mrs. Brown periodically, Kate?" she asked, her back to the room. "See if she gets anything else out of the brother?"

Skip's chest tightened. He opened his mouth to protest that she shouldn't go anywhere near that apartment complex again.

Kate shot him a hard look. "Yes, but I'll meet her on campus somewhere. And I was going to ask if we can spare a man or two to keep an eye on them, especially on Jared."

Then she shook her head, as if trying to get the pieces to come together better. "There was something off about that mugger. It's not like that area is all black. It's fairly low-cost housing, or as low-cost as Towson gets, so it attracts a lot of students and support staff, like Wanda, from the university."

"We saw a fair number of whites and Latinos there," Rose said.

Kate nodded slightly. "I think the place he was saying I didn't belong was the Browns' apartment. And something has been niggling at me ever since then." Her eyes glazed over for a moment as her focus turned inward.

Then they cleared. "I got it! His shoes. They were polished dress shoes."

"Hardly what a mugger would normally wear," Mac commented.

You really did miss your callin', darlin', Skip thought, but wasn't about to say out loud. No point encouraging her.

"Exactly," Kate said. "And he was well-spoken, also not what one would expect from a mugger."

"He could be some middle-class dude who's fallen low because of an opioid addiction," Dolph said.

"Maybe. I didn't see much skin. He wore gloves and a ski mask and came at me from behind, but I got the impression he was black. He kind of reminded me of Mrs. Brown's brother. I met him the first time I went over there. He was polite enough, even got his niece and her friends to back off. But I got the impression he thought I was intruding."

Rose added *Check out Wanda Brown's brother* under the second list she had started, titled *What We Need To Find Out*. She pointed to the item. "Dolph?"

"I'll see what I can do," Dolph said. "What's the guy's name?"

"Um, Jake, I think," Kate said. "Sorry, I don't remember his last name."

Dolph leafed through the papers in front of him and groaned. He looked up. "Wanda's maiden name is Johnson."

Rose shook her head. "There'll only be a thousand or two Jake Johnsons in the area. Let's focus on this issue instead, for now." She pointed to number one on the list—*Find older brother, Jimmy. What does he know?*

"What about protection for Wanda Brown and Jared?" Kate asked. "She can afford to pay, but can we give her a discount too?"

Rose looked at Skip, one eloquent eyebrow in the air.

He nodded.

"I can spare a man for today," his partner said. "And the case Manny Ortiz is working on should get wrapped up by this afternoon. Then I can assign him to them."

Kate's mouth curled up into her first full-blown smile of the day. "Manny would be a great choice."

Skip's heart melted at the sight of that smile.

Manny had been Kate's bodyguard on a few occasions, and they shared a special bond. She'd become the fierce protector of Manny's sobriety when the recovering alcoholic had gotten shot last year, during the Strategic Electronics case.

Skip gave a slight shake of his head. She might be infuriating sometimes, but the fact that his wife would go to bat for anybody who needed help was a big part of why he loved her.

Having secured the bodyguards, Kate now needed to see if Wanda would be onboard with the idea.

From her car, she called the math department's number. Wanda was in. When she came on the line, Kate asked, "Are you free for lunch, by any chance?"

A pause. "Yes, but today's really busy. I can only spare a half hour. And I brought my lunch."

"What's the best place to meet you on campus?"

"Freedom Square?" A brick courtyard midway between their buildings.

It was a pleasant day, and the outdoor tables were fairly far apart, providing a good bit of privacy.

"Sounds good. In twenty minutes?" That would put them in the middle of a class period, so fewer students would be wandering around campus.

"Okay."

Wanda was already there when she arrived. They had Freedom Square to themselves.

They exchanged pleasantries as Kate settled onto the opposite seat attached to the metal-mesh table.

Wanda made no effort to remove her lunch from its navy-blue insulated bag. "What's up?"

Kate took a deep breath and plunged in. "My husband's P.I. agency, they also provide bodyguards. I asked them to assign some to you and Jared, if you're willing. I think you're at risk."

Wanda's eyes went wide. "Why do you think that?"

Kate held out her hands, palms up. The scrapes were healing fast, but they were still visible. "I was mugged leaving your place yesterday."

Wanda's mouth fell open. Then she clamped it shut and made a soft growling noise. "So much for it being a safe neighborhood."

"Uh, I don't think the neighborhood is the issue. The mugger was dressed too nicely and talked too smoothly to be a common thug. And he warned me to stay out of places I don't belong."

"What the…?" Wanda shook her head. "I feel like I'm in the Twilight Zone. I take it you didn't see the mugger's face or this conversation would be moot."

"He wore a ski mask."

"How much are these guards gonna cost me?"

Kate quoted the daily rate Rose had given her, which was half the normal fee. But it would cover the actual cost of the guards. The agency wouldn't be out any money.

Wanda slowly nodded. "I can't afford that for long though, even with the GoFundMe money. Maybe a few weeks. It's gonna take longer than that before this cop is prosecuted."

The words *if he's prosecuted* hung in the air between them.

"Um, I'm not sure the cop is the issue either." Kate stopped and sucked in air. "My husband… Look, I need you to promise to keep something confidential."

Her instincts told her this woman was trustworthy, bu she couldn't risk Judith's career and Skip's P.I. license based on instincts. She was, however, pretty sure that Wanda Brown's code of ethics would require her to keep a direct promise.

Again, the woman nodded slowly. "Okay."

"My husband and his agency are investigating what happened, but they already had a client. So they couldn't take your money for that. It would be a conflict of interest. And they'll be in big trouble, if it comes out that they're poking around in what the police deem to be their business."

Wanda snorted. "Sure as heck is my business too."

"I agree. But somebody doesn't like the fact that we're investigating. I think the mugging was a warning."

"Who's your husband's client? The cop who's accused of killing my boy?"

"No, someone else, but I can't tell you who. That's confidential."

Wanda pursed her lips. "And your husband's not backing off because of the mugging?"

"No, although I'm sure Skip would like me to stay out of this from now on."

"Skip?" Wanda's face was still grim, but there was a slight twinkle in her eye.

Kate stifled a snicker. "Yes, that's his nickname. And don't you dare tease him about it, if you ever meet him."

Wanda gave an exaggerated shake of her head. "Never gonna understand white people."

Kate's snicker broke loose. "Wanda, you are a breath of fresh air," she blurted out.

One corner of the woman's mouth quirked up, but then her expression sobered again. "Are you gonna stay out of it?"

Kate hadn't really thought that through, but the answer came quickly. "No, but I'm going to be much more discreet."

"So you think the danger will be over when *Skip* and his people find out what really happened?"

"Yes."

"And what if this cop you know, what if he really did kill my boy?"

Tyrell's image sprang into Kate's mind. A fist squeezed her heart. "Then he'll go to jail for a very long time." The fierceness in her own voice surprised her. She shook her head slightly.

Wanda's eyes had gone wide again. "Why are you so passionate about this?" she said in a soft voice. "It's not your battle."

Kate stared at her for a beat. "Why shouldn't it be my battle? Because I'm white? Because it isn't my kids being shot?" Her voice caught. She swallowed hard. "Kids, and young people, are being killed. It's got to stop."

"And older men too," Wanda said quietly. "And sometimes girls and women."

Kate nodded, struggling to rein in her emotions. "When I see the families on TV, and they've lost a son, a brother, a father... I lost a husband to senseless violence." She choked up again.

Maybe the anniversary of Eddie's death was affecting her more than she thought. Could this be the way that she would finally find meaning in the pain? By stopping at least some senseless deaths. Something shifted inside her chest.

She leaned forward. "Don't tell anybody this just yet, but that task force I'm on, we're working on a plan that I hope we can sell to the governor. It will get the worst of the aggressive cops off the streets, *before* they shoot someone they shouldn't."

Wanda's eyes had gone wide again. "How?"

"It's complicated, and we haven't worked out all the details yet."

The other woman's brow wrinkled, then her lips pressed together. "So, we'll see." Her tone said loud and clear that she thought this was yet another promise from the white folks that would come to nothing.

"Yes, we will, and hopefully soon. It's a concrete plan and I'm positive it will work, if it's implemented properly. And I'm going to do my damnedest to see that it is."

Those last words were out of her mouth before Kate had actually processed them. But she realized she meant it. She had thought her job would be done when the task force produced their final report, but maybe not...

She groaned inside. She was supposed to be getting out from under responsibilities by closing her practice, not taking on some new cause.

"So how's this bodyguard thing work?" Wanda was saying.

"They'll have someone watching your apartment from a car outside, and an operative will follow you and Jared to his school—"

"He rides a bus."

"Then they'll follow the bus and watch outside the school."

"Okay. How do we handle the payment?"

"The agency will bill you when this is all over."

Wanda nodded yet again, and they both rose from the benches. Wanda picked up the lunch bag she'd never opened. "Guess I'll be eating at my desk."

Kate gave her a small smile and started to turn away.

"Kate..."

She turned back.

"Thank you for caring so much."

Kate almost burst into tears. She covered up the urge with a fake laugh. "Tell that to Skip. I suspect he thinks I care too much."

Wanda tilted her head to one side. "Maybe so. But it's refreshing. You don't just talk the talk, you walk the walk."

"Thank you." Kate quickly turned away, before the other woman could see the tears that were finally breaking loose.

It was fortunate there weren't many students around at the moment, because the tears wouldn't stop as Kate walked back to the parking lot where she'd left her car.

Her gut sense was that they weren't about Tyrell or Wanda Brown, though. Inside her head, Eddie's soft baritone echoed, *It's a good cause, my love.*

⟞◆⟝

Dolph blew out a frustrated sigh, as he and Skip meandered through the labyrinth of corridors in the Towson precinct that had once been his professional home. What a totally wasted day.

He'd spent several fruitless hours trying to track down the Jake Johnson who happened to be the brother of Wanda Johnson Whitmore Brown.

And now they had come up empty here. Judith, his former partner, was out of the office. The detectives hanging out in the homicide bull pen were a bit vague about where exactly she was.

And their inquiries in the Missing Persons Division regarding James Whitmore, Jr. had been met mostly with disinterested expressions. Nobody really seemed to care why a twenty-year-old black male hadn't shown up for school or work recently.

When Skip had pointed out that this kid was the older brother of the boy who had recently been shot by a cop *and* he had gone missing on that very same day, one of the detectives said he'd look into the connection. But he hadn't sounded all that eager.

What's wrong with this place? They're going to hell in a handbasket.

"Hey Dolph, wait up!" A voice from behind them.

They stopped and turned.

A slender man, average height, was jogging their way. He wore an impeccably tailored business suit and a big grin split his freckled, pale face, under a cap of closely trimmed hair the color of the Randolphs' cherry dining room table.

Dolph's mind flashed to the *Howdy Doody* TV show he'd watched as a small boy.

"Dolph! How ya doin', man?" The guy stopped in front of them, sticking out his hand.

Dolph shook the hand, trying to place the face.

"Crawley, Pete Crawley," the man said. "I'd just become a detective around the time you retired."

Dolph gave him a forced smile, trying to figure out why that name sounded familiar. He still wasn't recognizing the face.

"Hey, man," Crawley said, "I heard you were looking into the charges against my partner."

Ah, that's where he'd seen the name, on the crime scene log in the police report.

"I'm so glad," Crawley continued. "He's getting a raw deal."

Skip had visibly tensed. "Where'd you hear that?" His tone was carefully casual.

Crawley shrugged. "Around. I don't remember. I guess it was only a rumor."

"So, Andy Russell was your partner," Dolph said, trying to think of a way they could question this guy without confirming that they were investigating. He was coming up blank. "Who're you partnered with now?"

Crawley grimaced. "I'm flying solo for the time being. My former partner had already been reassigned. And I gotta tell you, I'm not fond of being on my own, without someone to cover my back. I hope you all can clear Andy soon, get him back on the job."

Dolph resisted the invitation to confirm that they were working the case. "I hope he gets cleared too. BCPD doesn't need a bad shoot on its record."

Would Crawley know about any enemies Andy might have? He didn't dare ask. If the rumor got confirmed that they were investigating, it wouldn't take long for the brass to connect the dots. Judith would be in water so hot, she'd be cooked in two minutes flat.

Crawley was nodding. "Wish there was something I could do to help?"

"Hey," Skip said, "did I see some vending machines around here? I could use a snack."

Dolph suspected Skip was trying to ditch Crawley, before one of them slipped and said something they shouldn't. But the guy wasn't taking the hint.

"Yeah," Crawley said. "I was headed that way. I'll show you."

Skip and Dolph hung back a little. "Is it just me," Skip whispered out of the side of his mouth, "or is this guy a tad too eager to please?"

"It ain't just you. It's finally coming back to me now. He's a bit of a kiss-up."

They rounded a corner, and sure enough, there were some vending machines.

Skip made a show of examining his choices.

Crawley reached in his jacket pocket and extracted a card. He held it out toward Dolph. "If you think of anything I can do to help."

Dolph hesitated, then took the card. "Sure, well, we're not working this case, but maybe we can call you if we ever need any info."

Crawley's face fell. "Yeah, sure. Uh, see ya around then." He turned and slowly walked away.

"Damn," Dolph whispered to Skip, "he's dying to talk to us, compare notes. What if he knows something that would help?"

Skip gave a slight shake of his head. "We don't dare."

"I know."

Crawley had stopped down the hallway a little ways, near some re-strooms. He was looking back at them.

Dolph sketched him a small wave.

Crawley waved back and moved on around a corner.

"Hey," Skip said, "They've got my favorite, trail mix with cashews."

Dolph looked at the snacks and chuckled softly. "I wouldn't trust anything in those machines, but you go right ahead and risk ptomaine poisoning, son. I've gotta answer the call of nature."

Dolph walked to the men's room and pushed the swinging door open.

He wrinkled his nose as the stench of stale urine and vomit assaulted his nostrils. He'd forgotten how vile the public restrooms in the precinct could be.

Trying to hold his breath, he stepped up to the nearest urinal, intent on doing his business quickly and getting out of there.

He thought he had the place to himself, until he felt movement behind him and caught a whiff of aftershave, not unwelcome as a cover for the less desirable smells. Dolph expected the man to step up to a nearby urinal.

Instead, an arm slid around his neck and yanked his head backward.

What the... His hands flew up, grabbing for the arm that was cutting off his air. A sharp pain erupted in his back.

Heart pounding, his fingers scrabbled at the arm still tight around his throat.

A second sharp pain. His legs went out from under him.

Then darkness.

CHAPTER TEN

Skip had re-examined the contents of the machine. Nothing better than the trail mix, so he fed his money in and punched the appropriate letter and number.

For a moment, it looked like the mechanism was jammed, but it slowly released his purchase.

Munching on the trail mix, he crossed the hall to wait near the men's room door. "You're a braver man than I am, Dolph Randolph," he muttered.

These were the restrooms accessible to the public, and the kind of "public" that frequented police stations wasn't all that high class. By the end of the day, the restrooms tended to be pretty scuzzy.

Then again, he'd been brave, or stupid maybe, to get anything that looked vaguely healthy from the vending machine. He chewed and swallowed a stale cashew, as he searched the small bag for its use-by date. Not finding one, he pitched the bag, still half full, into a nearby trash can.

Dolph had been in there for a while, even for an old man with prostate problems.

Skip waited another minute, then stepped to the door and nudged it open. "Dolph?"

Silence.

"In or out, Bud." A voice from behind him.

He turned to face a fat dude with a shaved head and multiple tattoos. From the odors wafting off his jeans and sleeveless denim shirt, he'd either spent the night in jail or didn't think bathing was a high priority.

Skip stepped aside and made an after-you gesture. He let the door swing shut behind the guy, deciding to give Dolph a few more minutes.

He'd taken one step away from the door when an ear-splitting scream erupted from the men's room.

Shoving the door open, Skip rushed in. The first thing he saw was tattoo dude, backed up against the stalls to the left, his eyes huge and his big paws covering the bottom half of his face.

Skip followed the guy's line of vision.

Dolph lay on the grimy floor in a pool of blood.

Kate had thought the plan might backfire, but not in this way. Edie was balking at going to her grandparents' house for an entire week.

"I've got friends, you know." Her voice was half whiny, half angry. "I wanted to hang out with them some during the break."

Kate's phone rang in her pocket. She pulled it out and glanced at the caller ID. *Rose.* She let it go to voicemail.

The phone still in her hand, Kate held her arms out in a placating gesture—Edie had resisted her efforts to get her to sit down at the kitchen table. "Look, I'm sorry, okay? I should have talked to you first before bringing it up with your grandmother, but now their feelings would be hurt if you didn't go." Secretly she didn't feel all that guilty. If Edie was already annoyed going into the visit....

"I can tell your grandmother that you already had plans for Easter weekend, that I didn't know about." She'd get an earful about her lack of parenting skills from Edith Huntington, but it would be worth it. She wanted to offer her daughter a compromise.

But the girl's face grew redder. "That's just 'cause you want me here for Easter."

"Is that such a terrible thing, to want my family together for a holiday?"

"Connie is going away on Tuesday, through Easter. If I'm gonna hang out with her, it needs to be earlier in the week."

Sheez Louise, who is this child and what has she done with my sweet Edie?

"Okay, then I'll tell her that you can only spend the end of the week with them."

Edie grimaced and opened her mouth, but Kate's phone buzzed in her hand.

She glanced down. A text from Rose.

Check your voicemail ASAP. Dolph's been hurt. Heart in her throat, Kate punched buttons on her phone as she stumbled to the table and sank down into a chair.

She put the phone to her ear.

"Dolph's been injured." Rose's voice was clipped and brusque, her way of holding in her emotions. "Knifed at the police station."

Kate gasped. Her hand flew to her mouth.

"I'm at the scene. Can you go to the hospital, St. Joseph's, as soon as you get this?" Rose's voice became hoarser, a little choked. "Skip's there. He's pretty shook up."

Kate stood up, her mind reeling. "We'll have to finish this later, sweetie. I've got to go."

"Go where?" Edie demanded, hands on her hips.

"To the hospital. Uncle Dolph's been hurt."

The girl's face fell. "Uncle Dolph? What happened?"

"I don't know," Kate lied. She wasn't about to tell her child that Dolph had been stabbed, not until she knew more.

"Can I go?" Edie's voice was now that of the child she still half was.

Her chest tight, Kate stepped over to her. She put her hands on either side of the girl's round face. "Not just yet. Let me see how he's doing, and then you can visit him later, okay?"

Edie stared up at her. "You look worried."

Kate wrapped her in a hug. "I am, but Uncle Dolph's a strong man. I'm sure he'll be okay." She held Edie away from her again. "Keep an eye on your brother for me, and I'll call you as soon as I know more."

Edie nodded, swallowing hard.

<hr />

Kate spotted Skip sitting on a beige couch in St. Joseph's ER waiting room. Knees spread, elbows resting on his thighs, head bent, he was staring at his shoes.

Kate had a disconcerting moment of *déjà vu*. Rob Franklin had sat on a similar couch in this same hospital, almost fifteen years ago, waiting to hear if a hit-and-run driver had succeeded in his efforts to kill Liz.

That driver *had* later managed to kill her Eddie. She shook her head to clear it of the bad memories and sat down next to Skip.

He looked up, his eyes shiny.

"How's he doing?"

"Don't know yet," he said in a monotone. "He's in surgery, to stop some internal bleeding."

"Is Sue here yet?"

"Yeah, she went to make some calls, to their daughters."

Kate tried, and failed, to imagine having to call a grown child to tell them their father had been attacked on the job, was in surgery, might not survive.

Sue Randolph had probably thought her days of worrying were over when Dolph retired from BCPD's homicide division. Private investigating wasn't nearly as dangerous as police work.

But this was the third time one of them had been seriously injured. Mac several years ago, and then Manny last winter, while undercover during that industrial espionage case.

And there'd been more than a few close calls through the years.

"Maybe–" She caught herself.

"Maybe what?" Skip said, his tone still dull.

Maybe you should look for a safer line of work, but she didn't say it out loud. This wasn't the time for that conversation.

"Never mind," she said. "Tell me what happened."

"He was stabbed twice, in the men's room at the Towson precinct. We were there trying to get a line on the older brother, but Judith was out of the office." Skip shook his head. "And Dolph's been out of there long enough now... We struck out."

"Did they catch who did it?"

He shook his head again. "Not a sign of him. But they found the weapon—a jailhouse shiv, a plastic knife filed into a point." He took a deep breath. It came out on a shudder. "Doc said that might've saved him. It wasn't long enough to go in all that deep."

"Can Dolph identify the guy?"

Skip looked at her, his eyes bleak. "He's been out cold since I found him. I should've gone in sooner, before he'd lost so much blood."

She took his hand. Her throat had closed, but she managed to get out, "It's not your fault."

His face sagged and his lips trembled. She wrapped her arms around him and he buried his head in her shoulder. "I can't lose him," he whispered. "I can't."

Kate resisted the temptation to say he wouldn't. There was no guarantee of that. She just held him.

He and Dolph were coworkers and good friends, but the relationship was more complicated than that. Dolph had adopted Skip as the son he'd never had. And he was a surrogate for Skip's beloved father, who had died of cancer way too young.

The clearing of a throat.

Kate looked up.

Rose stood nearby, her posture stiff, her face a stone mask.

She's trying not to lose it.

"Judith's on her way," Rose said. "She wants to talk to you, Skip."

Kate let him go and he straightened, swiping at his eyes with the back of one hand.

"About what?" he said.

"About what happened," Rose said. "She's investigating it herself."

Surprising, and yet not. Judith was a lieutenant in homicide. She didn't normally handle investigations directly, especially when the victim hadn't died.

But Dolph had been her partner, her mentor, for ten years, from the time she had been promoted to detective until his retirement.

"How did the guy get in there without my seeing him?" Skip said, anguish in his voice. "I was only at the vending machine for a couple of minutes, then I went on down the hall to wait for Dolph."

Kate's eyes stung. She swallowed hard, fighting back tears.

"My question is," Rose said, her voice gentle, "how'd he get *out* of the men's room without you seeing him?"

—◆◇◆—

Rob and Liz Franklin had received the bad news earlier from Rose. Now they were sitting down to a simple supper of soup and sandwiches—neither of them had much appetite.

Rob's phone buzzed. A text message from Rose.

Out of surgery but not completely out of danger. Condition has been adjusted to critical but stable. Lost a lot of blood. No damage to vital organs, but one of the knife thrusts glanced off hip bone. Too early to tell if permanent damage to the joint.

The message ended with, *Meeting at the agency in an hour. Come if you can.*

Rob pushed his phone across the table so his wife could see.

Without speaking they both rose and headed for the bedroom for their shoes. They left their dinner, pretty much untouched, on the table.

When they walked into the conference room of *Canfield and Hernandez, Private Investigations*, Rob assumed they were there to provide moral support. That is, until his wife plopped down in one of the leatherette chairs around the table and whipped her laptop out of the oversized purse she carried.

"I know I'm not as good as Dolph, but let me know what you need," she announced to the room full of senior staff, all of whom the Franklins considered friends—their closest friends.

Rob mentally added the absent Dolph and his wife to that list.

That thought kept his mouth shut. He didn't even bother to stick his fingers in his ears, as he usually did when she started talking about her hacking exploits.

"A list of all the lowlifes who got out of jail today," Mac Reilly growled, "or were arraigned and released on bail."

"And maybe anyone that Dolph arrested way back when who just got out of prison," Kate added.

Rose waved her hand in the air. She stood to one side of the table, next to a white board covered with her neat writing. "Judith's going to be looking into all that."

Liz nodded. "How about why you were there, at the police station? Could the attack be related to what you were investigating?"

Rose pointed to an item on the board—*Find older brother, Jimmy. What does he know?*

"He disappeared," Skip explained, "the same day Tyrell was shot. We were checking up on the missing persons case, but we struck out."

Liz made a show of flexing her fingers and poising them over the laptop's keys. "Name?"

"James Whitmore, Jr.," Rose said.

"We got a date of birth?" Liz asked, the keys under her fingertips already clicking softly.

Rose skimmed through a folder on the table in front of her. "August 10, 1998. Dolph found his juvie record already."

"Hmm," Liz said, "there's surprisingly little in the media about him. I'm only finding a couple of articles from last week that even mention him."

"Yeah," Skip said, "it's like his disappearance has been completely eclipsed by his brother's death."

"Which probably wouldn't be the case," Kate said, a touch of bitterness in her voice, "if it were a white boy or the alleged shooter wasn't a cop."

"What do you mean?" Rob said.

Her face was grim. "Everybody's so focused on this as a bad shoot, a white cop jumping to conclusions about an innocent black kid. They're not interested in any details that might confuse that issue. But why did Tyrell's older brother go missing the same day he was shot?"

"Could Russell have been after the older brother for something," Mac said, "and somehow the kid got in the way?"

Kate shook her head. "He swears he wasn't after anybody. He'd just gone off duty when he saw a uniform chasing a kid. He was closer to the kid, so he joined the chase."

"So why was the uniform chasing the kid?" Mac asked.

Rose shuffled through papers again. "Here's the full police report Dolph got his hands on. The uniform said the kid looked like someone there was a BOLO out on."

Skip reached out a hand for the report. "And the BOLO was issued by Russell."

Kate's mouth fell open. "But Andy swears he didn't know the kid. Had never heard of him."

Liz held up a hand. "Wait, here's something. I've been running a general search in the background, of all of BCPD's records. It pulls up everything. Even things that have been deleted."

She looked up, glanced around at all their faces. "Up until about a year ago, James Whitmore, Jr. was registered as a confidential informant with BCPD."

"Hmm, very interesting," Mac said.

"Who was his handler?" Skip asked.

Liz looked down at the screen. "A Detective JJ Walker."

"I remember Walker." Rose walked to Liz and looked over her shoulder. "He was still a patrol officer when I was with BCPD. Black guy, really ambitious. I'm not surprised he's a detective now."

"What's JJ stand for?" Rob asked.

Rose shrugged. "Don't know."

Mac said, "So the question is, why did this JJ make brother Jimmy inactive?"

"And what was the kid informing him about?" Rose leaned down, squinting at the computer screen. "Wait! It's not just marked inactive. The whole record that he was ever a C.I. was deleted."

"Which is why Dolph didn't find it," Liz said. "I didn't use the internal search engine. The program I use is, well, very thorough, designed to pick up deleted items."

And it's probably illegal, Rob thought, but kept to himself.

"Make a screen shot of that, please," Rose said.

Liz gave her a sidelong glance, then confirmed Rob's suspicions. "Um, we can't use it in any official way."

"I know, but we don't want all record of it to disappear somehow. Is there any way to tell how long ago the record was deleted?"

"Probably," Liz said without looking up from her laptop. "But this particular program doesn't produce that information."

"Anything else we can do tonight?" Kate said. She looked beat.

Rose shook her head. "But I'm going to assign a second person to the Browns' apartment, just in case Dolph's attack is related to this case."

She and Kate both glanced Skip's way. He nodded.

Rose turned to Mac. "I'm pulling you off that surveillance case, for tomorrow at least. Take Annette with you and see if you can locate Jimmy Whitmore's friends on campus, and talk to his roommates."

"Sure thing," Mac answered.

"And I'm going to check out this JJ Walker some more," Liz said.

Rob's insides clenched. *She's gonna investigate a cop?* But he managed to keep his mouth shut, reminding himself that his wife knew how to cover her electronic tracks.

"Me too," Rose said. "I'll give him a call tomorrow. Is there any reason why we can't admit that we're helping this kid's mom find him?"

Skip scratched the back of his neck. "I guessed we can say she hired us. That's not poking into I.A.'s case. And it's not unusual for a family to hire a P.I. to search for a missing loved one."

A cell phone rang. Skip reached in his pocket, looked down at the phone he'd pulled out. "It's Sue." He hit a button and put the phone on the table.

"You're on speaker, Sue."

"They've upgraded his condition to serious but stable." Sue Randolph sounded exhausted. "The doctors are confident he'll survive..." She trailed off.

A chorus of air being expelled. Smiles broke out around the table.

"His hip's another story." Sue's voice had turned firm, with something under the surface. Anger?

"He may or may not be able to walk again." A pause. "He's done, Skip. He won't be coming back to work."

The silence stretched out.

"Sue?" Rose said.

Kate shook her head. "I think she hung up."

The relieved smiles disappeared. Nobody made eye contact.

"Let's call it a night, gang," Rose said after a moment.

Several nods, a few murmured goodnights, as they all filed out of the room.

Once out on the sidewalk and out of earshot of the others, Rob asked his wife, "How'd you get into the Baltimore County police computer system that fast?"

She gave him a sideways look. "Do you really want to know?"

"Probably not but tell me anyway. For once curiosity has won out over good sense."

They reached the car. As he unlocked it, she rifled through her purse. He opened her door for her.

She handed him a dollar bill and climbed into the passenger seat.

He went around to the driver's side and got in. "You know I can't testify against you anyway, because you're my wife."

"The dollar's not from me. It's from Judith. You are now officially her attorney."

He raised his eyebrows at her and started the ignition.

"She gave me her user name and password."

Rob had been in the process of putting the car into gear. He jammed it back into park and turned to stare at her. "No way."

"Way," Liz said. "And yes, she does know she could lose her job–"

"And maybe her pension."

"Hon, her training officer is accused of murder, and the man who mentored her as a new detective and was her partner for years has been knifed, almost killed." Liz shook her head. "I don't think her pension is the main thing on her mind right now."

CHAPTER ELEVEN

Kate fought off guilt feelings, as she sat at the kitchen table grading papers. She hadn't gone to visit Dolph today, and it was unlikely she'd be able to take Edie to the hospital this afternoon to see him. She was so swamped right now, what with these essays to grade and now the task force meeting this evening—Amanda had texted that tonight was the only time this week that the majority of the members could come.

Kate had even cancelled her weekly lunch with Rob.

Skip went to the hospital this morning, she told herself. He'd called to say Dolph was doing better and seemed to be in decent spirits.

She blew out air. Who was she kidding? She was actually afraid of running into Sue Randolph. She had this irrational feeling of being responsible for Dolph's attack, even though she knew he was involved more for Judith's sake than because she, Kate, brought Andrew Russell's plight to their attention initially.

No, that wasn't exactly true. It wasn't just guilt that was gnawing at her gut and making it hard to focus on her students' essays—it was more a general restless anxiety, a feeling of being slightly out of control of her life.

How much of this is hormonal?

Maybe some of it, but her life had seemed to go off the tracks more and more in recent years. She felt burned out as a therapist, and while teaching was more fun than she'd imagined, it was also a lot more work.

And every time she turned around, they were involved in some dire situation, because of one of her clients or one of Skip's clients, or now because of one of the cops who had helped them in a previous dire situation.

The current mess was so confusing. It wasn't just a straightforward case of why and how Andrew Russell had ended up holding the gun that shot Tyrell Brown, but why did Tyrell's older brother go missing the same day? And then she was mugged outside the Browns' apartment, with the mugger delivering a cryptic warning, and now Dolph is knifed while at the police station investigating the case?

Her brain felt fuzzy. It felt like the puzzle pieces were on the verge of coming together, if only she could think straight.

Okay, that is hormonal. She was more than ready to be done with these damn perimenopause symptoms that made it hard to sleep, hard to think, hard to figure out how the hell she really felt about things!

Her phone rang, rescuing her from her fruitless reverie. *Wanda Brown* flashed up on the caller ID screen.

She picked the phone up and accepted the call.

After a quick exchange of pleasantries, Wanda said, "Jared's art teacher called. He drew a picture she says we need to see. You wanna come over later. She's sending it home with him."

"Um, that's probably a bad idea, me coming over, that is." Kate brought the other woman up to speed on Dolph's attack, when he and Skip had been asking questions about Jimmy.

"Dear Lord in heaven!"

Kate instinctively crossed herself.

"Somebody's trying to cover their tracks about something," Wanda said.

Kate's mind cleared, and her last shred of doubt about Andy's innocence evaporated. "Yes, and they're trying to be subtle about it, so the cover-up isn't obvious. Everything can be explained away as unrelated circumstances. I was robbed by a random mugger. Dolph was attacked by some pissed off criminal, maybe somebody he once sent to jail."

Despite the dire nature of the situation, a shiver of excitement ran down Kate's spine as she and Wanda bounced thoughts off of each other.

"You think Jimmy's involved in all this?" Wanda asked, a quaver in her voice.

"I think his disappearance must be," Kate said. "It's too big of a coincidence." She caught herself about to ask if Wanda knew her eldest had once been a police C.I.

Liz would be in big trouble if it ever got out how they came by that information.

"Okay, it's one-twenty now," Wanda was saying. "Jared's school lets out at three. I'm gonna call and ask his art teacher to keep him with her instead of putting him on the bus. Can you meet me there?"

Kate looked at the pile of papers in front of her.

Screw it, this is more important.

"Yes," she said into the phone, "and if my husband's available, I'll ask him to bring me. He knows how to spot a tail."

Wanda snorted on the other end of the line. "We sound like something out of a bad spy movie."

Kate answered with a soft snort of her own. "I'll text you when I know what time we can get there."

As she placed the call to Skip, she thought about how Wanda was holding up remarkably well in the face of Tyrell's death—probably because she was on a mission to find out what really happened. But if Jimmy didn't come home, or if something happened to Jared...

Kate shuddered.

Once Skip was on his way to pick her up, she wrote out a note to the kids saying she had to go out for a while, ending with, *We'll bring home pizza for dinner.*

She smiled, imagining both Billy's *Woot!* and Edie's frowning comment, *You know I don't eat carbs.*

<hr/>

Rose was in luck when she called the Towson precinct. JJ Walker was in.

When he came on the line, she said, in a fake perky voice, "Hey, JJ. This is Rose Hernandez. Don't know if you remember me."

A beat of silence, except for a phone ringing in the background. Then a low chuckle. "Sure, I remember you. Short, cute and mouthy."

"Mouthy?" She'd been called a lot of things before, but never mouthy.

"As in you wouldn't keep your mouth shut if you saw something that wasn't right." From his fairly neutral tone, she couldn't tell if he was irritated or was teasing her.

She dropped the perky facade. "Yeah well, that's why I went private. Hey, we've got a missing person case, a James Whitmore, and it's come to my attention that he was a C.I. of yours awhile back."

"Hmm, James Whitmore, lemme think... Oh, yeah, Jimmy. We caught him joyriding in a stolen car. Flipped him as a C.I. in exchange for getting the car's owner to drop the charges. But he never gave us anything all that useful. I think I deactivated his registration a year or so ago."

Rose was dying to ask him if he knew how the record then got deleted, but she couldn't, not without getting Liz in trouble.

"Anything you can tell me about him that might help us find him?"

"Nope. Didn't really know him all that well."

"Okay, thanks for your time."

"No problem. Wish I could've been more help."

<hr />

"This kid's got a long bus ride," Skip said as he drove out I-70 toward the private school that Jared Whitmore attended.

His wife didn't answer. She was busy looking over her shoulder.

"You sure we're not being followed?"

Seriously? He shot her a sideways, you've-got-to-be-kidding glance.

She gave him a small smile. "Of course we're not, but did anyone *try* to follow us?"

He shook his head, as he took the exit for Route 97. "And I didn't see any signs of anyone watching our house, which means if anyone is being watched, it's the Browns."

The school was only a half mile from the highway. His GPS told him to turn right. He swung into an entranceway next to a discreet sign for Spring Valley School. Under the name were the words, *Celebrating the positive and the possible.*

He parked and they climbed out of his SUV.

A short, curvy woman stood by the outside entrance of the square, fieldstone-faced school building. Skip assumed she was Wanda Brown, waiting for them.

Kate introduced them, and Mrs. Brown looked him up and down. "So you're Skip. Aren't you one tall, handsome dude?" She winked at Kate.

Heat spread up his cheeks.

Kate's mouth was hanging open.

Wanda Brown turned to her. "Close your mouth, white girl." Her tone was teasing. "I may be middle-aged and widowed, but I ain't dead."

Kate snickered, but then Mrs. Brown's face crumpled. "Bad choice of words," she mumbled.

Kate grabbed the woman's hand and gave it a quick squeeze.

Skip studiously looked away, and caught Manny Ortiz's eye, where he sat nearby in his car, waiting to follow the Browns home later. His window was closed, so he couldn't have heard the remark. But the sparkle in his eyes said he'd read the body language accurately.

Blatantly ignoring him, Skip strode for the door.

There was a good bit of hoopla to get into the school, the office staff checking with the art teacher, then they all had to show ID and Wanda had to vouch for them.

He was glad to see that security was decent.

They were slapping visitors' name tags on their shoulders, when a slender, thirty-something woman—with light brown skin, a big smile, and a head full of shoulder-length dark braids ending in colorful beads—came down the hall toward them.

She greeted Wanda and stuck out her hand to Kate, and then to him. "I'm Taneka Fields, the art teacher here."

She turned and led them back along the hallway to a spacious class-room. There were only a few desks at one end. Easels were scattered around the rest of the space, along with small tables holding a variety of art materials, from watercolor paint sets to chalk and pencils.

"The students haven't been dismissed yet, but Jared should be here soon. I asked his teacher's aide to bring him here just before the final bell. Do you have any questions in the meantime?"

"Do you use the art as therapy?" Kate asked, "or are you just encour-aging the kids to express their creativity?"

The teacher's smile broadened. "Both. I have a master's degree in art therapy. In Jared's case, he has real talent. I'm hoping I can help him develop that. But art isn't a sideline subject here. We are constantly looking for ways to help the kids communicate. Our policy is to *not* focus on limitations but rather on the kids' talents and interests, and we expand from those talents and interests, using them to help the kids develop as many of the skills as possible that they will need in life."

It could have sounded like a canned speech, straight out of a brochure, but the woman seemed to enthusiastically believe in what she was saying.

And Kate was smiling. "You said Jared has real talent."

"Yes, I'll show you in a moment, but first, Mr. Canfield, can I ask you to sit down." She turned toward a corner of the room. "Maybe over behind my desk. Your size is likely to be overwhelming for Jared, not to mention there are at least two people too many in the room for his comfort level."

"Do you want me to sit down too?" Kate asked.

"Yes, but over here, and Wanda..." Ms. Fields gestured toward a stu-dent desk next to where she had just ushered Kate. "You said he's already met Mrs. Huntington-Canfield, correct?"

"Yes," Kate said, before Wanda could answer. "And please call me Kate. Much less of a mouthful."

"And I'm Skip," he said from his position behind the desk. He, by far, had the most comfy spot, with a full-sized adult desk chair.

In the next minute, it became obvious why the teacher had taken such pains with the set-up. A lanky black teenager entered the room, a middle-aged white woman behind him. At the sight of them, he began flapping his hands in the air and tried to turn back toward the door.

The woman, the aide no doubt, held her ground in the doorway, blocking it, but talking to the boy in a soothing voice. "It's okay, Jared. Your mom's here. See her." She pointed to Wanda.

The boy's eyes darted around the room, landing everywhere but on human faces.

"Jared," Wanda called out, in a firm but kind voice. "Come here, son." She gestured for him to come to her.

The boy complied, walking toward his mother, the aide following, perhaps still not sure that he wouldn't bolt.

"Come sit down, son." Wanda patted the empty desk on the other side of her from Kate. "Jared, do you remember Miss Kate? She was at our house the other day."

The boy's eyes seemed slightly out of focus. He picked up speed, almost running the last few steps and sat down at the desk.

Ms. Fields now had a large piece of white paper in her hands. She walked to the front of Jared's desk and turned it around, showing the other side to him. No sign of recognition in his eyes.

"I'd like to show this to Miss Kate and your mom. Is that okay?"

He looked away from her, seemed to be staring into space, but he tapped a finger twice on the desk.

Ms. Fields stepped to one side and slipped the paper onto the desk in front of Kate.

She looked down at it. First, her expression was confused, then she gasped.

Jared started making strange noises. His hands were flapping again.

Kate slid the paper over to Wanda. Her eyes went wide, as she studied it.

She took one of Jared's hands in hers. "Son, is this back behind our apartment?"

He tapped the back of her hand with his free index finger, twice.

"Is it that last day we saw Bear?"

Jared looked away from her, across the room. But he tapped her hand again, two times.

"Do you know these people?" Wanda gestured toward the drawing.

His face tightened, his eyes scrunched closed. He tapped her hand twice, then once on the desk.

Wanda took a deep breath, and pointed to something on the drawing. "Is this Bear?"

A clear two taps that time.

She pointed again. "Do you know these two people?"

Jared screeched and flapped his arms in the air.

"Okay, son," Wanda quickly said. "Would you like to go back to your regular classroom now? I'll be along to get you in a little while."

He made a fist and banged it on the desk, twice.

The aide stepped forward. "Was that a yes, Jared?"

He looked up at her. Then he stuck out his index finger and poked the desk twice, hard.

Wanda let go of his hand. "Go along then. I'll come get you soon."

He got up and scurried to the aide's side.

She patted his arm. "I'll keep him in the classroom after the bell rings."

"Thanks, Ms. Harris," Wanda said. "We won't be long."

As if on cue, a soft chiming began in the hallway beyond the classroom door. It slowly rose in volume but never got particularly loud.

The aide ushered Jared out the door and closed it behind her.

Skip let out a breath he hadn't realized he'd been holding. He got up and went over to Kate's side. Looking down, he expected to see people, but it was an abstract drawing, all triangles of different sizes.

They were also different configurations, some with equal sides—what was that called? He tried but couldn't resurrect the name from his memories of high-school geometry class.

But most had one side that was shorter. Some were so long and skinny, they looked like daggers. And they were all various shades of brown or tan, with a touch of orange here and there.

Except for a couple of triangles that weren't colored in—they had been left white. And a few small ones that were black.

One of the dagger-like shapes was orange.

Skip had to agree with the boy's art teacher. Jared had talent. The overall effect was intriguing.

"Do you see it?" Wanda asked him. His wife looked up.

He shook his head. It was just triangles.

Kate traced some of the shapes with an index finger. A human figure emerged. The triangle that was the face was medium brown, with its point slightly blunted—the chin. A darker triangle represented a hood on the back of the head.

Skip crouched down and squinted. There were two tiny white triangles in the face, with even smaller black triangles inside of them. A slightly lighter brown triangle under them was a nose. It was the face of a wide-eyed boy.

Other details came into focus. A black triangle on the boy's arm was the hand of another figure standing behind him—taller, also with a brown face, darker than the boy's. It had no features. A darker still triangle gave the impression of a hood, pulled low over the top part of the face.

Two white triangles were the head of another figure, taller than the boy, shorter than the person behind him. Standing a few feet away, an arm extended toward the other two. Several small dark triangles created the shape of a gun in his hand.

The dagger of orange was coming from its barrel.

Skip glanced up at Wanda's face. Her eyes were shiny.

"Can we take this?" he said quietly to the teacher. "It could end up being evidence."

It would have been better to get Judith to come to the school and get it, but he didn't want anything happening to it, nor did he want to draw attention to the school. Hopefully, his testimony would be sufficient to substantiate a chain of evidence.

But what was this evidence of? It showed there was a black person, probably a man, in the alley with the boy and his white shooter. And at the time of the shooting, not later when the uniformed officer arrived or his back-up.

Had that other man shown a weapon? Had Andy Russell shot at him and hit the boy by accident?

Kate tapped his arm. He looked up.

The art teacher was standing in front of them with two large pieces of posterboard, taped together on two sides. "A makeshift portfolio, to keep it from getting messed up," she said.

"Let me take a couple photos of it first." He took out his phone and snapped several shots, some of them close-ups of parts of the drawing.

The teacher then slid the paper in between the sheets of posterboard.

Skip's stomach hollowed out as he considered the implications. "I want to assign a guard to Jared, even in school."

Ms. Fields shook her head. "I doubt the director or his teacher would go along with that. It would be too disruptive to the whole class."

"How about a short female?" Kate said. "Introduced as Jared's new personal aide."

Skip grinned at his wife. "I'll ask if she's willing."

The teacher nodded. "That might work. Some of our kids have one-on-one aides."

Outside the classroom, Wanda Brown stopped, an odd expression on her face. "I can't afford another guard. Maybe I should just keep Jared home."

"The guard will be my business partner," Skip said. "We won't–"

Kate put a hand on his arm, but she was looking at Wanda. "You said Jared's doing so well here. And whoever's doing all this..." she waved her hand in the air, "they've attacked one of Skip's people, a dear friend of ours."

Wanda was watching her intently.

Skip wasn't at all sure what was going on between these two women, but he adjusted the makeshift portfolio under his arm and kept his mouth shut.

"It's personal now," Kate said, "even more than it was before."

Wanda glanced at him, then back at Kate. "I'm paying until the money runs out."

"You got it," Skip said.

———◦———

Billy grabbed a fourth slice of pizza and stuffed a third of it into his mouth.

"Hey!" Edie objected.

"Whadda you care," Billy said around the wad of pizza, "Miss I'm-Only-Eating-The-Toppings."

"Don't talk with your mouth full," Kate said. She resisted the temptation to tell Edie that the three pepperoni slices she'd just devoured probably had more calories than the crust of an entire piece of pizza.

"Why are you worried about your weight?" she said instead. "You're fine."

Edie stuck her nose in the air. "Grandmother says one can never be too careful about what one eats."

Kate hid a smirk. *We'll see how you feel about that after she serves you fish three nights in a row.* Edie hated fish.

"Where'd you go this afternoon, Mom?" Billy asked.

"We went to a special school, for kids who have autism. Do you know what that is?"

"Sure. Some kids at my school have that. Most of 'em are in a special classroom. They don't talk much, and the ones that do, they talk kinda funny."

"How so?" Skip asked.

"Well, this one kid talks pretty good, but he's... I don't know, kind of fake with it."

"Stilted, like he's reading a script for a play?" Kate said.

Billy nodded.

"That's because it's hard for people with autism to interact socially," she said. "They don't know what to say, and they don't pick up on the signals that we all give off for how we're feeling or reacting to things."

"Whaddaya mean?" Billy said around another bite of pizza.

Kate let the bad table manners slide this time. She picked up a piece of pizza, stared at it, and frowned.

"What's the matter?" Billy asked.

She smiled at him. "Exactly. You noticed the look on my face and figured there was something wrong with the pizza. What would the kid at your school say?"

"Probably 'I like pizza' or something dumb like that."

"But you see, that's not dumb to him, because he doesn't get what my expression means. He only sees that I'm eating pizza. He's trying to be sociable, but he's not reading my emotions accurately."

"We've got kids like that at my school," Edie said, in the obnoxious tone she had perfected lately. "They're in the dummies class."

"You mean the special education class," Skip corrected.

Edie shrugged.

Kate wasn't sure if Edie was trying to get a rise out of her, or if her daughter really was that insensitive. She opened her mouth, but Skip held up his hand.

He'd pulled out his phone and was scrolling for something. He turned the phone to Edie. "What do you see?"

She tilted her head to one side as she stared at the image on her father's phone. "Is that from a museum?"

Skip smiled. "You think it's good enough to be in a museum?"

Edie nodded.

Still holding the phone out to her, he said, "Let your eyes go out of focus some."

Edie stared at the phone another few seconds. Her eyes went wide. "Oh my God, it's people!"

Kate stifled the urge to reprimand her for taking the Lord's name in vain.

"What are they doing?" Skip asked.

"It's a black man and his son and a white man is handing them a flower, like the tiger lilies we have out back."

He made eye contact with Kate over their daughter's head.

"It's all in the eye of the beholder," she murmured, but her chest had warmed at Edie's assumption that the drawing represented a gesture of goodwill.

"Do you think the person who drew that drawing is a dummy?" Skip asked.

Edie shook her head slowly, her eyes wary. She suspected this was a trick question.

"It was drawn by a boy who has autism," Kate said. "He can't talk, but he uses his art to communicate."

"Lemme see," Billy demanded.

Skip looked at Kate. She shrugged, figuring it wasn't much more graphic than some of his video games.

Skip held out the phone so Billy could study the drawing.

"It's just a bunch of triangles."

"Let your eyes go out of focus a little," his father instructed again.

Slowly Billy's expression shifted. His eyes widened and his mouth dropped open. "It's a shoot out, from some cop show."

Skip met her gaze again over the kids' heads. A shiver ran down Kate's spine.

CHAPTER TWELVE

Kate would have given anything to get out of going to the task force meeting. It had already been an incredibly long day.

But she sucked it up and went.

Indeed, since she was acting chair, she figured she should get there early, to make sure everything was organized and to greet the others as they arrived, as Ben would normally do.

Ben Horowitz's assistant was a total godsend. Amanda Hudson, a petite blonde in her late twenties, had already placed legal pads, pencils, glasses of ice water and packets of papers at each place around the polished wood table that took up most of the conference room in Ben's suite of offices. The packets contained an agenda for this meeting, the minutes from the last one, and several attachments, including the list of PTSD symptoms that Kate and Cheryl Mendez, the other mental health professional in the group, had developed, and the initial report everyone had agreed on last time.

Amanda had also placed a list of names on top of Kate's pile of goodies at one end of the table.

"Thank you." Kate sighed as she sat down.

Amanda gave her an enigmatic smile and continued prepping a large coffee urn with ground coffee and water. "I ticked off the names of those who will be here tonight. Only three couldn't make it."

Kate scanned down the list. Two of the unchecked names were low-level politicians who had contributed little to the previous meetings.

Unfortunately, Cheryl's name was missing a check mark as well. *Damn!* Her best ally wouldn't be there.

But the Baltimore City police chief would be in attendance. Kate wouldn't have been surprised if he'd bow out, considering that he had a lot on his plate. His force was still dealing with some protests downtown.

Her eyes caught on one of the other names, Jasmine Jackson. An image of the African-American woman's forty-something face popped into Kate's mind. She liked the way Jasmine had spoken her mind at previous meetings, never deferring to the men's opinions unless she actually agreed with them.

"What's Ms. Jackson's background?" Kate asked.

"I believe she is the principal at an inner city middle school."

"Oh lordy, I do not envy her *that* job."

Amanda smiled again, a little more naturally this time. "Me neither."

"How much did you tell people over the phone?" Kate asked.

"Not much, just that the governor asked that the task force reconvene and give him any additional findings as quickly as possible."

"Hmm, do you happen to know what Ben told the governor verbally, when he met with him to deliver our initial report?"

Now Amanda's expression turned sly. "I believe he asked the governor about expanding the parameters of the task force's charge."

Kate smothered a chuckle. Those sounded like Ben Horowitz's own words.

"And do you know what the governor said?"

"No, ma'am, but I can make an educated guess."

Kate nodded. "So can I." Another thought struck her. "Did Ben recommend me as the acting chair?"

"Yes, ma'am."

Okay, now I know what I need to do. Despite her fatigue, Kate felt a lot more grounded than she had when she'd first walked into this room.

The others began to trickle in and she greeted them, then suggested they skim over the minutes from last meeting. "We're not going to read them out loud. I'll explain why once we're convened."

When everyone had arrived, Kate convened the meeting and thanked them for coming out on short notice. "Now to the reason I asked you to read the minutes yourselves. When Ben delivered our initial report, he told the governor that we were considering expanding the focus of our group. That, combined with the governor's rather dramatic call for us to, excuse the expression, get our butts in gear, tells me that time is of the essence tonight."

A chuckle from the sheriff of a rural county in southern Maryland, and the medical doctor, Todd Anderson, smiled.

Kate drew in a deep breath. "I believe the governor wants us to do exactly that, expand our focus to look at how to identify and deal with officers who are at risk of using excessive force or making bad judgment calls that can end in tragedies like the one this month. Especially since at least some of those officers are suffering from PTSD, which is contributing to their anger issues."

The rural sheriff's face was now red, the black Baltimore police chief looked conflicted, and Jasmine Jackson's expression was carefully neutral, except for the upward twitch of one end of her mouth.

"I don't believe," the sheriff drawled, "that we came to a consensus on all of that." The sharp look in his eye belied the easy-going implications of the drawl.

"Which is why we are here tonight," Kate countered. "But personally, I don't see any other explanation for this particular sequence of events than that the governor wants us to pursue this, and give him a plan to prevent more mothers from having to go through what Wanda Brown is now."

Kate cringed a bit inside, since she now believed that Tyrell's death was not the result of a bad shoot by an officer with PTSD. But she wasn't above using the current tragedy to drive this agenda forward.

Joe Lourdin, a county councilman from a western Maryland county, snorted. "And if the plan doesn't work, he'll disavow all responsibility," he said *sotto voice*.

Jasmine Jackson turned to him. "So be it, if he blames failure on us. It's about time somebody tried to do something to stop black boys from being killed."

"Easy for you to say," Lourdin responded. "Your career won't be affected."

He had a point, even if protecting his political backside was all he was interested in. This was the first time Kate had ever heard him speak.

The roundabout way that the governor had delivered his message could mean he was preparing to distance himself from the task force if their plan was a bomb. But they had to try, for all the other black kids out there who might not make it to adulthood otherwise.

"Chief Bourdeau." She was more than ready to get the focus off of herself for a while. "I believe you and Sheriff Thompson had given us the beginnings of a plan for identifying overly aggressive officers, the last time we met. Something about their resisting arrest numbers."

The Baltimore chief cleared his throat. "Overly aggressive officers will likely have higher than normal resisting arrest charges added on to other charges for their collars, uh, their arrests. It's an indication that they are rough and abrasive–"

Jasmine coughed. "Abusive," she muttered.

Kate wondered if there was some history between these two, both employees of Baltimore City.

"They escalate the situation," the chief continued, acting as if he hadn't heard Jasmine, even though she was seated next to him, "instead of de-escalating like they're supposed to, and when the perp gets pissed off and talks or fights back, the officer slaps on the resisting arrest charge."

"In other words," Jasmine said, "they are deliberately provoking the suspect."

The chief turned to her, was quiet for half a beat, then said, "Yes, but some of those men are still basically good cops."

Kate jumped in. "So let me recap. In our initial report, we identified several signs for supervisors to look for, indicators that an officer might be suffering from PTSD." She held up her left hand and ticked off fingers. "First, indicators of nightmares and insomnia—dark circles, dull expression, drooping posture and, obviously, fatigue. Second, jumpiness, easily startled. Third, indicators of excessive anger, such as confrontations with supervisors... Are you getting all this, Amanda?"

Ben's assistant, sitting off to the side, nodded. Her pen flew over the legal pad in her lap. Next to her was a small table which held a state-of-the-art digital recorder.

The other reason Kate hadn't wanted to read the previous meeting's minutes out loud—Amanda was a little too thorough. The minutes tended to include almost every detail of their discussions and had often taken half the meeting time to read and vote to approve.

But now Kate was glad for that thoroughness. And in the next moment, she was even more pleased.

"Yes, ma'am," Amanda said, "and the point was made in the last meeting that angry confrontations with supervisors meant more angry confrontations with the public as well."

Kate resisted the urge to jump up and kiss the young woman. "Note that in tonight's minutes as well under number three."

Dr. Anderson raised a finger in the air. "Excessive alcohol or other drug use."

Kate nodded. Amanda scribbled.

Kate scanned the faces at the table. She knew she was steam-rolling over them some, but she felt an urgency to get this proposal ironed out and approved tonight.

"So now we make those items the first few points on a new list, indicators of officers who may use excessive force, and we add high number of resisting arrest charges to that list. Now, what remedies do we suggest?"

Chief Bourdeau held up a hand in a stop gesture. "As I started to say earlier, some of my better officers can get a little rough sometimes. I don't want my best..."

Kate's tired mind zoned out and flashed instead to one of her favorite TV shows. One of the main characters, Danny Reagan, definitely got "rough" at times, in his efforts to catch the bad guys. But she had trouble imagining him charging someone with resisting arrest, when he had provoked that resistance. Then again, he was a fictional character.

She tuned back in.

"I can't have my people hamstrung," the chief was saying.

"Chief, are you familiar with the show, *Blue Bloods*? Do you think Danny Reagan files resisting arrest charges after he's been 'a little rough,'" she made air quotes, "with a suspect."

Both the sheriff and the chief stiffened in their chairs.

Guess they don't like being compared to a TV drama. She didn't blame them. Skip refused to watch most of the shows she loved.

"Think about it," she said. "Those good but rough cops, you know they're rough with suspects because...?"

A beat of silence. Sheriff Thompson broke it. "Because of the brutality complaints against them."

"Yes, *not* because of their resisting arrest records. Because they're using some excessive force as a means to an end, not because they are getting off on the power or need to vent their PTSD anger."

Thompson and the chief slowly nodded their heads, but Jasmine Jackson leaned forward. "Wait a G-D moment. Are we justifying police brutality as the ends justify the means?"

"No, not at all," Kate said. "But we need to stay focused on the goal here. We are trying to stop out-of-control angry cops from killing unarmed, innocent citizens."

Jasmine sat back in her chair, but she didn't look happy.

Kate quickly added, "Excessive force in general is not what we've been charged to address here. The governor wants a plan to stop senseless deaths."

Another member leaned forward and cleared her throat. Mary Cho was Asian-American, and also a physician. She had never spoken at a meeting, best Kate could remember.

"But don't you think that excessive force in general *is* part of the problem?" she said now in a low, melodic voice.

The city police chief gave her a small smile. Jasmine bristled beside him.

Chief Bordeau said, "Sheriff Thompson, what would you say is an excessive number of brutality complaints in your jurisdiction?"

"Heck, we only get a dozen or so a year for the whole force."

The city chief nodded. "Where as I'm dealing with that many each month, and what's gonna seem excessive for any given officer depends on what part of town he or she is policing. That's why I think the high resisting arrest to over all arrests ratio is a better indicator."

Mary Cho cleared her throat again. "Perhaps we could include excessive brutality complaints as grounds for reviewing whether or not an officer has to go through this program, but leave the definition of *excessive* up to the jurisdiction."

"Chief?" Kate said.

He was quiet for a moment, then he nodded again.

The sheriff chuckled. "Heck, the fear of havin' to go to a shrink might be a better deterrent than the suspensions they usually get when a complaint seems valid."

Dr. Anderson ran a big hand through his blond hair. "So, are those all the indicators we want to list, and what do we suggest the supervisors to do about them?"

"*Obviously,*" Joe Lourdin said with a slight sneer, "refer them for counseling, as the good sheriff implied."

Kate nodded slightly in Amanda's direction.

She nodded back. She was getting this down.

And in the written minutes, snide tones and sneers wouldn't matter.

Chief Bordeau heaved a sigh. "Additional training in how to de-escalate a situation."

He's probably wondering how much that's going to cost.

Sheriff Thompson snorted. "Additional training? The academy I went to hardly gave us any trainin' in that at all, and not much more in how to subdue a perp without drawin' yer weapon. I'd suggest makin' it *substantial* additional training."

Kate nodded at Amanda. She scribbled away.

"Anger-management classes," Jasmine said, then added, "And if they still push the limits?"

Kate took a deep breath. "Termination."

Sheriff Thompson shook his head. "Probation, *then* termination."

Kate paused as if she were thinking about that, and then nodded. She'd planned for probation to be a step in the process all along, but she'd learned from the best, Ben Horowitz. You don't begin negotiations with what you want, you aim higher and "compromise" on what you wanted in the first place.

"And what if they kill somebody," Jasmine said, "while they're on probation?"

Kate had no good answer for that, at least not one that she was willing to say out loud.

But Chief Bordeau was. "Look, innocent lives matter, but our officers also need a chance to recover from the trauma the job inflicts on them. They put their lives on the line every day. They deserve a few chances to straighten themselves out before we cast them aside."

"So these bigoted, aggressive cops get multiple chances?" Jasmine said. "How many chances did Tyrell Brown have?"

Kate held her breath. She wasn't about to get between two black people, one of them a chief of police, on this issue.

Bourdeau sighed again. "It's hard enough to get good people for this dangerous job that pays crap. If we start firing every cop with anger issues without giving them a couple of chances to straighten out..." He trailed off, shaking his head.

Jasmine opened her mouth.

The chief held up a hand. "This isn't the perfect solution, but it's a damned good step in the right direction."

"The chair will hear a motion," Kate quickly said, "to adopt these indicators and courses of action as our plan to present to the governor."

"I so move," Todd Anderson said.

When the chief seconded, Kate was only a little surprised. Sheriff Thompson said, "I second," a beat behind him.

Kate hid a smile. "Ayes?" she asked.

Everyone responded except Jasmine Jackson.

"Nays?"

Jasmine was still silent, her face set in stone.

Damn!

Kate looked at Amanda. "Please note in the minutes that we have seven ayes and one abstention. The motion has carried."

Kate thanked everyone for their time and adjourned the meeting.

Chief Bordeau lingered as the others filed out.

Kate approached him, her hand extended. "Thank you, Chief, for your support."

He shook her hand. "Don't mind Jasmine. She takes it personally when kids get hurt."

"So do I. I'm a mother. ...Um, it's probably none of my business, but do you two have a history?"

One end of the chief's mouth turned up. "You might say that. She's my ex-wife."

At the house, Kate had never been more delighted to rid herself of her tailored suit and pinching shoes and replace them with sweats and her fuzzy slippers.

As she and Skip settled on the sofa for their evening *tête-à-tête*, he said, "Judith's having one of their lab techs work with the photos I took of the boy's drawing, to bring out the details more and see if there's anything else recognizable."

"Good. Did you ask Rose about going undercover at the school, to protect Jared?"

"She wasn't fond of the idea." He stretched, then settled his arm back around her shoulders. "But she'll do it. She wants to find out who attacked Dolph as much as I do."

"So you think it's all related?" She did herself, but she wanted to hear his reasoning.

He nodded. "I might not think that if you hadn't been mugged, and the guy hadn't given you that cryptic warning. We'd probably be assuming it was someone from Dolph's past, a perp he put away. And Judith is looking into that angle."

"Does she have Andy's case now?"

"No, that's Internal Affairs. She can't officially get anywhere near it. She signed the drawing into the evidence room under the case number for Dolph's attack. And by the way, that detective, JJ Walker. Liz couldn't find any dirt on him, either personally or professionally. No blemishes on his record."

"How's Dolph doing?" Kate asked. "I was planning to go see him today, but then I got the call from Wanda." That wasn't totally true, but it appeased her guilt some to assume she would have eventually talked herself into going to the hospital.

"He's a lot better. They're sending him to an orthopedic rehab center for a few days, to evaluate his hip. He may need an artificial one."

Kate's stomach knotted. "Was Sue there?"

"She came in as I was getting ready to leave."

"How was she?"

Skip shrugged. "Pleasant enough. I think she's gotten over blaming us for him getting hurt, but I doubt she's going to back away from making him retire completely."

He squeezed her shoulders. "You can let go of the guilt now about dragging us into this case. Judith told me this afternoon that she would have reached out to Dolph, if I hadn't come to see her that day."

The knot relaxed a good bit in her stomach.

This was probably the best opening she was going to get. She turned slightly toward him in the circle of his arm. "You know, I've been thinking. I'm getting tired of all the chaos and danger in our lives. And I'm really enjoying not feeling the pressure of responsibility for clients so much." The few she had left were winding down, except for a couple of tougher cases that she would have to refer to another therapist.

Skip lifted a questioning eyebrow. "Responsibility?"

"That might not be the best word. I'm not responsible for my clients' lives, I know that. And I have to stay somewhat detached in order to do my job. But when I take on a new client, I'm essentially promising to do my best to help them. I hadn't realized how... *heavy* that felt until the weight lifted some."

She was letting herself get sidetracked. She took a deep breath. "Maybe it's time for you to consider a different profession too."

Both eyebrows went up. "Say what?"

"Sweetheart, neither of us really needs to work. Eddie's insurance money has almost doubled over the last ten years, thanks to his former partner investing it so well for us."

"Yeah, but I'm not ready to retire."

"Not retire completely, maybe just leave the fieldwork to your younger staff."

He gave her a mock glare. "You sayin' I'm old, darlin'?" he drawled.

She sighed and nestled against his shoulder, then lifted her head to kiss his chin. "No, I'm saying I'm getting too old for this adrenaline roller coaster we end up on every few months or so, usually because of something that's happening to one of my clients or one of yours."

She kissed his chin again. His five o'clock shadow tickled her lips. "I'm getting rid of my clients," she said softly. "Maybe you should consider getting rid of yours too."

He blew out air. "I'll give it some thought, but my first reaction is that I'm not ready to give up the agency, or even be tied to a desk. But maybe I can be more selective about what cases I become personally involved in."

They sat in silence for a few seconds. Then he nudged her away slightly so he could look down into her face. "But I've got a lot of friends in law enforcement, as do you. And you've got a lot of former clients. Do you really think, if any of them comes to us in trouble, like Andy Russell did, we'd be able to turn our backs on them?"

She shook her head slightly. He had a point. "Probably not, but I want to try a little harder to keep the chaos of other people's problems out of our lives."

He smiled. "That sounds like a worthy goal."

She frowned.

He tilted his head. "I thought that was what you were hoping I'd say."

"Oh, it is. Just something happened at the task force meeting this evening."

She gave him a synopsis of the plan they'd come up with.

Skip nodded. "I like it. The reality is that cops know which of their brothers in blue are likely to go too far one day, but they won't report them. And the supervisors probably already know anyway. But the blue code keeps anybody from doing anything about it."

"And you think that's okay?" Her voice ended on a slight screech. She clamped her mouth shut.

But Skip didn't seem to take offense. "Yes and no. Of course, it's not okay when innocents get hurt because of an overly aggressive cop. But that blue code is critical. When you're in a tight spot, you can't be worried about whether or not your fellow officers will really have your back. So any officer that rats another out, over anything, is ostracized—"

"Because they can't be trusted."

"Exactly," Skip said. "The plan didn't pass, huh?"

"Oh no, it passed. Almost unanimously."

"So why the frown?"

"One member... I can't totally figure out what's going on with her. She's a black woman, and at first, she seemed happy with the direction things were going, but she ended up being the only abstention. She objected to the next to the last step, the final probation before the officer is fired."

She shook her head. "Turns out the city police chief is her ex-husband. He stayed after to tell me not to worry too much about her reaction..."

When she trailed off, Skip said, "But?"

She turned her whole body to face him. "I can't help wondering if Jasmine felt like her voice wasn't heard tonight, that she was being steamrolled over. Heck, I *was* steamrolling the proposal through, but I wasn't intentionally trying to silence her. And Chief Bordeau agreed with me."

"As did everybody else. You said it was almost unanimous. You're just feeling guilty because you couldn't make everybody happy. Don't ever run for office."

"Why not?"

"'Cause politicians don't get things done by worrying about everybody's feelings. And it will be politicians who decide what parts of your proposal end up in the final program."

That reality check did nothing to improve Kate's mood.

She flopped back against the sofa and blew out air. "We'd be able to sell this much better if there were a bit more diversity on the task force."

"I'm sure the governor would have gone for that, if he'd known y'all were gonna be addressing this particular issue."

"True, he mostly picked people who had expertise and/or a vested interest in the police PTSD issue." Kate shook her head. "But it's gonna be hard to sell this program, with a bunch of mostly white people coming up with a solution for a black problem."

"From where I'm sitting, it's more of a bad cop problem. We white people have the power and the privilege, why not use it to make the world a safer place for kids like Tyrell?"

Kate nodded. "I just wish... I hope I didn't offend Jasmine."

Skip put a finger under her chin and tilted her face up. "Darlin', sometimes you worry a little too much about what's going on inside other people's heads."

"Probably." But she couldn't shake the feeling that she had reason to worry about Jasmine Jackson.

CHAPTER THIRTEEN

On Thursday, Kate had a normal day for a change. After her one morning class, she made considerable progress getting caught up with grading and class prep. She even tossed some healthy ingredients into the crock pot to start their slow simmer for dinner.

When the kids got home from school, she took them to the hospital to see Dolph. He was being transferred to rehab the next day.

He was delighted to see them and was quite animated, despite having to lie on his stomach.

"So, what are you hoping the Easter Bunny will bring this year?" he asked Billy.

The boy scoffed. "I don't believe in the Easter Bunny anymore, Uncle Dolph."

"What? You think the Tooth Fairy brings that basket of goodies?"

Edie giggled, and Kate's heart warmed in her chest.

At four that afternoon, Amanda called with an update. "I've got a rough draft of the report almost done, but Ben called with a list of statistics he wants me to research, to back up what you all are saying in the report."

"That sounds like a good idea." Kate didn't have to ask what statistics. She could make an educated guess.

"Problem is I'm not sure I can get all this done by end of day tomorrow. It might be Saturday before I can get it to you."

"That's okay," Kate said. "I should probably run the final report past the members before we submit it. Send me the rough draft when you have it done and I'll go over it. Then we'll send it out to them while you're doing the research."

"What if they change their minds?"

That had occurred to Kate, but it was a chance she'd have to take. She didn't want to be accused later, if this whole thing blew up in their faces, of ramming the report through. "Even if one or two of them do, we should still have a majority."

"But the governor wanted—"

"Amanda, how slow do the wheels of government normally turn?"

A low chuckle. "Pretty darn slow most of the time."

"Then I think getting a report to the governor one week after he asked for it will be fine. We're aiming for delivery to the State House on Monday, okay?"

"Okay, I'll get this draft to you and get going on the research."

⬦

Friday morning, while Kate was in session with a client, Carol Foster left a message on her office voicemail.

"There've been three more suspicious deaths, in under a month." Carol's voice sounded slightly frantic. "I don't know what to do. Call me, please."

Kate had forgotten all about Carol's concerns. *Okay, this was what we were talking about the other night. Don't get involved, just listen and advise.*

She returned the call. After a brief exchange of pleasantries, she asked, "These deaths, are you sure they aren't to be expected, considering what ailments or injuries the patients had?"

"Maybe. At least nobody else is questioning them, that I know of. You said that woman, the social worker, was going to investigate. Have you heard anything from her?"

"No, but that doesn't mean anything. She wouldn't necessarily get back to me, especially if she found something wrong. She'd want to be discreet about it, not damage the reputation of the hospital."

"That's part of what I'm worried about. I like my job here. I don't want the hospital to be harmed or any more patients..." Carol trailed off.

"Okay, what are your options?" Kate said.

"I've been thinking about that. I don't think my supervisor would do anything. She's the kind who always wants to believe everything is fine. I could go right to the top, to the hospital's CEO. I'm sure if there's a mercy killer running around the hospital, he'd want to know about it."

"Is that what you think is going on? It's not someone's carelessness or malpractice?"

"I don't know. All the cases are patients who were in really bad shape. Most weren't expected to survive, but they were still hanging on. One of them, there was a battle going on among the family, about taking them off life support. But some of them were stable, but in a coma and they had brain damage. One guy's brain was okay but he was paralyzed from the neck down, and I heard his fiancée dumped him."

"You've been looking up their charts?"

"Discreetly, as I can, when my supervisor's not watching." Carol paused, cleared her throat. "Um, I was wondering if maybe I should talk to the social worker myself, tell her what I'm seeing."

"If it gets out, you could lose your job. Whistle-blowers aren't always appreciated."

"I know, but I can't turn a blind eye," Carol said.

"Okay, lemme give you Theresa's cell phone number. I'm sure she won't mind you calling her this evening. She was very concerned." Kate looked up Theresa's number on her own cell phone and gave it to her client.

Former client!

She was silently congratulating herself for not getting involved, when Carol said, "Maybe I should go directly to the CEO. If I'm right, the publicity could be really bad, especially with this one case?"

"Why's that?"

"It was that black boy that the cop shot."

Kate's hand flew to her face. Her insides clenched, as her mind scrambled for the best course of action.

"Kate, are you there?" Carol said.

"Yes, I'm just thinking."

They'd been working under the assumption that someone was trying to cover up something about Tyrell's shooting, that they were trying to discourage her and the agency from pursuing the investigation, without being too obvious about it. The shooter going into the boy's hospital room to finish him off, so he could never tell what really happened—that fit the same pattern.

But what about the earlier suspicious deaths at the hospital? They'd been happening for some time, long before Tyrell was shot.

Kate shook her head. Her immediate problem was keeping Carol safe. If it got out what she suspected about Tyrell's death....

But she might be safer if others knew about her suspicions. There'd be no point in silencing her if she'd already talked. "I think you should definitely call Theresa, maybe not even wait for tonight, but meet with her away from the hospital, where you can't be overheard."

A half-beat of silence. "Why the change in your tone, Kate? It seemed like you didn't think it was so urgent before."

Damn, Carol knew her too well, after all their years of working together.

"Well, I think you're right, that the boy's death does make it a bigger problem. You probably should go ahead and talk to the CEO as well, but be very discreet."

"Of course I will, but I doubt I'll be able to get in to see him today. That will have to wait until Monday."

"Have you told your husband?"

"Yeah, but he thinks I'm over-reacting. Maybe if I tell him you're taking me seriously, he will too."

"Hopefully, but make sure he knows to keep all this to himself for now. And call me if there are any other developments."

"Will do. Thanks for listening, Kate."

They signed off, and Kate flopped back in her desk chair.

"Holy crap!" she said out loud to her empty office.

A surge of emotions erupted inside of her, bringing tears to her eyes. Had Wanda lost her son unnecessarily? Could he have possibly survived and at least been partially okay again? Maybe there would have been brain damage, or motor damage, but...

If there was a mercy killer loose at Dulaney Valley Hospital and they knew Wanda's situation, they might have concluded that she would be better off without a second disabled child.

Kate suspected Wanda would feel differently about that.

Anger burst forward, leading the stampede of jumbled feelings. How dare someone take that woman's child away from her! It wasn't their choice to make.

Her hands clenched, and her mind darted to Dolph. Thank God he was in a different hospital, and was awake and alert.

She knew her mind was spiraling off into irrationality, but she couldn't seem to rein it in.

She called Skip, got his voicemail. "Call me asap," she said. Then she followed up with a text with the same message.

What did all this mean? And how could they even begin to investigate what was happening at Dulaney Valley Hospital?

And what if Tyrell really didn't die from his bullet wound?

———◦———

Over the weekend, Kate managed to convince herself that everything was under control.

Jared's drawing was in Judith Anderson's hands, and she was investigating both Dolph's attack and, unofficially, Tyrell Brown's shooting. Meanwhile, Rose and Manny were keeping Wanda and her kids safe.

And Carol Foster would be okay, once she had shared her observations with Theresa and the hospital's CEO.

Kate and Skip had discussed whether they should tell Judith about Carol's concerns, but Judith would want her name, which would mean Kate was breaking confidentiality. They'd decided to wait, to see what action the hospital took to look into the matter.

Both children had sleep-overs Saturday night, Edie at Connie's house. Kate could relax, knowing that Maria, their former nanny/housekeeper and now Connie's stepmother, would keep a sharp eye on the girls.

Kate and Skip had a taste of what an empty nest would be like. Skip cooked Saturday evening, which meant the meal was not only edible, it was downright tasty.

Afterwards, they set out to make love in the middle of the living room rug, just because they could. This turned out to not be a great idea, when first Peaches the cat and then Toby the dog decided to join in on what no doubt looked like rough-housing to them.

Laughing, they adjourned to the bedroom. Things went much smoother after that.

They went to church Sunday morning. Their pastor, Elaine Johnson, asked about the kids. Skip assured her they were fine, just visiting friends.

They came home with fresh palm branches. Kate tucked them above a picture on the wall of the living room, putting the old ones from last year aside, to be burned along with the remnants of last fall's leaves that were still scattered around their yard. One wasn't supposed to throw Palm Sunday palms in the trash, but burning them was acceptable.

At six that evening, Kate's tranquility was shattered when she and Skip settled into their recliners in the TV room to watch the local news.

The second story was about an "exclusive early report on a proposed plan to combat police shootings of unarmed civilians." A toothy female anchor quickly summarized the basics of the task force's plan, then concluded with, "One party familiar with the proposal, who wishes to remain anonymous, expressed concerns about the plan because, quote, 'already known-to-be-aggressive officers will get multiple chances before they're terminated.'"

Kate felt like she'd been punched in the stomach. "Jasmine Jackson." Those were practically the woman's exact words.

"Hmm," Skip said, "seems like you did have reason to worry about her."

The land line rang in the kitchen. Kate hurried into the room and turned up the volume on the answering machine. She let it answer the call, in case it was a reporter.

Her own voice droned on, inviting the caller to leave a message. Then a male voice she had only heard on TV before.

"Ms. Huntington, this is Governor–"

She grabbed up the phone. "Yes, sir. I'm here."

"Ms. Huntington, did you see this evening's news?"

"Yes, sir. Just now."

"And is that the plan that you were going to propose to me?"

"Yes, sir. More or less. Mr. Horowitz's assistant is preparing the final report."

"More or less how?"

"They kind of skimmed over how we would identify the aggressive officers, for one. And a few other specifics were left out."

"Harumph." A couple of beats of silence. "It's not a bad plan, but now I'll have to implement all of it, whether the state can afford it or not."

"Sir, I have an idea for how to offset some of the costs. Cheryl Mendez and I have talked privately about organizing a group of our colleagues who are willing to provide some *pro bono* hours each month to counsel officers with PTSD and/or anger problems."

"You think you can pull that off?"

"Yes, sir. Nobody gets into our field solely for the money." *Because there isn't much in this profession.* "I think we'll be able to get enough volunteers."

She and Cheryl had conceived the plan partly because they could guess who the state would hire to counsel the officers—the cheapest counselors they could get, i.e. those fresh out of graduate school with no experience, or mediocre ones who were hungry for clients. For this plan to work, the counseling had to be high quality, with specialists in the anger management and PTSD recovery fields.

"Hmm," the governor said. "Get me that report asap."

"Yes, sir. I'll do my best. Uh, and sir, I apologize for this leak. I should have emphasized to the others that we were to keep everything confidential until–"

"No need to apologize, Ms. Huntington. I've heard rumors that one of your task force members has plans to run against me in the next election." The governor disconnected.

Maybe not Jasmine Jackson then, although the anchor's quote sure sounded like her. Who else could it be, and what was their agenda?

Kate shook herself. *Not my job!* She'd let the politicians duke it out. Her job was to get that report into the governor's hands.

"Darlin'," Skip called from the living room. "Your cell phone's buzzing."

She ran out of the kitchen and grabbed it up. A text from Amanda. *Calling u now. I am not a reporter.* Followed by a smiling emoji.

Really? A smiley face?

The phone rang. She fumbled it, then answered the call.

"I saw the news," Amanda said without preamble.

"The governor called me."

"I figured he would. Ben is horrified, by the way."

"It's going to be a lot harder to sell this to the public now. The gov–"

"Already working on it," Amanda said. "The last of the responses came in last night, but I didn't want to bother you with it on a Saturday night. Councilman Lourdin's changed his vote, but he was the only one."

Hmm, maybe he was the leak.

"And Ms. Mendez voted yes," Amanda continued, "so she cancels him out. The other two abstained on the grounds that they weren't there. And Ben's a yes, of course."

Kate breathed out a heavy sigh of relief. Three abstentions, one nay, and eight ayes.

"Do you have a secure email account?" Amanda asked. "Just to be on the safe side."

"Good idea." Kate wouldn't put it past some reporter to try to hack her email account. It had been done before. "Send it to Kate at C&HPI dot com." It was her encrypted email account through Skip's agency.

"I'll send the final draft for you to look over while I proofread it for typos."

"Thank you!"

"Once you approve it, I'll get it to the governor by courier this evening."

Amanda disconnected before Kate could thank her again.

"You're smiling," Skip said.

"If you ever need an office manager for the agency, I can recommend someone." But they'd have to wait until dear Ben either passed away or retired.

By seven-thirty, they had the report on its way.

At nine, the doorbell rang. Skip went to answer, in case he needed to chase the press off the front lawn.

But it was a guy with a florist's name on his hat and a huge bouquet of flowers. "From the State House, sir."

Skip tipped him, took the bouquet and turned to Kate, grinning. "Looks like you came up smellin' like roses, darlin'."

She grabbed the card, searching for the phone number of the twenty-four-hour florist.

"What are you doing?" he asked.

"Passing along the gratitude." She called and ordered flowers to be delivered to Amanda at Ben's office address the next morning.

CHAPTER FOURTEEN

Monday morning, Kate smiled at the memory of the flowers from the governor as she scanned her classroom, looking for heads that were not bent over their tests, for roaming eyes searching for answers on their neighbors' papers.

Then her mind wandered to worries about Carol Foster. She was supposed to meet with the hospital's CEO today. Would he take her seriously?

Kate made a mental note to call Carol later to touch base.

The sound of a trapped bee came from her pocket. A few students in the front row glanced up. They'd all been instructed to turn their phones off, but Edie and Billy were at Maria's house, so hers was on vibrate.

Another quick scan of the unnaturally quiet classroom—those students who had glanced up were now bent over their tests again. She pulled the phone out slightly and peeked down.

A text message from Judith Anderson. *Call my cell phone* was all it said.

Curiosity won out over appropriate test proctoring. She got up and left the room.

Out in the hall, she called Judith.

"Can you come over to the precinct this afternoon?" the detective said without preamble. "I've got the enhancement of that drawing to show you."

"That was fast."

"Yeah, the tech put in a couple of hours over the weekend on it, for free. I think he was kinda fascinated by the idea of an autistic kid drawing something like that." She dropped her voice. "I'm glad he was willing to do that. Andy's I.A. hearing is next week."

"Hmm, it would be better if I could show it to the boy's mother. Actually, it might be interesting to see how he himself reacts to it. Can you email it to me?"

A brief pause. "I don't want it falling into the wrong hands."

Kate gave her the secure email address. "It's through the agency and it's encrypted."

A low chuckle. "Something tells me Dolph was responsible for that."

"Of course."

"Okay, image has been sent. Oh, and I'm officially hiring you as a consultant on Dolph's case, if anyone ever asks."

"Cool. What am I getting paid?"

Judith snorted and disconnected.

Kate smiled to herself.

She felt the need to get back into the classroom, but first she dashed off a text message to Wanda Brown, to see if she could meet her at Jared's school at dismissal time.

<hr />

Less than three days in and Rose was having very mixed emotions about this gig. She really wasn't all that good with kids to begin with, and these kids didn't react as you would expect.

Jared wasn't so bad. He got upset sometimes and flapped his hands, or even yelled nonsense syllables for no apparent reason. But most of the time, he was pretty cooperative.

He seemed to have a lot of passive language and understood most of what she said to him, even if he didn't always acknowledge or react to it.

She had just gotten the boy settled in for his art class when her cell phone vibrated. She pulled it out. Kate, asking for an escort to the school, to meet with the art teacher and the boy's mother.

Kate's text ended with *Sorry for all the cloak and dagger.*

She texted back. *Totally necessary, a boy is dead. I'll set it up.*

The art teacher was glaring at her.

Rose waited until all the kids were occupied with projects and then slipped out of the room. She texted Manny to pick Kate up at two and bring her to the school. There was no need to tell him to watch for tails.

He would.

———◆———

By late morning, Skip had plowed through the most pressing of the paperwork on his desk—with Rose out of the office, his in-box was overflowing. Then he turned his attention to the Tyrell Brown case.

The previous week, Mac and one of their young female operatives had tracked down a half dozen of Jimmy Whitmore's friends on the university's campus. They'd all claimed they hadn't seen him in over two weeks and had no clue where he was.

Skip called Mac, who was on a surveillance case, to run through all of it with him again. He needed to find some thread to tug on. "Did these kids seem to be telling the truth?" he asked.

"Seemed to be," Mac said in his gravelly voice. "We both thought so at the time. And Annette thinks this one girl has a crush on him and was hurt that he hadn't called her or answered her texts."

"What was your take on the girl?"

"She didn't seem no different from the rest of 'em. They all seemed kinda confused and worried. A couple of 'em commented that he was usually more reliable."

Skip decided to trust young Annette's instincts on the crush. As observant as Mac was, he sometimes missed the signs of love.

"What twenty-year-old doesn't have any contact with his friends for over a week?" Skip said. "Every kid under twenty-five these days is either talking or texting on their phones."

A pause, then Mac said, "A very scared kid."

"Or a very dead kid." His chest tightened at the possibility that Wanda Brown had lost another son.

"Dolph had checked his phone records. As of a few days ago, there weren't any new calls since the day his brother died."

"He probably ditched the phone and got a burner."

"Ya know, one kid did say somethin' else. She and Jimmy are in the same psychology class and she said he stopped a lot after class to talk to the teacher. Maybe that prof knows somethin'. Hang on."

The rustle of paper, as Mac rummaged through the pages of his old-fashioned pocket pad. "Her name is Dr. Ramirez," he finally said.

"I'll check it out. You can get back to your surveillance now."

"Much rather be your backup," Mac grumbled. "These insurance scams ain't my favorite cases."

"Potential scams, and they're our bread and butter. I'll call you if I need backup."

———— ◆ ————

At a few minutes after three, Rose and the art teacher sat in the front of the art room, in vaguely uncomfortable silence. They hadn't totally hit it off.

The teacher had set Jared up with drawing paper in the back of the room. The boy seemed absorbed, as he had earlier in art class.

Was he one of those *savants*, who was incredibly talented at one thing, while otherwise unable to negotiate life without a keeper?

"How does this *savant* thing happen, anyway?" she asked the teacher in a low voice.

The woman bristled slightly, or perhaps it was Rose's imagination. "People on the autism spectrum run the whole gamut of intelligence. It's just that they have no way to readily express their intelligence most of the time."

"So Jared could have an IQ of 140, and we wouldn't know it."

"Not for sure. It's hard to test the IQs of children on the spectrum, since they don't perceive things nor communicate the same way typically developing kids do." She paused. Her voice had softened some. "But Jared is very artistically talented, and since that's the only way he can excel and express himself readily, he focuses a lot of energy into it."

Rose nodded, as Kate walked in the front door of the classroom. She moved quietly toward them, watching Jared, presumably trying not to disturb him.

Wanda Brown and a teenage girl, a thinner and lighter-skinned version of her mother, entered the room.

Jared looked up at the girl. His face lit up in a big toothy grin.

The boy's teacher smiled. "And sometimes he communicates just fine." She rose to greet everyone.

Kate introduced Rose to Wanda and her daughter. The girl, Clarissa, had what looked like a permanent sour expression on her face.

Rose didn't think much of it. She was a teenager, after all.

Kate had brought her laptop. Rose watched over her shoulder as she set it up on the teacher's desk and opened her agency's email account. Wanda leaned over Kate's other shoulder. The girl and the teacher stood on either side of their little group, also staring at the computer. Kate clicked on an attachment and a brown abstract image filled the screen.

Rose blinked. It wasn't abstract, at least not completely. Thick black lines outlined three figures, the windows of a brick building behind them, and some trash cans. Thinner black lines delineated details within the figures.

Everything was made up of triangles, in shades of brown, orange and tan, with a few white or black ones. A brown-faced figure stood behind a boy. His hand gripped the boy's arm. The kid looked scared.

A white person faced them, arm extended. Fire shot from a dark brown blob at the end of the arm. Rose squinted. Wait, it was several small triangles forming a pistol.

Kate gasped and pointed at the shoes of the brown-skinned figure behind the boy. They were abnormally large, almost like clown's shoes, and one of the few black objects in the picture. A tiny white triangle rested on the toe of each one.

"Shiny black dress shoes," Kate whispered.

Wanda Brown, leaning over Kate's other shoulder, nodded agreement.

Kate looked up at Rose. "The guy who mugged me, he wore shoes like that."

"You were mugged?" the teacher, Taneka said.

Kate nodded. "And we think it's related. The mugger warned me to stay away from, quote, 'places I don't belong.'"

Rose glanced over at Clarissa. Her eyes had gone wide at the mention of the mugging, indicating it was news to her as well. But she stood with her arms crossed over her chest, legs spread in a defiant stance.

Kate stiffened a little in her chair, then looked back over her shoulder at Wanda Brown. "Your brother has shoes like that."

Wanda's face closed but she otherwise didn't react.

But the teenager reared back. "What? You think Uncle Jake is the only black man who's got good shoes?"

"No, of course not," Kate said, but the girl wasn't listening.

She was stomping toward the back of the room, apparently bent on collecting her brother and leaving.

"Stop, Clarissa," her mother ordered.

The teen slowed but she didn't stop.

"If you get that boy upset, I'm gonna tan your hide, girl. And don't think I can't still do it."

I'll help, Rose thought, but of course didn't say out loud.

Clarissa stopped but kept her back to the adults.

Wanda turned back to Kate, her face stony. "What exactly are you implying?"

"Not a thing. It was just an observation."

Kate rose and gestured toward the teacher's desk chair she'd been occupying. "Why don't you sit and see if any other details jump out at you?"

Wanda Brown gave her a wary look but took the seat. After a moment, her back stiffened, but she said, "Nothing, except that it definitely looks like the alley behind our place."

"You sure there's nothing else?" Kate said in a gentle voice.

Wanda shook her head hard. She looked up at Rose, not Kate. Her eyes were shiny with tears. She pointed to the screen.

Rose leaned forward and squinted at where she was pointing. A series of tiny rusty-red triangles ran down the boy's front, almost invisible against the dark brown of his jacket.

Rose swallowed the lump that suddenly clogged her throat.

"Do you think there's any point in getting Jared to look at this?" Kate asked, her tone implying she hoped they didn't have to.

"That could be a bad idea," Taneka said. "There's a reason why he hides upsetting things in geometric patterns."

They all looked at Wanda. It was her call.

"It'll probably upset him, but finding out what really happened to his brother..." She trailed off, stood and picked up the laptop.

Carrying it to the back of the room, Wanda sat at the desk next to Jared's. She touched his arm, then slid the computer on top of the drawing he was working on.

He stared at the screen and said "Bear," as clear as could be.

Then he flapped his arms and yelled, "No jay, no jay."

"Okay, you're okay," Wanda said, but the boy's agitation grew.

Wanda snapped the laptop closed and removed it from Jared's desk. It took some effort on her part, but she got him back to working on his current drawing.

Then she stood and shuffled over to the teacher's desk, sat down heavily in the chair and let out a sigh. She opened the computer again in front of her but seemed to avoid looking at the image.

Rose cleared her throat. "Who's Jay?"

"Probably himself. We all refer to him as J sometimes around the house."

"Could Tyrell have seen his brother looking out the window?" Rose asked. "And maybe was warning him to get back?"

Wanda shook her head, but then said, "Maybe. Jared sometimes echoes what he hears." Tears had pooled in her eyes.

"Unfortunately," Rose said as gently as she could, "this won't be admissible as definitive evidence of what happened. And it doesn't tell us who the shooter is–"

"It's that white cop, obviously." This from Clarissa, who was now standing in front of the teacher's desk, hands on her hips.

"It's a white person," the teacher said, from behind Rose, "Probably a man."

Kate frowned. "Could be a wo–"

"That's good enough for me," the girl interrupted, crossing her arms again.

Rose took a second to steady her voice. "It doesn't tell us anything more about the shooter, but it does tell us that another person was there, an African-American or Hispanic male most likely."

"Thus says the token brown friend of the white lady."

"Enough, Clarissa!" Wanda said. "Mind your manners."

Rose pretended to ignore them both. "A defense attorney would shred this as official evidence, but it tells us that there was more to what happened than a simple bad shoot." She pointed to the blood trail. "It's unlikely this is an exact representation of what happened either. If the man was standing behind the boy, the bullet would have struck him too."

"And that wasn't where he was hit," Kate said softly, reminding them all, without saying it out loud, that Tyrell had been shot in the head, not the chest.

"So, it's artistic license," Clarissa said.

"Which is fine for art work," Taneka said, "but not so much for evidence."

"Exactly." Rose laid a hand on the mother's shoulder. "Mrs. Brown, please don't take this the wrong way." She used the formal name intentionally, even though the woman had said to call her Wanda. "Just to rule him out, could you check on your brother's whereabouts the day Kate was mugged?"

The police had already checked his alibi for the day of the shooting. It wasn't much of one. He was an electrician, and he'd said he was on the road, between calls, at the time.

The shoulder tensed. Rose removed her hand.

Then the woman seemed to deflate in the chair. "I'll see what I can find out."

Out at the cars, Rose told Manny she'd take Kate home, so he could follow Wanda and the kids.

Kate got into Rose's car and buckled her seatbelt, feeling unsettled and vaguely guilty about the whole interchange they'd just had with Wanda and Clarissa.

"It's not an unreasonable scenario to raise," Rose said, as she started the car. "Uncle Jake could have been the man in that alley. It's behind his sister's place, and he doesn't have a good alibi for that day."

Kate gave her a small smile. "You know me too well. You knew I was feeling guilty about even bringing him up."

Rose shrugged as she pulled her car into line behind Manny. Wanda's car led the parade, with both her kids in it.

"The question is," Rose said, "why would he be in that alley? Did he and some white guy have a beef, and Tyrell just happened to get in the middle. And now Jake can't come forward without admitting to whatever he was doing there?"

"And keep in mind," Kate said, "whatever happened, it went down in just a few minutes, from the point where Andy went into that alley, and the uniformed officer heard gunshots."

"No, from the time the kid went into the alley. You said that was the last thing Andy Russell remembered clearly."

"True," Kate said. "So assuming it wasn't Uncle Jake in the alley, maybe it was some random black guy. He's holding onto Tyrell. Maybe he was threatening him in some fashion and Andy was trying to shoot him, and his feet went out from under him, so the shot didn't go where he was aiming."

Wanda pulled out of the school's parking lot, Manny close on her bumper.

Another car was coming down the road, so Rose had to wait. "You really think you can sell Andy to either Wanda or the people of Baltimore as a hero instead of a bad cop?"

Kate sighed. "Still, there are a dozen possibilities for what that other guy was doing there."

Rose made a noncommittal noise.

By the time they got to I-70, Wanda's and Manny's vehicles were the size of matchbook cars on the horizon. "That woman has a lead foot," Rose commented.

"No wonder Manny didn't let that other car get between them," Kate said, with a slight chuckle.

The car in front of Rose turned off and she accelerated. She took the entrance ramp for I-70, headed toward the Baltimore Beltway.

Rush hour was beginning but the traffic was moving well, traveling at the speed limit or slightly above. But Manny and Wanda were both moving farther away in the distance. They had to be doing at least five miles over the limit.

Kate resisted the urge to say more about the case, letting Rose concentrate on her driving.

The whoop-whoop of a siren behind them. Rose let up on the accelerator. "Damn," she muttered under her breath.

A dark, unmarked car whipped by, lights flashing on its dash.

Rose slowed further as the police car veered into her lane, racing toward Manny's and Wanda's cars. "Uh oh, Ms. Leadfoot is about to get a ticket."

But the unmarked car pulled off just ahead of Manny, where he had pulled over on the shoulder.

A text from Manny flashed up on Rose's Bluetooth screen. *You back there? You got them?*

Rose pushed a button on her steering column. "Text Manny," she instructed her Bluetooth. "Yes, we've got them."

She stayed at a sedate sixty-five, five miles below the speed limit, until they were past the flashing lights of the unmarked car. Then she accelerated, slowly closing the gap between them and the Browns' car in the middle lane.

But other cars kept getting in the way. Rose had to do some weaving in and out. "Keep an eye out for other cops," she told Kate.

"I am."

They were about four cars back when the car in the fast lane, next to Wanda's, veered toward her front fender. She swerved and almost hit a pickup truck that was racing up the right lane toward the next exit.

Kate held a hand to her chest, over her racing heart. She took a deep, calming breath as Wanda moved over into the right lane behind the truck. In the next second, Kate's heart was pounding even harder.

The car that had originally veered into Wanda's lane had *not* gone on down the road as one would expect.

Instead, it was once again riding beside Wanda and edging slowly over.

"Damn!" Rose yelled.

CHAPTER FIFTEEN

Wanda's car slowed. Her right tires went off a little onto the shoulder.

"Hold on!" Rose gripped the wheel and stomped on the accelerator. They surged forward, weaving in and out, until their car was right on the tail of the offending vehicle.

Rose hit the brake, jolting Kate forward against her seatbelt. The horn blared as Rose rode right on the guy's bumper.

At least Kate thought it was a guy. The back window of the car was tinted. She could only make out a vague outline of the driver's head.

"Call Wanda," Rose yelled. "Tell her to keep going, no matter what."

Kate scrambled for her phone. It almost flew out of her hand as Rose's front bumper none-too-gently nudged the back of the car in front.

The outline of the guy's head shifted. He was now looking in his rearview mirror.

Wanda's phone was ringing in her ear. "Hello?" Clarissa's voice, scared.

"Rose says to keep going, no matter what. Tell your mom, even if her car is damaged. And stay on the line with me."

"Okay." The girl's voice was small. Gone was the angry bravado from earlier. She repeated Kate's words to her mother.

Rose was yelling at her Bluetooth screen as she drove, "Call 911." She nudged the guy's bumper a second time.

"What is the address of your emergency?" a disembodied voice said from her dashboard.

"I-70, eastbound, just east of 32. Driver acting very erratic. Either road rage or he's high. He's trying to run another car off the road."

"Your car?"

"No, the one in front of me, but we know the occupants. They're the vic's family in a recent homicide."

"Help is on the way."

The dark car in front of them was now riding alongside Wanda's car. Unfortunately she was hemmed in by an eighteen-wheeler in front of her.

Wanda slowed. The car slowed with her, forcing Rose to ease up on her speed as well.

Kate glanced back over her shoulder. There was no traffic right behind them. People were moving over a ways back, swinging into the far-left lane to get around these slow-pokes in front of them.

"Hit the brake," Rose yelled.

Clarissa yelled the orders to her mother, without Kate having to relay them.

Wanda's front end dipped down as she slowed abruptly.

The dark car slowed and Rose's bumper hit his again, only this time she didn't back off. The screech of metal against metal.

Rose's engine roared as she accelerated and shoved the other vehicle down the middle lane.

The guy glanced over his shoulder. Once the truck had gone on down the road, his car moved toward the right.

Rose stayed with him, bumper to bumper, pushing him into that lane.

Kate looked back. Wanda was keeping her car well behind them. Other drivers were slowing behind her, finally catching on that there was something going on.

The dark car veered off onto the shoulder. Rose let him go there.

"Floor it," Rose yelled. "Get in the middle lane."

Wanda's car shot past Rose's window.

Kate watched out the back window as the dark car's driver's side door swung open.

Rose pulled over behind Wanda and floored it too, throwing Kate off balance. But she thought she'd seen a man get out and raise his arm.

A loud ping.

"What was that?" Kate yelled at Rose over the straining engine.

"Not sure. Might have been a bullet."

A part of Kate's brain had been praying all along. Now it just kept repeating, *On my God! Oh my God!*

She had almost forgotten the phone next to her ear and jumped a little when Clarissa said, "Mom wants to know what to do?"

"What should they do?" she repeated to Rose.

"Keep going, but she can slow down some now."

Kate passed that along.

Sirens behind them.

"Finally," Rose said.

The unmarked police car came up beside them, lights flashing on the dash. The black uniformed officer in the driver's seat pointed to Rose and then to the shoulder.

"Tell Wanda to pull over."

Kate relayed that.

The two cars pulled off onto the shoulder, Wanda's in front. The unmarked police car pulled in behind Rose's car.

Then the officer jogged past Rose's door as she was in the process of lowering her window. "What the–"

Something's off here! Kate threw open her car door and jumped out.

"Lock your doors," she yelled into the phone.

She could barely hear Clarissa repeating her words over the road noise of the traffic that had now resumed its break-neck rush to get home.

The officer had reached Wanda's door. An eighteen-wheeler careened past, not more than three feet away from his back. He jogged around to Clarissa's side and knocked on the window.

The delay had given Rose and Kate time to get to the back end of the car.

"Officer," Rose called out, "that maniac back there tried to run us all off the road."

The officer barely glanced her way. "Miss, I need you to keep your hands where I can see them and step out of the car." He seemed to be directing his words at Clarissa.

Kate couldn't see the girl from where she stood, but Wanda's door eased open. She stepped out carefully, closed the door and edged along the side of the car toward the back where Rose and Kate stood.

Kate was still holding her phone in her hand. She put it to her ear. "Clarissa, you there?" she said quietly.

"Yes."

"Is your mom's door locked?"

"It is now. I just locked it."

"Something is off here. Stay in the car with the doors locked for now."

"Lady, you're just seein' what it's like to drive while black."

Kate ignored her and returned her attention to the officer, who was standing by Clarissa's door, looking undecided.

Rose raised a hand and gestured for him to come back to where they were.

He didn't move for a couple of seconds, then he took a few steps forward.

"What seems to be the problem, Officer?" Kate raised her voice to be heard over the traffic noise.

He stopped next to Wanda's back fender, legs spread, and put his hands on his belt, but his head was down, his eyes shielded by the bill of his hat. "Man back there with a seriously damaged car, says this lady ran him off the road." He put his hand on the fender.

"Well, that's weird," Rose said, "because my car is the one that's banged up." She gestured toward her front end, with its dented bumper and partially caved-in grill.

"He's the one who tried to run *us* off the road," Kate said. "It took some fancy driving for us to turn the tables on him without anybody getting hurt."

The cop waved a hand dismissively. "I need to see your driver's license, ma'am," he said to Wanda, "and I need everyone out of the car, to make sure no one is armed."

Wanda gave a slight shake to her head.

Kate took a step toward the cop. "Officer, that is a very bad idea. The boy in there has autism. One, you will freak him out, and two, he might wander out into the road."

Something was happening to the man's mouth. It twisted to one side. But Kate couldn't see the rest of his face, his hat was pulled so low.

He stepped back a pace and rapped knuckles against the back-passenger window.

The muffled sound of a shriek from inside the car.

"Stop," Kate said, "you're upsetting the boy."

Wanda opened her mouth, but Rose held up her hand in a stop gesture.

"Enough. I'm an off duty BCPD officer and I can see by your uniform that you're Baltimore County as well. Since we're in Howard County at the moment, you are out of your jurisdiction. And you have no right to insist that the boy get out of the car if that would put him in danger."

The cop puffed up his chest and his hand went to his gun holster. "I have that right if I have reason to believe there are guns in the car."

"And you believe that why?" Kate snapped. Her heart was pounding and her stomach queasy. This could all go south so fast.

Rose held up her hand in Kate's direction, but she kept her eyes on the officer. "I repeat, you are out of your jurisdiction."

It had barely registered in Kate's peripheral vision that another vehicle had pulled up behind the unmarked police car.

"What's the problem, Officer?" Manny's voice.

Kate turned partway around. He was trotting toward them, his empty hands out in front of him. She was half relieved, half scared for him, another person with non-white skin that this officer might decide to harass. What didn't make sense was that the officer himself was black.

She turned back toward the cop and her stomach dropped.

His lower face had turned into a growling mask. "This isn't any of your business, mister. Clear out."

"But it is, sir. These are my friends. We were all traveling together when you stopped me."

Kate wondered if they should try to explain about who Wanda was and why they were following her. She caught Rose's eye and raised her eyebrows questioningly.

At that moment, they heard sirens in the distance. The cop's head snapped up and Kate caught a quick glimpse of one eye, before he pulled his hat's bill even lower over his face.

She had seen fear in that eye.

He took two long strides to the back of the car and, turned half away from them, used his shoulder to shove past her and Rose. He grabbed Wanda by the arm. "You're under arrest, for leaving the scene of an accident." He tried to drag her around Rose's car to his own, but Manny blocked his way.

Kate held her breath. They were all dangerously close to the traffic now.

The cop stopped, still hanging onto Wanda's arm.

Manny held his hands up in a confused gesture. "I don't understand, Officer."

"Get out of the way," the man snarled. He jerked and Wanda almost stumbled out into the road.

Manny lunged for her, and the cop swung an arm back, as if to punch him.

Then the sirens were on them and two Howard County police cruisers made a wide arc around them and pulled over in front of Wanda's car.

Now the traffic was moving over, giving them room. *People are probably thinking it's a drug bust or something.*

When Kate turned her attention from the cruisers' blue lights back to the scene in front of her, the Baltimore County cop had let go of Wanda and stepped away from her. She quickly moved back to where Kate and Rose stood between the cars.

Uniformed officers stepped out of both cruisers and flowed back toward them, on either side of Wanda's car. Kate's chest fluttered with anxiety when she noted they were all white, three males and one female.

The woman stopped beside the car and shone a flashlight into the interior. Another wail from the backseat.

"The boy has autism," Rose yelled. "You're upsetting him."

The officer must not have seen anything scary because she joined her comrades.

An older officer, carrying an air of authority, stepped forward. "What's going on?"

Rose said, "That guy back there, on the shoulder. He tried to run this lady off the road." She gestured toward Wanda, then at her own car. "I finally managed to get behind him and turn the tables on him. I used to be on the job, by the way."

Kate looked around to see what the original officer's reaction would be to that. Rose had pretended she was *still* on the job earlier. But she didn't see the black cop.

"What guy on the shoulder?" the Howard County officer said.

"This other policeman, from Baltimore County," Rose said at the same time, "pulled us over and tried to blame... Wait, you didn't see a guy with his rear end bashed in back there?"

Manny gave a slight shake of his head. Kate hoped Rose had seen it.

"Anyway." Rose shrugged. "That's what happened. The guy must have been high or something."

"Or a racist," Kate said. "Could have been a random attack, a hate crime." She didn't believe that any more than Rose believed the guy was high, but apparently the agenda now was to throw up a smokescreen.

The lead officer nodded. The other cops looked on, impassive.

"You wanna file a complaint?" the lead one asked.

"Yes," Rose said, "but I didn't get his license plate number. I was too busy trying to keep from wrecking my car, and keeping him from wrecking Mrs. Brown's here."

Kate let out a breath and sucked in another one. These officers apparently believed their version of events. She looked around, wondering what had happened to the aggressive cop. She glanced back to where his car was.

It was gone.

She caught sight of a dark car pulling past them, the hatless driver looking away. She craned her neck, trying to see the back plate. It was partially obscured with mud. She could only make out two numbers.

Wait! The license plate was muddy but the car was otherwise clean.

Skip had sweet-talked the psychology department secretary into giving him the professor's schedule, and as her final class of the day was letting out, he stood outside her classroom. When the last of the students had filed out, he stepped into the room.

"Ma'am, are you Dr. Ramirez?" he asked the plump, middle-aged, Hispanic woman who was gathering books and papers from the table in the front of the room.

She wore a loose-fitting green dress, and she was giving him a wary look. "Yes."

She would barely come up to mid-torso on him. Yet he suspected from her demeanor that the students didn't give her any grief.

"Has Jimmy Whitmore been in class the last week or so?"

Her eyes lost their sharp edge. Her lips turned down, and she shook her head. "Did you hear about his little brother?"

When Skip nodded, she continued, "I assumed he was needed at home. I sent him an email, expressing my condolences, but I didn't get a reply. I hope he comes back soon. He's missed a lot of material already."

Apparently, she hadn't heard that the kid was missing. "What kind of student w... is he?" He'd caught himself at the last second, about to use the past tense.

"I can't discuss grades, but I can say that he's one of the best in the class."

"How well do you know him?"

"Better than most students. He's come to my office hours a few times. He wants to pursue a career in psychology." Her wary look was back. "Who are you anyway?"

He swallowed a sigh, hating to be the bearer of bad news. "My name is Skip Canfield. I'm a private investigator. Jimmy Whitmore has been missing since the day his brother was shot."

Her eyes went wide. "Oh my!" She patted her chest with her hand. "You don't think he hurt his brother, do you? I thought a police officer was the shooter."

"No, we don't think he was involved in the shooting." Which wasn't entirely true. It had occurred to Skip that Jimmy could be the black guy in Jared's drawing, and that the bullet that struck the boy had been intended for his older brother. "But it seems a strange coincidence that he went missing the same day. Can you tell me anything else about him?"

She took a deep breath and let it out slowly. "The things he's said to me aren't strictly confidential, but still..."

Skip shrugged. "I understand. My wife is a psychotherapist." He didn't mention that she taught part-time in the woman's own department. He didn't want to derail the conversation. "But is there anything you can tell me that might help me find him? I'm afraid he could be in trouble."

The woman shook her head again, but gestured toward the front row of student desks, with chairs attached.

He managed to fit his large frame into one of them as Dr. Ramirez settled in another. She left one empty desk in between them, which he interpreted as a lack of complete trust in him still.

"I know that he was very angry with his father," the professor said, "for leaving the family. He's saving his money to get his last name changed to Brown. He adored his stepfather. He wanted to change his name when he was younger, but his mother was afraid they'd lose the child support payments. But now, his father is dead, and he's on a full scholarship here."

"He's that good a student then?"

"Oh yes, he was starting to apply to graduate schools. I wrote a couple of reference letters for him."

"Did you ever see any sign that he does drugs?"

"Absolutely not. I don't think he even drinks. He told me he'd gotten into trouble a few times, shortly after his stepfather was killed. But then he realized that his mother didn't need any more stress in her life, so he went to his high school counselor. She referred him to a grief counselor with a sliding scale."

"And he got himself straightened out?"

Dr. Ramirez nodded.

Skip plastered on a smile to cover his confusion. This prof's version of Jimmy meshed with what Mac and Annette had gotten out of his college friends, but it didn't jive with what Rose had found out when she'd canvassed the Browns' neighborhood. The neighbors' descriptions of the kid fit better with the getting-into-trouble part.

But it wouldn't be the first time that a black kid had a wild youth and then tried to make a better life for himself. Actually, any kid was at risk of going down the wrong path, especially when things went haywire in their world. He'd seen it often enough in his line of work. Some succeeded in getting themselves back on track, and some didn't.

Skip's chest tightened again. The fact that Jimmy was missing said he was probably now in the latter category.

"Anything else you can tell me about him?" he asked the professor.

She paused for a moment, apparently thinking that over. She shook her head.

He extracted a card from his pocket, handed it to her. "Please, can you let me know if you think of anything else, or if Jimmy contacts you."

She stood and extended her hand. "I certainly will."

He shook her hand, being careful not to squeeze too hard. "Thanks, Dr. Ramirez."

She smiled. "Call me Juanita."

Outside the classroom, Skip checked his phone. He'd missed a call from Kate.

She'd left a voicemail. "Can you pick the kids up at Maria's? I've gotten tied up. We've had some excitement this afternoon. Tell you about it when we both get home."

Skip groaned softly. He suspected *excitement* was code for something that would make his stomach churn.

CHAPTER SIXTEEN

They gathered at Wanda Brown's kitchen table. Whoever was doing this now knew that Kate was still in touch with her, so there was no point in going elsewhere. And Jared needed to be in his own space.

Wanda had gotten him settled in his room, with his drawing pad and colored pencils. Clarissa was in her room across the hall, both doors open so she could keep an eye on him.

"Coffee?" Wanda asked the group. They all shook their heads.

She pulled a pitcher of iced tea out of her fridge and held it up. "I drink this stuff year round."

"I'll take some," Kate said, forgetting that it was sweet tea. She was thirsty enough that she drank it anyway. *Fear'll do that to you.*

Rose opened her mouth, but Manny held up a hand. "First, let me tell you what happened to the guy in the banged-up car. He was backing up on the shoulder, to the previous exit, when I went past him. He must've gotten off the highway before the other police cars came along."

"Did you get a look at his face?" Rose asked.

"Not enough to tell anything but that he was white. He had a baseball cap on, pulled low."

"That cop wasn't a real cop, was he?" Kate asked.

Rose shook her head.

"He did the traffic stop by the book," Manny said.

Manny would know. Like Rose, he had been a police officer himself once upon a time.

Now he was saying, "So the guy may have once been on the job, or he's just watched a lot of cop shows."

"Or he's been stopped a lot himself," Wanda said, her tone a bit caustic.

Manny nodded. "Didn't dawn on me until he was driving away that he was wearing a Baltimore County uniform and we were in Howard County." He grimaced. "That's when I got a sick feelin' in my gut."

"Did you catch his plate number?" Rose asked.

"He was too far down the road before I thought to look. I really thought he was stopping me for speeding. It was a Ford though, but I couldn't make out the model."

"I tried to see his plate while he was sneaking off," Kate said. "It had some mud on it, but two of the numbers were 1 and 5."

"So the whole thing was a set up," Rose said. "The cop stops Manny to get him out of the way, while the other guy goes after Wanda's car, to run her off the road."

Wanda, sitting next to Kate, shuddered. "But they didn't know you and Kate were back there too." She gestured to the pitcher of tea and then to Kate's glass.

Kate shook her head.

"The guy trying to run us off the road," Rose said, "it was a dark plate, not Maryland, unless it's one of those vanity plates. And the car was an older model."

"Did you see a front plate, Manny?" Kate asked.

"There wasn't one. And yes, it was an older car, a Subaru. I recognized the symbol on the front grill. Used to have one—those suckers go on and on forever. Body finally rusted so bad I had to get rid of it."

Kate wriggled her phone out of her pants pocket. "Let me call Judith." She placed the call.

"Anderson." Judith's voice was clipped.

"This is your consultant. Can you check on a couple of vehicles?"

"Um, wait a sec." A half beat of silence, then a door closing. "What's this about?"

"Hang on." Kate put the phone on speaker and laid it in the middle of the table. She identified the people present.

Then Rose succinctly reported on what had happened. She concluded with, "The two cars involved were a dark Ford sedan. Kate caught two digits, 1 and 5. Might be an unmarked police car. The other is now damaged in the rear, dark-colored plate, no plate on front, an older-model black Subaru."

"I'll check them out. You get anything out of the picture?"

"Not much that we didn't already know," Rose said. "That there were two adults, one black, one white, in the alley with the boy. And it was from the day he was shot. He's got blood on his jacket."

"Hmm, I hadn't noticed that," Judith said. "Anything else?"

Rose glanced at Kate, one corner of her mouth twitching. "The black adult has big feet and was wearing dress shoes."

Kate gave her a small smile. *Time to earn my "pay" as a consultant.* "I think, from the body language, that the black person was hanging onto the boy, to keep him from getting away."

"Not my brother then." Wanda's tone was completely caustic now. "He wouldn't put my kids in harm's way."

"Maybe he saw the boy running," Rose said, "and stopped him, figuring the cops would be less likely to hurt him if he wasn't running away."

"But he would've said somethin' after my boy was shot," Wanda said, heat in her voice.

"What if he knew the shooter," Manny said, "and for some reason he didn't want to acknowledge knowing him?"

Wanda rolled her eyes, her lips pressed together in a grim line. "Why you all tryin' to hang this on my kin? You just wanna get that white cop off."

Kate held up her hand. "No, we do this. We brainstorm like this all the time, throwing out ideas to see what fits and what doesn't."

"Gotta go," Judith said from the phone on the table. "I'll let you know what I find out about the cars."

Kate pocketed her phone and opened her mouth to reassure Wanda that they weren't trying to railroad her brother.

Wait! They'd forgotten to tell Judith what Jared had said when he saw the enhanced picture.

Could the boy have been trying to say, "No, Jake?"

"Mama?" Clarissa's voice was that of an upset child.

They all turned.

She stood in the open doorway to the living room, holding a large piece of paper in her hands. Her face was wet with tears. "It could be Uncle Jake."

She took a step into the kitchen and turned the paper around.

This one was all rectangles, or at least four-sided shapes, and all in shades of purple.

Kate squinted and faces erupted all over the abstract drawing, some large, some small. Dark, matching faces with square jaws, a thin, straight line for a mouth, a wide nose, and no eyes. A hood was pulled down over the forehead.

Wanda was shaking her head. She stood up abruptly and crossed the kitchen, plucked a framed photo from the group on the shelf above the sink. She brought it back to the table.

Sitting down, she put it flat in front of her and covered the top half of a man's face with a hand. Then she covered the hood of one of the images in the drawing.

Kate leaned to the side to peer over her shoulder. Her insides went cold at the sight of Wanda's brother's face next to the images. It could be a match.

She spotted something. "Wait!" She pointed to one of the smaller images.

Now that Kate had seen one, she spotted more of them. About half of the smaller images had a hat pulled down over the top of the face, rather than a hood.

It looked a lot like the brim of a police officer's hat.

"It's not Uncle Jake," Clarissa breathed out on a small sob.

"Of course not," Kate said. "You or your mom would have recognized him today, even with his hat pulled down."

Rose pulled her phone out and snapped a photo of the drawing. "I'll send this to Judith. She needs to know that our fake cop is probably the same dude in the drawing of the crime scene."

They said their goodbyes, and Rose and Kate went out to Rose's car. Kate patted its front fender. "Poor baby."

Rose winced. "I hope the insurance company doesn't decide to total it."

I hope the insurance company doesn't raise the agency's rates through the ceiling, Kate thought.

She started to open the passenger door, but Rose waved her toward the back of the car. She pointed to the back fender, near the taillight.

There was a small round hole in the metal. "Remember the pinging noise?" Rose asked.

Kate nodded, her chest tight. "Is that...?"

"Yup. Bullet hole. I didn't want to say anything in front of Wanda and the girl."

"I'll text Judith," Kate said, her voice sounding grim in her ears, "and have her add shooting at us to the list of these guys' crimes."

<hr>

Skip had been right. Kate's news of her day made his stomach churn.

After dinner, they settled on the sofa while the kids did their thing upstairs. By the time Kate was finished telling him about the harrowing drive back from Jared's school, he was regretting eating so much of the pizza she'd brought home.

"Hmm, so y'all are interpreting the boy's new drawing to mean the black dude in the first drawing and the fake officer today are one and the same." He rubbed the stubble on his jaw. "That lets out Jimmy as the black guy in the alley. His mother and sister certainly would have recognized him today."

"Not to mention," Kate said, snuggled up against his side on the sofa, "he would have absolutely no reason to try to fake arrest his mother."

"So these guys were trying to get rid of Wanda or kidnap her?"

"Wanda and/or Jared. Either kill them..." A slight shudder ran through her shoulders, beneath his arm. "Or maybe incapacitate them. Running people off the road isn't a surefire way of eliminating them."

"Maybe they planned to *make sure*, once the car ran off the road."

Kate twisted her head to stare up at him. "By shooting them? Then it wouldn't look like an accident."

"More likely by breaking their necks," he said gently.

She shuddered again, harder. "How did they even find out about Jared's drawings?"

"Good question. We've been keeping a tight lid on that. But maybe they didn't find out about him. Maybe they're just afraid that Wanda or one of the kids saw something that day—something they might not even realize is relevant."

Her eyes went wide. "They'd take out a whole family, just in case? That's pretty ruthless."

"Yup, and everyone would've thought it was a tragic accident."

Kate shook her head. "The fake traffic stop says they knew Manny was guarding her."

"They could've figured that out by tracking her movements for a few days."

And maybe I should put a guard on you. He kept that thought to himself for now. Kate wouldn't like it. But tomorrow morning, he'd ask Rose to assign someone that Kate had never met, someone good at being invisible.

Kate was shaking her head again. "That poor woman cannot lose another child."

"Speaking of her lost children, we're getting conflicting stories on her eldest. In his neighborhood, he hangs with a rough crowd, but his teachers and friends at school describe him as an A student and squeaky clean. Do you know a Professor Ramirez?"

"Only in passing," Kate said.

"Jimmy's apparently talked to her a good bit. She said his earlier scrapes with the law were a reaction to his stepfather dying overseas. And that he got himself straightened out when he realized he was just making Wanda's life more miserable."

Kate turned slightly in the circle of his arm to look up at him again. "Juanita strikes me as a straight-shooter. I'd be inclined to believe her."

"So why is Jimmy still hanging with a bad crowd around his mother's neighborhood? A couple of neighbors said they've seen him with the 'thugs,' as one guy called them, even after he got his own place near campus."

"Maybe they're his friends from way back and he feels a sense of loyalty?"

"I need to look into them more. Maybe they know what happened to him." He paused. "Or maybe they made it happen."

Kate's eyes were shiny. "I pray every day that he's somehow okay, even though I know that's probably not reality."

"Keep praying anyway." He leaned down and kissed her, more as a distraction than anything else.

It worked.

After a second or two, she deepened the kiss. When they finally broke for air, she said, "I've been thinking that an empty nest won't be all that bad. This past weekend was fun."

He grinned. "It certainly was." He lowered his lips to hers again.

<hr />

Kate hadn't scheduled any clients for this week, anticipating that the kids would be home. She'd had an idealized fantasy that they would do some fun things together, but Edie had spent the first three days of spring break with Connie Pérez, and now they had just dropped her off at her grandparents' house.

Kate looked in the rearview mirror at Billy in the backseat. As happened on a regular basis lately, it hit her that he wasn't a little boy anymore. He was growing fast and she suspected he would be Skip's height or taller before he was done. He had her blue eyes, but his straight brown hair was Skip's. As she watched, he skimmed it out his eyes in a practiced move that echoed his father's.

She glanced at the road, then back at the mirror. "How about we stop for ice cream on the way home?" It would probably spoil his appetite for lunch, but what the heck.

He met her gaze in the mirror and broke out a toothy grin "Yay!" he yelled at the top of his lungs.

Okay, in some ways, he was still a little boy.

She shook her head slightly but didn't say anything. She and Skip had spent the last eleven years reminding this boy to use his "inside voice," with minimal results. She figured he'd probably end up as a sports announcer or referee.

Her cell phone rang, with the unique ring she had assigned years ago to Carol Foster.

Relieved but also a tad guilty—she'd forgotten to call Carol last night, understandable after the day she'd had—she hit the button on her steering wheel to accept the call. "Hey, Carol, how'd it go with the CEO?"

"The who?" A male voice.

"Uh..."

"Kate, this is Richard. I'm on Carol's phone."

A chill ran down Kate's spine. "Is Carol okay?"

"Depends on your definition of okay. She's alive."

Kate's stomach twisted. "What happened?"

"She made another suicide attempt, only at work this time."

The chill spread through Kate's body. "When?"

"Yesterday afternoon. They found her in a supply cabinet. She'd–"

"Uh, Richard, I'm not alone." She glanced in the rearview mirror. Billy's eyes were wide, his expression intent.

"I'm in my car, and my son is with me."

A beat of silence. "Okay, well Carol wanted—no, she insisted that I call you. She said she had to talk to you, but she didn't have her phone with her." The tension in his voice was palpable. "I had to go back to her office to find it–"

"Where is she?"

"St. Joseph's but they want to transfer her to Shepard Pratt."

Air whooshed out of Kate's lungs. Thank God it wasn't Dulaney Valley.

"She's fighting that tooth and nail," Richard added.

"Okay, stall them. I'll drop my son off at home and be there as soon as I can." She disconnected.

"Mooom, you promised ice cream!"

"I know, but this is an emergency." She met his gaze again in the mirror. "I'll bring some home with me. And maybe you and Dad and I can go out to dinner tonight, to Chuck E. Cheese."

"Mom," his tone was a little less strident, "I'm too old for Chuck E. Cheese."

"Okay, whatever you want then."

"Pizza."

Kate gave an exaggerated groan. "Two nights in a row."

"Hey," he grinned at her in the mirror, "you said whatever I wanted."

She chuckled as she pulled into their short driveway. "You got your key?"

"Yeah."

"Okay, lock the door behind you and don't answer it for anybody, and if the phone rings, don't let on to the caller that you're home alone."

Billy rolled his eyes and climbed out of the backseat. "I know the drill, Mom."

"Love you," Kate called out.

"You too," he yelled back over his shoulder as he climbed the front porch steps.

"Don't forget to throw the deadbolt!"

He waved a hand in the air without turning around.

She backed out of the drive, turning her car toward St. Joseph's Hospital.

CHAPTER SEVENTEEN

On St. Joseph's psych ward, Kate showed her counseling license and convinced the staff to let her in to see Carol.

Richard must have heard her voice. As she headed down the hall, he came out of Carol's room and met her halfway. "Thank you for coming. She's been pretty hysterical ever since she woke up. Kept insisting that I had to get you here." His tone was apologetic.

"It's okay, Richard. You did the right thing. Tell me what happened."

"She was in a supply room, passed out. She'd apparently broken into the narcotics cabinet and taken an overdose of oxycodone. She had the empty pill bottle clutched in her hand." He paused, took a deep breath. "She's never done anything like–"

"Wait, how'd she end up here?"

"They gave her an antidote and she came to some, enough to insist that the paramedics bring her here. But she was hysterical, kept insisting that she hadn't tried to kill herself. The doc here sedated her last night, to get her calmed down."

He stopped, took a deep breath. Tears pooled in his eyes. "I don't think I can go through this again."

Kate rested her hand on his arm. "Richard, it's not what you think. She really *didn't* try to kill herself."

Richard looked at her like *she* needed to be committed. Kate walked past him. "Let's go talk to her."

Carol sat up in bed, her hair sticking out in all directions, a too-big white hospital gown sagging off of one shoulder. "Thank God you're here."

Kate hurried over and sat on the edge of the bed to give her a hug. Carol clung to her for several seconds. Her shoulders were shaking. "Shh, you're safe now," Kate whispered.

She glanced over her shoulder at Richard. "You look exhausted," she said in a gentle voice.

He stared at her in confusion for a second, then sank into the visitor's chair near the bed. Kate suspected he'd slept there last night.

Carol pulled back, swiping at her eyes with the backs of her wrists.

"Tell me what happened," Kate said.

"I was working at my desk, and I started feeling funny, kind of woozy. I thought about getting a cup of coffee, and that's the last thing I remember before waking up on a gurney." Carol stopped, gulped in air.

"I was still really out of it, but I was terrified. I knew what had happened and knew I had to get out of there somehow. I threw a fit, threatened to sue the hospital if they didn't let me come here, told them my insurance wouldn't cover Dulaney Valley because they weren't a preferred provider for my plan—"

Richard sat forward in his chair. "What? That's crazy. Your plan is *through* them."

"I know. I told them I was on your plan and it was an HMO. I was desperate to get out of there."

Richard opened his mouth, but Kate raised a hand in the air. "Let her finish."

You'll see soon enough why she did what she did.

"But when I got here, the staff didn't believe me when I said I hadn't tried to commit suicide. They must've put something in my IV, because the next thing I knew, I woke up in bed here, with Richard snoring in that chair." She stopped, shook her head slightly.

Kate took her hand and squeezed it. "Take your time. You're safe now."

Carol gave her a lopsided smile. Richard still looked confused.

"I didn't have your cell phone number because my purse and phone were still back at my office, in my desk drawer. I sent Richard to get them and call you..."

"Okay," Kate said, "back up and tell me what happened yesterday, before you felt funny. Did you talk to the CEO?"

Carol shook her head. "When I called on Friday to make an appointment I couldn't get past his admin. She kept insisting that I tell her why I wanted to see him. So yesterday morning, I called her again, from my car in the parking lot, and told her what I suspected. He was out of the building, so the earliest she could get me in to see him was at four."

Kate had been watching Richard in her peripheral vision. His expression had morphed from confused to grim to horrified. "My God, this is about the deaths at the hospital. They tried to kill *you*."

Carol nodded and suddenly she was sobbing.

He struggled out of the low chair and sat down on the other side of the bed, gathering his wife into his arms.

Carol sobbed harder.

Kate wished she could give them some privacy, but she needed to know more. She quietly moved from the bed to Richard's abandoned chair and perched on its edge.

When Carol had quieted, Kate said, "Go back to well before you felt weird. What were you doing?"

"I did my normal morning routine, checked email and such. And then I got a call from the mailroom around ten. I went down to sign for a package for my boss. It was about twenty minutes after I got back that I started to feel funny."

About the time it takes for roofies to kick in.

"Did you have any food or drink at your desk that you left unattended?" Kate asked.

Carol pulled back a little bit in Richard's arms and closed her eyes. After a moment, she opened them again. "I had a donut I'd grabbed earlier but hadn't eaten yet. I ate it after I got back from the mailroom."

Kate thought for a moment. "It has to be the charts that you pulled. Somebody saw you with them or somehow they–"

"It's all computerized now. I called them up on my desktop."

Richard nodded. "Then the killer must have done something to them electronically, flagged them somehow, so that they were notified if anyone accessed those files."

"That's got to be it," Kate said.

A token knock on the half-open door and a middle-aged, balding doctor walked in. "So, how are we doing today, Mrs. Foster?"

He stopped, taking in Carol's additional visitor. "This is a restricted floor."

Kate rose and held out her hand. "I'm Mrs. Foster's therapist. I believe she is stable now. If you feel she's okay physically, she needs to be discharged."

At an earlier point in her career, she would have tread more lightly. Doctors didn't take it well when psychologists questioned their supreme authority in the health professions' pecking order.

But at this point, she didn't really care about the doctor's ego. They needed to get Carol out of the hospital. She was too vulnerable here.

The doctor ignored her extended hand. "What kind of therapist?" His tone was suspicious.

She let her hand drop. "My apologies. I'm Dr. Kate Huntington." She rarely used the doctor title, even though she had a doctorate in counseling psychology. The paradigm she'd been trained in tended to eschew hierarchies and see the therapeutic relationship as a partnership between client and therapist.

But if hierarchal creds were needed here, so be it.

She could tell that the doctor was waffling.

Then Richard jumped in. "Put her down as leaving against medical advice if you want, but I'm taking her out of here."

The doctor stiffened. He glared at Richard and turned to Carol. "Are you a victim of domestic violence, Mrs. Foster?"

Kate didn't know whether to laugh or cry. Bless this doc for thinking of that, but if Carol were a DV victim, that definitely wasn't the way to ask her about it, so abruptly and in front of her husband.

Kate held up both hands. "I assure you, that is not the situation. Can we speak privately for a moment, Doctor?"

After a brief hesitation, he nodded.

Her mind scrambled for the best approach as she grabbed her purse and followed him out of the room.

Once in the hallway, she said, "Look, this is a complicated situation." She pulled her counseling license out of her wallet and handed it to him. "But I can assure you that Mrs. Foster is *not* suicidal. And her husband is not abusing her. However, it is not safe for her to stay here."

She wasn't sure how much more to say or what exactly would convince this guy.

She took a deep breath. "We have reason to believe that someone tried to kill her yesterday. My husband is a private investigator, and he and I are both working in conjunction with the Baltimore County Police Department on this case. I'm an official consultant. You can call Lieutenant Judith Anderson of BCPD to verify that, if you wish."

She made herself shut up, figuring that was more than enough to overwhelm this guy.

His eyebrows had migrated halfway up his forehead. After a few seconds, he said, "I will arrange for Mrs. Foster to be released AMA. I'll get a nurse to bring the forms."

Of course he'd go for AMA—against medical advice—to cover the hospital's ass.

"Thank you." She waited until he had turned and walked away before letting out pent-up air. Thank heavens he hadn't taken her up on her offer. She wasn't at all sure what Judith would have said to the man, since she hadn't yet told the lieutenant, or anyone for that matter, about the possible link between Carol's situation and the Tyrell Brown case.

As she had promised, Kate stopped at the grocery store for ice cream on the way home. She got one tub in Billy's favorite flavor, strawberry, and a chocolate one for herself, and picked up a few other things as well.

As she rounded one end of an aisle, she spotted a man who seemed vaguely familiar. In a faded tee-shirt and sweat pants, he was juggling two boxes of cereal—perhaps trying to decide between them.

She pushed her cart closer, then jolted to a stop. It was Andy Russell.

She was stunned by the change in him. Even right after he'd been accused, he was well-dressed and still taking care of himself.

Her chest tightened. The man before her was a shell of that cop. The thickness around his waist had become a full-blown paunch and his shaggy beard went well past fashionable stubble. Under it, his face was pasty.

He looked up, and recognition dawned on his face as she approached.

"Hello," he said in a dull voice.

"Hi. How're you doing?"

He shrugged, focusing again on the cereal boxes in his hands. "Uh, I hear your husband's agency is looking into the shooting."

She hesitated. "Unofficially."

"I don't have much money right now, but tell your husband, if he manages to clear me, I'll pay him back someday, somehow."

"That's already being taken care of," she said without thinking.

He narrowed his eyes. "What do you mean?"

She took a deep breath. "I mean don't worry about paying for the investigation right now. Just... take care of yourself."

He nodded slowly, his eyes back on one of the cereal boxes. "My kids used to love this crap."

Grateful for safer ground, she said, "How old are your kids?"

He looked at her, his eyes watery. "Thirteen and fifteen. They live with my ex-wife. They won't visit me now. They think I'm a racist."

Oh dear God!

Kate resisted the urge to gather him into her arms. Her own eyes stung.

"This will eventually get resolved, Andy. You just need to hang in there for a while."

He shrugged and threw both boxes of cereal into his cart. He turned it and started to move away. "Tell your husband what I said."

Kate shook her head and hurried to finish her shopping and get home to Billy.

As she stood on her front porch, fumbling one-handed for the keys in her purse, while holding the paper bag of groceries in the other arm, she said a little prayer that both Andy Russell and Carol Foster would be okay.

She'd left her former client in her husband's capable hands, and had promised them that she herself would get in touch with Dulaney Valley Hospital's CEO.

She managed to get the doorknob lock undone, then juggled the key chain, searching for the deadbolt key.

The door drifted open.

CHAPTER EIGHTEEN

Kate shoved her heart from her throat back down to her chest. No point in panicking... yet. But she'd specifically told Billy to lock the deadbolt.

She pushed the door the rest of the way open and looked in. The living room was empty. She speed-walked around the corner into the empty kitchen and put the grocery bag down on the table.

The house was eerily quiet. Now her heart was pounding in her chest. This was not right.

She poked her head in the study and looked around the corner of the L-shaped living room into the TV area. No Billy.

She debated whether or not to call out his name. If there was someone in the house, she would be announcing her presence. But then again, she'd probably already made enough noise to do that anyway.

"Billy," she yelled.

No response.

Creeping up the steps to the second floor, she was wishing she had gotten back to an *Aikido* class or two recently.

The upper hallway was empty. Most of the doors were closed, except for the bathroom, and Billy's room. No noise came from there.

Kate's stomach clenched. Her brain was producing a horror slide show of what she might see when she entered that room. "Billy!"

No answer. She moved to the half open door, took a deep breath and shoved it all the way open.

Billy sat at his desk, back to the door, his computer screen full of fighting aliens.

Air rushed out of Kate's lungs and her body went limp. She grabbed for the doorframe to steady herself.

"Billy!" she yelled louder.

His ears were covered by earphones. He must have put them on out of habit, even though he was the only one home.

Relief shifted to annoyance. She walked over and grabbed one side of the ear phones.

Billy jumped in his chair and whirled around. "Mom, you're home."

"Yes, I am. Why didn't you lock the deadbolt like I told you?"

His face clouded. "I did."

"It wasn't locked."

"I thought I did."

She stifled a sigh and let it go. She pointed to the screen, where the aliens, without Billy at the controls, were now wandering around with stiff movements, randomly firing their weapons into space. "Is that on your approved list of games?"

They did try to control what TV and video games their kids were exposed to, but sometimes it was a losing battle.

"Joey lent it to me."

"Uh-huh." Kate didn't know much about game technology, but she was pretty sure they did not come with a lend feature. "As in, he made a pirated copy for you."

"Uh, I don't know. He just gave me a flash drive with it on it."

"Well, finish your game, then take it off of your computer and give him back the flash drive."

He screwed his face up. "I don't know how to take it off."

This time she let the sigh surface. "Okay, I'll get your father to do it. And if you want a copy of the game you can either earn the money to buy it or put it on your Christmas list next year."

"Next year?" he screeched. "That's months away."

"Then I guess you have some additional chores in your future to earn some money."

She ruffled his hair and left the room.

Down in the study, she got on her own computer and looked up the phone number for Dulaney Valley Hospital. She punched the number into her cell phone and waded through multiple menus, until finally the canned voice said, "If none of these options meet your needs, please hold on the line and someone will be with you shortly."

It took another five minutes to get past not one but three staff members before she got to the CEO's admin assistant, who informed her that his schedule was extremely tight.

"May I ask what this is about?" Her tone said it wasn't really an option to say no.

Kate was prepared for this. She wasn't about to give the real reason, not after Carol's experience.

"I'm on the governor's task force on PTSD in police officers. We're talking to all the heads of the local hospitals about certain aspects of the issue." *There, that sounded official enough, but also vague enough.*

"Can you send a list of questions, please?"

"Um, it's a little more complicated than that. I will need to ask follow-up questions, based on his responses."

"I understand," the woman said with a bit of a strain in her voice. "But if there are figures or other things that need to be researched, it would be much more efficient if I looked those up ahead of time."

Kate shook her head slightly. She had to give it to this woman, she was good at her job—the protector of the realm part of it at least.

Okay, she'd make up some bogus questions and waste the woman's time. "Sure, I'll send you the list. But time is of the essence, the governor is about to announce the new program, and we need to be sure we have everything ready."

A brief pause. "The earliest I can get you in is Thursday at two-thirty, and he will only have a half hour for you."

Kate let out pent up air. She was in. "That should suffice."

The woman gave her an email address to send the questions to. Kate repeated it back to her. "Abritton at Dulaney Valley Hospital dot org. Got it. Thank you, Ms. Britton."

"You're welcome. Have a great day." Ms. Britton nearly sang the last part. Kate suspected she enjoyed doing battle with those peons who dared to try to breach the CEO's castle walls.

Kate disconnected and then debated if she should try other avenues to get through to the powers-that-be at the hospital sooner than Thursday.

Carol wouldn't really be safe until others knew about what was going on.

Skip blew out air. It had been a frustrating morning.

Rose had informed him that they were out of operatives, until she could interview and hire some more. "The only way I can put somebody on Kate is if I pull them off of a paying case, or I can pull Manny from the Browns."

"No," Skip had told her, "don't do that."

They'd finally decided to pull Mac and have him shadow Kate. "He's got plans for tonight, but I'll go over to the house, while you're wining and dining that new client. And if Kate spots Mac, we'll just have to deal with her wrath."

Skip had chuckled. "Nice of you to say 'we' but you know darn well, it'll be me she'll get mad at."

Rose had flashed him a smile.

And now he'd hit a dead end with Jimmy Whitmore. They had the two conflicting images of him, but no one seemed to have a clue where he might be.

He spread his palms out on his desk and tried to think of another approach to finding him. Nothing came to mind.

To the best of their knowledge, the kid didn't have any credit cards in his name. Dolph's initial look at the young man hadn't turned up any credit at all, except a small car loan.

The car itself, a black Toyota Corolla, bought secondhand, was also missing in action. There was a BOLO out on it, but so far it hadn't been spotted anywhere.

Had the kid left town, maybe even the state?

"Speaking of cars," he mumbled to himself. He grabbed his cell phone and punched the speed dial number for Judith Anderson. Maybe she had something on the cars involved in the attempt yesterday to run Wanda off the road.

He got her voicemail.

Hmm... he drummed his fingers on the desk. How could the kid be surviving with no credit? Had he been involved in something with his lowlife friends in the neighborhood and had a stash of cash as a result?

Of course, if he's dead, he doesn't need any money.

But Skip wasn't ready to admit defeat. How else could the boy be getting funds?

Hmm, maybe a fake credit card, or one in a fake name. He grabbed his phone and called Liz.

"Hey, Skip. What's up?"

"Are you still willing to pinch-hit for Dolph on this case?"

"Of course," Liz said. "I don't like people hurting my friends."

"Can you see if a young man recently applied for a credit card in the name of James Brown?"

"Sure, if you've got a year to wade through the results."

He chuckled. "Yeah, hadn't thought about how common that name would be. How about James Whitmore Brown?"

"That narrows the search nicely. I'll get back to you."

"Thanks, Penelope."

Liz's booming laugh erupted in his ear. "I can't believe you're a *Criminal Minds* fan. Isn't that a busman's holiday for you?"

"Pretty much. I watch it under duress. Kate loves it."

Another hearty chuckle. "Sometimes I wonder about that girl. Okay, I'll let you know what I find." She disconnected.

Skip called Judith again, and this time he got her. "Anything on those cars?" he asked, after a brief exchange of pleasantries. Very brief with no-nonsense Judith.

"The unmarked is probably not a real police car, or at least not with BCPD. We've got three with plates that have 1 and 5 in their numbers, and they're all signed out to detectives, not uniforms, and none of them seem to have anything to do with this case. I checked with them anyway. They all said the cars have not been out of their possession since they signed them out.

"The other car—we found an abandoned Subaru, PA plates, in the northern part of the county. Bashed up rear end. It was reported stolen in Lancaster a week ago. It had been wiped clean inside. Except for the backseat. All prints back there belonged to the family who owns it."

Skip let out a small groan. "Hey, when Missing Persons looked for credit in Jimmy Whitmore's name, did they look for James Brown or James Whitmore Brown?"

"Lemme check the MP file." A couple of beats of silence. "Here it is. Nope, just James Whitmore."

"Okay, I've got someone double-checking on that angle for us. I'll let you know if we come up with anything."

"Good," Judith said. "I'm digging deeper on that unmarked car. It could be stolen too—a regular old car decked out with added lights and siren—but I don't think they would have bothered to put mud on the plate if that's the case. I've got feelers out in other jurisdictions' car pools."

"Great. Keep me posted."

Judith disconnected, and Skip paused for a moment to contemplate the irony of the situation. Usually getting the police to share information with private investigators was like trying to get Billy to eat peas.

———◆○◆———

Kate spent another hour attempting to get through to someone in the up-per echelon of hospital administration at Dulaney Valley. She even stooped to lying and pretending to be a reporter about to break a scandalous story regarding the hospital and seeking a comment.

That got her transferred to the public affairs office. She almost told the director there why she was really calling, but she decided against that move for now. If whoever she talked to told the wrong people...

Which brought her around to Theresa Barlow. Who had she told?

She called Theresa's cell phone.

"Hey, Kate, what's happening?" She sounded downright cheerful.

Which kind of plucked at Kate's nerves, but then again, she may not know what happened to Carol.

"Um, did my client come to see you?"

"Yes, she did." Theresa's voice was now appropriately subdued.

"Have you heard what happened?"

"Just that she tried to kill herself. Was she that unstable?"

"No." Kate resisted the temptation to say more—that at times in the past, yes, she'd been that unstable, but not this time. That, however, would be a breach of confidentiality. "It was a set-up, intended to look like that when–"

"Dear God," Theresa gasped. "Someone tried to kill her?"

"Yes. In the course of investigating, have you told anyone what we sus-pect?"

"No one. I just pulled up the charts of all deaths in the hospital due to heart failure in the last year. I've been going through them, eliminating the obvious ones where a heart attack was not unexpected. I've got six so far that could be suspicious."

"Hmm, my client pulled them too." Even though Theresa was on her cell phone, not her desk phone at the hospital, Kate still wasn't comfortable using Carol's name. "I'm guessing that's how whoever's doing this found out that someone was on to them."

A pregnant pause, then, "Okay, that makes sense. You sure she didn't accidentally take too many of her antidepressant pills?"

"I'm sure." Kate wasn't willing to tell her how it really went down. No doubt, the hospital was trying to keep it hush-hush that one of their employees broke into a narcotics cabinet and tried to kill themselves on the hospital property. If Theresa admitted to the wrong person that she already knew that... Well, it would be a long shot, but they could possibly put things together and realize Theresa was in on the investigation.

Sheez, it's exhausting being this paranoid.

"Did my client give you any names?"

"No, I told her not to just yet. I figured if I pulled the same cases that she already suspected, that will tell us that we're really on to something."

"Good thinking," Kate said.

"And now I'm really glad I didn't just pull the cases she suspects. That would have flagged the killer again. Did she get in to see the CEO?"

"No, but I've got an appointment with him. Unfortunately, the earliest I could get in to see him was Thursday at two-thirty."

"Okay, I'll keep you posted on what I find in the files."

"Great."

Kate had no sooner disconnected than the landline rang. She got up from the kitchen table and grabbed the phone from its charger. She groaned when she saw that it was her former mother-in-law.

After a stiff exchange of greetings, Edith Huntington said, "I may have to come over and get some additional clothing for Edie. Does she have something that is appropriate for a formal luncheon?"

Huh?

"I don't think so. I'd have to go through her closet." Edie had once had a black dress, bought for the funeral of a great aunt, but Kate suspected it was now too small.

"Do check on that right away, please. If she doesn't have anything, I'll have to take her shopping tomorrow. The luncheon is Thursday."

"How formal is formal? What kind of luncheon is it?"

"It's the Junior League's annual luncheon to honor the women who have volunteered at the thrift shop, you know the one we run to make money for the homeless. I don't want to miss it, and I thought it would be an excellent opportunity for Edie."

To do what, be bored silly?

Kate shook her head. Edith, no doubt, wanted her granddaughter to be "seen," as a precursor for her to eventually join such things as the Junior League.

Holy crap, I hope she isn't thinking of a coming-out party.

Then she told herself to get a grip. Edie was definitely not debutante material, and if her grandmother tried to force that on her, she would be guaranteed to run the other way.

A big grin spread across Kate's face.

Edith sniffed on the other end of the phone line. "And on the subject of clothing, you really should have taught her by now to respect her clothes. She throws them all over the place. I told her to pick them up off the floor, and the next time I went in her room, they were in a heap on the chair!"

Kate's grin grew wider, but she pressed her lips together to resist responding to the criticism. Instead, she said, "I'll go look right now in her closet, and call you back in a few minutes."

Once Kate had dutifully rummaged through Edie's closet and had called her mother-in-law back with the negative results, she sat down again in the kitchen to grade some papers.

When she put her phone down on the table, she accidentally hit the photo icon. An image of Jared Whitmore's latest drawing came up.

She picked the phone up and scrolled back to the crime tech's enhancement of the first drawing. Pouring over it to see if she'd missed anything was much more fun than paper-grading—actually most things were more fun than paper-grading. After a half-dozen or so papers, even scrubbing a toilet seemed enticing.

Kate closed her eyes for a moment and visualized the view from Wanda's kitchen window. As alleys went, it wasn't horrible. A few trash cans, but mostly the pavement of the alley itself and sidewalks on both sides. And the back walls of the apartments facing the next street over. Did the backs of the buildings also alternate brick-front and stucco veneer?

She looked at the photo again. Apparently so. On one side, the background had more reddish-brown triangles, while the other side had more yellowish-brown ones. The brick wall versus the stucco one.

The boy and the other figure holding onto his arm were in front of the red brick section, the shooter in front of the stucco.

Wait, then why were there two red brick sections just above the shooter's head?

She stared at the image for a few seconds. Maybe there was a patch of stucco missing there, letting the brick underneath show through.

Or–

Her phone rang, making her jump in her chair.

Why am I suddenly a bundle of nerves?

She laughed at herself. Might be because she was in the middle of not one but two murder investigations, where people were still being threatened.

The phone rang again. The caller ID said *Judith Anderson.*

"Can you come down to the precinct?" the lieutenant asked before Kate could even say hello.

"Uh, sure. What's up?"

"I need you to listen to some voices and see if you can identify your mugger's."

A jolt of adrenaline ran through Kate's body—excitement with a frisson of fear. "You have a suspect?"

"Yes, ma'am." Judith's voice sounded excited as well, a rare occurrence.

CHAPTER NINETEEN

Kate was still rattled by finding the front door so poorly secured when Billy was home alone. The rankest amateur of thieves could pop a doorknob lock. She'd watched Skip do it once or twice.

So she brought Billy with her to the Towson precinct, figuring he'd get a kick out of seeing the inside of a real police station.

She made sure her car was locked before they walked away. At a few minutes after five, the parking lot was bustling with workers and officers headed home. But most of them would be gone by the time she and Billy came out.

Just because you're paranoid... Her brother Jack's voice, teasing, as he'd loved to do when they were kids.

Better safe than sorry, she countered with one of their mother's favorite sayings, usually uttered when she was making them take a jacket or sweater they didn't think they needed.

Billy broke into her nostalgic thoughts. "Why can't I have some special time with my grandparents?"

She put an arm around his shoulders. "I think we can arrange that for this summer, but don't be assuming your sister is having a great time."

He turned his head and looked up at her, his eyes wide. "Why wouldn't she be? They're rich. She's probably getting three desserts and lots of toys and..." He trailed off.

"You know your sister would not eat three desserts. She might not even eat one, with her new no-carbs rule." Kate paused, choosing her words.

"And her Grandmother Huntington isn't an easy person to get along with."

Billy's expression was still skeptical as they reached the precinct's door. Kate pulled it open for him to go through, then stopped in the lobby. "Tell you what, I'll bet you ten dollars toward that video game you want that your sister will call and want to come home early."

He narrowed his eyes at her. "I haven't got ten dollars."

"Okay, your end of the bet is that you have to rake up the remnants of last fall's leaves out back, and without complaining or having to be reminded."

He nodded.

Kate grinned at him. "Prepare to get some blisters from that rake, young man."

Judith found a uniform to keep an eye on Billy. "Come on," the officer said. "I'll show you some mug shots. Wanna see what bad guys look like?"

"Yeah," Billy said, his eyes round.

Judith chuckled, then her face sobered as she ushered Kate to a small conference room. A male technician was fooling with some electronic equipment.

She and Judith took seats at the end of the table opposite the equipment. "We're recording this whole session," Judith said, "for validation later."

Kate nodded.

The guy clicked his mouse and a red light came on at the top of his monitor.

Judith identified herself and Kate, then noted that the witness had agreed to having the session recorded.

"Now I want you to listen to each of these," Judith said, "all the way through. Then we'll play them a second time and see if you can identify your mugger."

Kate nodded again, and Judith raised an eyebrow to the guy.

He moved his mouse and clicked.

A male voice filled the room. "Learn to stay out of places you don't belong."

Kate opened her mouth. Judith held up her hand and nodded to the guy. He moved the mouse and clicked again.

A second voice, "Learn to stay out of places you don't belong."

At the fourth voice, Kate knew. A shudder ran through her, but she kept quiet.

After the sixth voice, Judith said, "Okay, John. Play them again. Kate, hold up your hand if you think one of them is your mugger."

She dutifully listened to each of the first three again. Number one was too high pitched, two and three, had the wrong cadence. Number four once again sent a chill down her spine. The words were said with less vehemence, but it was her mugger's voice. She held up her hand.

"Are you sure?" Judith said. "Do you want to hear the last two again?"

"No, I'm sure. It's number four."

Judith's face was impassive. "Play the last two, John."

He did so, but neither came close to being right.

"It's number four," Kate said again.

"Thanks, John. That'll be all." Once he was out the door, Judith's shoulders slumped. "Four was a police detective."

Kate's own body deflated. "The suspect was five or six, wasn't he? Who is he?"

Judith didn't answer her first question, which Kate took as a yes.

"He's the leader of a group of young people who buy and sell drugs in the area around the university's campus. Also a known associate of Jimmy Whitmore. And he likes to dress nice, including fancy dress shoes. Even his sneakers are made of Italian leather."

"So, does this eliminate this guy as a suspect, the fact that I couldn't identify him?"

Judith shrugged. "Voice recognition is always a long shot. He may still be the mugger, but we've got no evidence. We'll have to cut him loose for now."

Kate's chest and stomach tightened. "Can you wait to do that until Billy and I are out of here?"

"Sure." Judith rose and placed a hand on Kate's shoulder as she walked past her. "Thanks for coming in."

⸺ ◆◯◆ ⸺

On the way home, Kate was trying to convince Billy that Chinese carry-out was a much better dinner option than yet more pizza.

Her phone rang through the Bluetooth. The screen told her it was Rose. "Hey there."

"Hey yourself," Rose said. "I tried the house first but got no answer. Any news yet on how our plan is working–?"

Kate quickly cut her off. "Um, yes, but I have Billy with me at the moment."

"Oh." A brief pause, road noise in the background. Apparently Rose was driving as well. "Hey, Mac is meeting up with some old Army buddies tonight, and I know Skip has that dinner meeting with a new client. You want me to grab some carry-out and bring it over?"

"That would be great," Kate said.

"Chinese okay?"

"Perfect." Kate laughed as Billy scowled.

"What's funny?"

"Long story," Kate said. "We'll see you at the house in a bit."

Even though he'd resisted the idea of Chinese food, Billy made short work of an egg roll, a bag of fried wontons and an order of General Tso chicken. With some pressuring, he even ate some of the broccoli from Kate's chicken with cashews.

Once he'd asked to be excused, Rose turned to Kate. "Any cage rattling from Edie or your ex-mother-in-law yet?"

Kate couldn't stop grinning as she told her about the phone call from Edith Huntington.

"I'd love to be a fly on the wall," Rose said with a chuckle, "when Edie finds out where they're going for lunch on Thursday."

Kate laughed. "It could get ugly."

"How's Billy enjoying his spring break?"

A pang of guilt tightened Kate's uncomfortably full stomach. "Not as much as I'd hoped he would. The downside to this set-up with Edie is that I now have no one to stay with Billy when I can't be home."

"Isn't he old enough to stay by himself for short periods?"

"Yeah, I guess. Edie did at his age..." She trailed off.

"But?"

"Edie was more mature, and she didn't have the flightiness that comes with ADHD. Earlier today I had to leave him alone for a little while. When I came home, he hadn't thrown the deadbolt on the front door."

Rose cocked her head to one side and raised an eyebrow.

"Okay, that doesn't sound all that awful, but when I dropped him off, I specifically told him to lock it." Butterflies fluttered in Kate's chest. "And I guess I'm being paranoid, but with everything that's been happening lately—kids getting shot in broad daylight and fake cops chasing us on the highway and Dolph getting stabbed, in a police station of all places."

Not to mention my client being set up to look like she tried to kill herself. But Kate *didn't* mention that. It was confidential.

"When do you need coverage for Billy?"

Kate wondered why Rose was asking, but she answered anyway. "Tomorrow I have classes from nine to noon, and Thursday eight-thirty to ten." Originally her classes were to be the only times that Edie and Billy would have been on their own.

Kate shook her head. *Best-laid plans and all that jazz.* "And now I've got an important meeting on Thursday, at two-thirty."

Rose raised her eyebrow at right angles again. She had very expressive eyebrows.

Kate waved a dismissive hand in the air. "Nothing related to our case." Well, it might be, but again she wasn't ready to get into the mercy killings, not until she saw if Theresa pulled Tyrell's case, independent of Carol's suspicions.

Rose nodded and picked up a fortune cookie. She broke it in half and pulled out the slip of paper inside. Tears pooled in her eyes as she read the fortune.

Alarmed, Kate said, "What?"

Silently Rose passed the paper to her.

You will have great influence on the younger generation.

Rose made a choking sound, then waved her hand in front of her face. "This is ridiculous," she muttered.

Kate grabbed her other hand on the table and gave it a squeeze. She let go quickly—Rose hated overt displays of affection. "Biological clock?"

Rose nodded, staring down at the table.

"It can be a powerful thing," Kate said.

Rose looked up, her eyes still shiny. "No way I'm having a baby. I'm already in my forties and Mac and I..."

"Would make lousy parents. Uh-huh, I've heard that song before, but I'm not so sure it's true."

Rose snorted. "Yeah, we'd be great, if the kid needed tough love, but all that cuddling and goo-ga stuff when they're little." She actually shuddered.

"And you'd be in your late fifties and Mac would be pushing seventy when you hit the teenage-rebellion-slash-juvenile-delinquent stage."

Rose gave her a mock glare. "No kid of ours would dare become a delinquent."

Kate laughed, but then sobered. "You don't know that. There are so many influences on kids today. You pray that they'll turn out okay, but..."

"So why did you have kids?"

Kate shrugged. "We were young and dumb."

"Not that young," Rose pointed out. "You were only three years younger than I am now when you had Edie."

That gave Kate pause. Rose's math was correct, she'd been in her late thirties when she'd had her children. But the circumstances were so very different.

"I married Eddie in my twenties, and we tried for *years* to have kids. But it didn't happen." She paused, took a deep breath, recalling the hollow longing in her chest. "And then I found out I was pregnant after he was dead."

Rose now grabbed *her* hand and squeezed it, then let go. "I know, I was there." Her voice was tight.

"You were the third person I told that I was pregnant."

Rose gave her a lopsided smile. "And you hardly knew me at the time."

Kate chuckled at the memory of that stilted conversation between a young widow and the rookie cop who had been assigned to protect her.

Then she took a deep breath. "When Skip and I got together, I assumed I wouldn't be able to get pregnant again. So, um, I kind of tricked him into not using protection."

Rose's cheeks flushed to a tawny peach color.

Kate resisted the temptation to laugh. "But lo and behold, Billy happened. So, in our case, young and dumb kind of extended a bit into our late thirties."

Rose's face twisted into a grimace. "Please tell me that this biological clock thing eventually lets up."

"It does. Hey, I read an article recently about it, debating if it's just societal pressure or is there really a last-ditch hormonal effort by Mother Nature to get women to reproduce." She pushed herself to a stand. "Lemme see if I can find it again and send it to you. It was pretty interesting."

She headed for the study. Rose followed her.

Kate sat down at the desk and jiggled the mouse to wake up the computer.

Nothing happened.

"Skip must have turned it off last night. We usually leave it on, but maybe he heard a prediction of thunderstorms."

She hit the power button on the hard drive unit and waited, then clicked on the browser's icon and typed *biological clock* in the search box. "Or maybe the operating system updated."

Rose had wandered over to Skip's gun safe. "When's the last time you cleaned in here?"

Kate turned in her desk chair and stared at her friend. Rose could be obtuse sometimes when it came to social skills, but she wasn't usually rude.

But Rose wasn't looking her way. She was wandering around, examining the bookshelves like she'd never been in the room before.

She turned and mimicked putting on gloves.

Totally confused, Kate blurted out, "What?"

Rose put two fingers against her lips, then pointed to the top shelf of the bookcase next to her.

Kate squinted up at it but didn't see anything out of place.

Meanwhile Rose was babbling away. "You got any *rubber* balls that Toby doesn't play with anymore. Our dog has chewed up all his."

Has she lost her mind? She doesn't have a dog.

"I had to put on *gloves* to pick up the last one, it was so slobbery. I threw it in the trash."

Partial understanding dawned. She wanted rubber gloves for some reason.

"Yeah, I think I do have some. Let me get them."

Still quite confused, Kate gestured for Rose to follow her to the kitchen, but instead Rose went to the desk and grabbed a square of blank post-its. She wrote on the top one, tore it off and held it up.

Listening device. May be more.

Kate's mouth fell open. A hand flew to her chest, where her heart was pounding erratically.

She gasped. "That's why–"

Rose quickly shook her head and again held a finger to her lips.

CHAPTER TWENTY

That's why the deadbolt wasn't thrown, Kate finished in her head, as she rushed into the kitchen. Someone had picked the lock, but without a key there was no way for them to relock the deadbolt when they left.

She dug under the sink for a pair of rubber gloves. Her hands shook at the thought of someone being in the house with Billy earlier.

Back in the study, Rose donned the gloves, then dragged the desk chair over to the bookcase. With Kate steadying it, Rose climbed up and stretched to reach the top of the books on the uppermost shelf.

She brought down a small box, about half the size of a ring box. Putting it carefully on the desk, she grabbed the post-its again. Kate leaned over her shoulder.

Anything moved or missing in here?

Heart thumping and stomach queasy, Kate looked around. The legal pad next to the keyboard was shifted slightly, cocked in the wrong direction for a right-handed person sitting at the computer. Trying to be quiet, she checked the desk drawers, then scanned the room again.

She saw what had first alerted Rose. An empty ammunition box Skip had apparently forgotten on top of the gun safe. It had been moved slightly, leaving a dust-free spot on the otherwise dusty surface. If she or Skip had touched it, they would have thrown it away, and the kids knew to stay well away from the gun safe.

She pointed to the pad and Rose handed her a pen. *Things have been moved but I don't think anything is missing*, she wrote.

Rose nodded and took the pad, scribbled on it, then handed it back. *Going outside to call Mac, get him to bring the debugger over.*

Kate headed for the stairs and took them two at a time, desperate to check on Billy, even though she knew there was no current threat.

He was in his room, contentedly playing video games on his computer. Kate backed away from the half open door, leaving him to his innocent bliss.

She and Rose sat in the kitchen and made idle chit-chat, acting like nothing was wrong, until Mac arrived.

He swept the downstairs of the house with his debugging device and found two more tiny boxes, one on top of a kitchen cabinet and one taped on the underside of an end table in the living room.

Silently, Kate got three baggies from the kitchen. Rose dropped the boxes into them and set them on the floor by the TV. Then she turned it on.

Kate let out a nervous laugh. In a low voice, she said, "You probably ought to put them on top of the TV. Toby may try to eat them."

She glanced over to the corner, where the dog was lying on his bed, his head raised, watching them.

Why didn't he bark when someone was in the house earlier, planting listening devices?

Maybe he had, and Billy hadn't heard him because of his earphones. Kate shuddered. Thank heavens he'd put those earphones on. If he'd come downstairs... She couldn't even let herself think about what might have happened.

Rose gestured for them to go into the kitchen. "I need a cup of tea."

Toby rose and followed, probably hoping for a treat.

Once there, Kate looked down at him. "You're the world's worst watchdog." The dog looked up at her adoringly and wagged his tail.

The tea kettle slipped from Rose's grip and banged onto the burner.

Kate jumped, but the dog didn't react.

Rose caught her eye. "Toby," she said at a normal volume.

The dog kept looking at Kate.

Rose went to the cabinet under the sink, where the dog treats were kept. She pulled out the box and rattled it.

The dog didn't look her way.

"Toby," Rose yelled. Still nothing. Then she stepped toward him and waved her arms around, the box of treats still in one hand.

Toby's head jerked around and suddenly he was sitting in front of Rose, tail sweeping back and forth across the floor. Rose laughed and gave him a treat.

"And all along I've thought he was getting stupider," Kate said. She heard the shakiness in her voice.

As did Rose apparently. "Sit. I'll get the tea."

"I'd rather have wine." Kate pointed at the fridge as she sank onto a kitchen chair. Rose tossed her the treat box.

Toby watched it arc through the air and was at Kate's knee by the time she'd caught it.

She gave him another treat and ruffled the thick hair on his head. "I'm so sorry, boy. I've been maligning your intelligence, when all along you've been slowly going deaf."

Mac walked past her and ruffled her thick curls. "Don't feel bad, sweetpea. He is kind of a stupid dog."

"Hey," Kate objected but she felt her mouth tugging upward at the teasing.

Mac smirked. "I'm gonna check the upstairs."

Rose nodded and brought Kate a glass of white wine.

Kate took a big gulp, then sank back in her chair. "This has been the longest day of my life."

She stared into her wineglass. She'd just remembered what day it was, the anniversary of Eddie's death.

That *was the longest day of my life, but today is in second place.*

"I'll have to cancel classes tomorrow. No way I'm leaving Billy home alone." For the umpteenth time, she wished Towson's spring break coincided with the public schools, but it didn't.

Rose sat down with a mug of tea. "I've got some paperwork I can do at home tomorrow morning. I'll pick him up around eight-thirty, and he can spend the morning with me."

"What about Jared?"

"He stayed home today. Clarissa's off from school so she's watching him, and Manny's guarding them." Rose paused, shook her head slightly. "I suspect Wanda will keep him home the rest of the week. I think what happened yesterday rattled her more than she's willing to let on. Can't say as I blame her."

Kate silently agreed. She considered protesting further. She doubted Rose had really planned to do paperwork tomorrow. But the end of the semester was looming, and she had a ton of material still to cover in her classes. "Thank you."

Mac came back into the kitchen. "Upstairs is good. And I dusted the bugs. No prints."

"Probably no point in checking the study then," Kate said. "They must have worn gloves."

"What's this about babysittin' the rug rat?" Mac asked.

Rose looked up at him. "While Kate has classes tomorrow and a meeting on Thursday."

Kate's throat suddenly closed and her eyes stung. She was so grateful to have these two in her life.

Okay, I really am tired if I'm getting this sappy. But she knew it wasn't only fatigue or even menopausal hormones. Being scared out of her wits one time too many the last couple of days was taking its toll on her emotional control.

Liz called bright and early Wednesday morning, while Skip was sitting in the kitchen sucking down his first cup of coffee.

"Found him," she sang into the phone.

Suddenly Skip was wide awake. "You did?"

"Well, I found his credit card. It's in the name of James Whitmore Brown. He produced an affidavit saying he had legally changed his name. Don't know if it's legit or not—it looks good if it's a forgery. Anyway, the credit card company accepted it."

"How'd you see the affidavit?" Skip caught himself. "Wait, I'm with Rob on this one. I don't want to know."

Liz chortled. "But you gotta sing 'la, la, la, la,' off key or I'll tell you anyway."

"Nope, way too early for that."

Liz's laugh boomed from the phone, then she said, "He hasn't used it much since the day he disappeared. But yesterday afternoon, he bought a hundred and five dollars' worth of stuff at Luis's Groceries."

"Alright! You got an address?"

"You bet." She gave it to him.

He repeated it as he wrote it down. "Thanks, Liz. Don't tell Dolph I said this, but I think you're a slightly better hacker than he is."

"Dear sir, I am most flattered." Her laugh boomed again and she disconnected.

Rose had arrived to pick up Billy while he was on the phone. "You got a lead on Jimmy Whitmore?"

"Yeah." Skip filled her in.

"Damn, wish I could go with you," Rose said.

"I think I can interview a grocery store clerk on my own."

She shook her head. "But if you find out anything, then you'll want to pursue it. I don't think any of us should be poking at this hornet's nest without backup, especially once they figure out that their bugs have been deactivated."

She and Mac had taken them with them last night. Mac was going to examine them further and turn them off.

"So you're convinced it's two or more perps?" Skip said.

"There were two of them involved in trying to drive us off the road, and two guys in Jared's drawing."

"It could be one guy and an underling," Skip said, playing the devil's advocate.

Rose cocked her head to one side as she poured herself a mug of coffee. "I guess. I'll call Mac to go with you."

"What about Kate?"

Rose glanced at her watch. "I'll have him meet you there after he follows Kate to school. She should be okay once she's in her classroom. These bozos aren't likely to try anything in front of a room full of witnesses."

Skip snorted. "I don't know. They've been pretty bold so far."

"But they are trying to stay under the radar. Look, I've got two interviews this afternoon. At least one of them's a strong candidate. I'll put him on Kate as soon as he can start."

⎯⎯◄O►⎯⎯

Luis's Groceries turned out to be a ma-and-pa corner store—not a big surprise—in a neighborhood just over the line in Baltimore City.

And "pa" was Luis, who stood sentinel behind the register, while two pimply-faced teenagers, one white, one Latino, stocked shelves from multiple open boxes scattered around the floor.

Luis nodded a greeting. "Sorry for the mess," he said in a thick Spanish accent. He waved at the boxes and the boys. "Wednesdays are delivery day." He pronounced the *nes* in *Wednesday* as a separate syllable.

Mac hung back as Skip gave the man a big smile. "No problem." He flashed the photo of Jimmy Whitmore. "Have you seen this young man?"

Luis's face closed. "You a cop?"

"No, private." Skip held up his P.I. license in its thin leather case. "I'm working for his mother. She's worried sick."

Not a total fib. Judith might be footing the bill, but at this point, Skip was really hoping he could reunite Wanda Brown with her lost son.

Still frowning, Luis said, "I see him yesterday afternoon. He get some stuff."

"One hundred and five dollars worth of stuff," Mac growled. "I'll bet that's a pretty big tab here."

"*Sí*, sixty was cash back."

Skip gave Luis a skeptical look. "This wasn't the first time he came in then. I'm assuming you don't give cash back to just anybody."

"No, it first time. But a regular customer, she vouch for him."

"You know this woman well?" Mac said.

"*Sí*, she live right down the street."

"Her name?" Skip said.

Luis eyed him suspiciously.

Skip raised his hands in the air. "As God is my witness, I mean these people no harm."

The grocery store owner sighed. "Juanita Ramirez."

The name had slammed Skip in the solar plexus. He could have sworn the lady professor had been telling the truth when she'd said she didn't know where Jimmy Whitmore was.

Now he stood on her porch, ringing the bell for the third time, and steaming. Mac had gone around the back of her house, in case the kid tried to take off.

The front door flew open, and Dr. Ramirez stood in the doorway, a burgundy robe wrapped tightly around her plump form. "Mr. Canfield, what are you doing, ringing my bell so early?"

He glanced at his watch. It was nine-ten.

She raised an eyebrow at him. "I had a night class last night, and my first class this morning isn't until eleven. I repeat, what are you doing on my porch?"

"I'm still looking for Jimmy Whitmore. Or should I say, James Whitmore Brown."

She didn't blink or flinch. "And I told you that I had no idea where he is."

"I believe that was true then. But Luis down on the corner just told us you vouched for him yesterday, so Jimmy could use a credit card to get cash."

"I did, but I have no idea where he is staying."

"You mind if I come in and look around?" Skip asked.

Her cheeks flushed. "Yes, I mind. Now go away." She slammed the door shut.

He texted Mac with the bad news.

They were almost back to where they'd left their vehicles, parked at the curb near Luis's Groceries, when one of the stock boys, the white one, approached them.

"Hey, is there a reward or something for info on that guy?"

Skip said, "There might be. Have you seen him?"

"How much?"

"Twenty."

"Fifty," the kid countered.

Damn, I should've started at ten.

"Twenty-five."

The kid hesitated.

"I'll make it thirty if the info's worth it."

"I've seen him, goin' in and outta that lady's house yesterday and today."

"When was the last time?" Mac asked.

"This mornin'. He came out in a bathrobe and got her newspaper."

Which means he's probably in there now.

"I remember thinkin' that old lady must be hot in bed, to snag a young hunk like him."

Skip resisted the desire to slug the kid. Mac growled low beside him, apparently fighting the same urge.

"That *old* lady," Skip said, "is probably about the age of your mother. Show some respect."

The kid grinned and held out his hand.

Skip fished out his wallet and extracted a five and a twenty.

"Hey, you said thirty!"

"You lost the extra five with that dirty crack." He held up the bills. "Take 'em or leave 'em."

The kid snatched the money and took off running, back to his place of employment.

"So we know he's alive," Mac said.

"Yup." Skip texted Kate with the good news, adding *Let Wanda know.* He'd give her the pleasure of making the woman's day.

Then he called Judith and filled her in, giving her Juanita Ramirez's address.

"No luck finding the fake cop's car," Judith said. "Might have been the guy's own car, and that's why he put mud on the plate."

Skip sighed. "Or could've been stolen plates on his own car, and the mud was just an extra precaution." They signed off and he pocketed his phone.

"Ya think the cops will have better luck getting past Dr. Ramirez?" Mac asked.

Skip gave him a small grin. "If Judith comes herself, I'd say fifty-fifty odds. If she sends somebody else, unlikely."

"Unless she can drum up some charge against him and get a warrant."

Skip shrugged. "It's not illegal to disappear."

Mac chuckled. "Wish I could stick around and watch her and Judith go at it."

Kate was wondering why she'd made such an effort to hold her classes. Attendance was usually poor anyway, the class period after a test. Plus it was only two days from a holiday weekend. Half her students were probably out of town by now, either headed home to spend Easter with their families or turning the long weekend into a second spring break.

She was half tempted to hit them with a pop quiz on today's material when they came back next week.

Walking out of her last class, she pulled her phone out and glanced at its screen. And stopped in her tracks when she read the text from Skip. It was all she could do to keep from shouting out loud.

She should wait until she was out of the building to call Wanda. She didn't want anyone overhearing her end of the conversation. But as she was moving past the canteen area on the psych building's ground floor, headed for the double doors that led to the sunny day outside, she spotted Wanda sitting at one of the tables.

The woman waved her over.

"I left a message on your office phone, hoping you'd be free for lunch." The words sounded light, carefree, but Wanda's body language was anything but. Her face was grim. She rubbed her hands nervously up and down her arms.

"I was in class," Kate said.

"I figured. That's why I didn't call your cell. I just came on over. I thought you'd go back to your office and check your messages before you left."

Kate sat down and leaned forward. "What's going on?" she whispered.

"Somebody's been in my place," Wanda said in a low, tense voice. She rubbed her arms again. "This morning, when nobody was home."

Kate's heart raced. "Are the kids okay?"

Wanda nodded. "Jared got restless, so Clarissa took him for a walk. Was it your people?"

"No, the bodyguards wouldn't go inside. They're supposed to keep a low profile and not let on that they have any connection to you all. But Manny would have discreetly followed the kids, which would have left the apartment unguarded. Tell me what happened."

"Clarissa called me 'cause things had been moved in his room. He's compulsive about his space, gets upset if anything's out of place."

Kate took a deep breath. "Someone was in my house too. They planted listening devices. We found them last night."

Wanda's eyes went wide. Her lips pinched together.

"I'll have one of our guys go over and check your place for bugs." Kate looked around the canteen, which was filling quickly with students and faculty seeking their lunch. "But I'd better wait to call until I'm outside."

Then she smiled. "That's where I was headed just now, to go out and call you. I've got some good news." She leaned in even closer. "They haven't found Jimmy exactly, but they think they know where he is and that he's okay."

Wanda's mouth fell open and she jumped up. In the next second, she had grabbed Kate out of her chair and was giving her a bear hug. "Thank you, sweet Jesus!"

Kate gave her a squeeze back and whispered in her ear. "We're drawing attention."

Several people had turned their way, distracted from their sandwiches and chips.

They let go of each other, made eye contact, and both started laughing.

Once they were seated again, Kate leaned across the table. "They think he's been staying with one of his professors. A friend of ours in the police department is going over to check it out."

Wanda's eyes clouded. "They won't hurt him, will they?"

"No, of course not. He hasn't done anything wrong, except scare the crap out of you." Kate gave her a small smile. "Worrying one's mother is not against the law."

"Maybe it should be," Wanda muttered.

Kate chuckled. "We could start a petition. Get it added to the legislature's agenda next session."

Wanda grinned at her. "Every mother in the state would sign it."

CHAPTER TWENTY-ONE

Rose and Billy had just finished lunch when she got the call that Kate was headed home from the university.

"Did you get the good news about Jimmy Whitmore?" Rose asked.

"Yes, and I passed it on to his mother. But apparently somebody broke into her apartment earlier today. Some things were moved around."

Rose shook her head, even though Kate couldn't see her. "Somehow I'm not surprised. I'll send Mac over to check things out." *Once he's followed you home.*

"I'll roll by to get Billy."

"No need," Rose said. "I'll bring him to your house. I need to run an errand over that way anyway."

Earlier, while Billy played games on her computer, she'd done phone interviews with the two prospective operatives that had been scheduled to come in that afternoon.

One was on the young side, not very experienced, but she hired them both over the phone. *Beggars can't be choosers*, as her cousin Maria liked to say.

They were already on their first assignment, and Rose wanted to check on them.

She spotted the guy out front fairly easily, sitting in his car half a block down, on the other side of the street.

He was hunched down some, and a casual observer probably wouldn't notice him.

But then again, whoever was behind all this was *not* a casual observer—not if they had both the skills and the hutzpa to break into Kate's house while her son was upstairs.

Then again, maybe they hadn't known Billy was there when they first broke in. There had been no cars in the driveway or out front at the curb. Nonetheless, they had professional skills, she had no doubt of that. She also suspected that they'd looked through the contents of Kate and Skip's computer, maybe even copied everything to a flash drive.

She cruised on past the house and her new operative.

"Where ya going, Aunt Rose? That's our house," Billy said.

Rose made eye contact with him in the rearview mirror. "You never miss a trick, do you, kiddo?"

He grinned at her.

She turned right to go around the block. "I've got a little game for you. I'm testing two new people I hired. I've got them watching your house. See if you can spot them."

She drove slowly down the alley behind Kate's house, past the small garage that they used for storage. She spotted the second guy, but only after a careful perusal of the backyard.

In dark clothes, he was standing up against the trunk of a tall pine tree, deep in the shadows of the wooded yard.

Billy was silent in the backseat, staring intently out his side window.

She slowed to a crawl, giving him plenty of time. Still no outcry of success.

She smiled to herself and made another right out of the alley, then turned onto Kate's street again.

Now the operative's car seemed to be empty. Had he seen her and figured out that she was checking on him? But how would he recognize her? They'd never met in person.

He'd better not be off peeing on a neighbor's bush.

"Hey, I see him," Billy yelled from the backseat.

"Where?"

"He was in that car we just passed. I saw the very top of a baseball cap, sticking up a little in the driver's window."

"Very good. Only the one guy?"

"Yeah." The boy's voice deflated. "I couldn't find the other guy."

"That's good too, for him." She met his eyes again in the mirror. "He gets to keep his job."

The boy's grin came back.

She went around the block one more time and stopped in front of Kate's house. She called each of the new guys before she and Billy got out of the car. "You just saw a car go around the block twice. It was me, your new boss. I'm about to go into the house with the client's son."

She hadn't told them they were guarding their other boss's house, figuring that would make them too nervous.

A little anxiety keeps your people on their toes, too much makes it hard for them to think in a tight spot.

Once inside, Rose told Kate about the guards outside. She didn't want her freaking out if she happened to spot them.

Kate objected, but Rose kept talking. "I'll come here tomorrow to stay with Billy while you're at your meeting. That way the guards can watch over the house and us."

That shut Kate up.

Kate called Carol Foster to check on her.

"I'm doing much better," Carol said. "I think the drugs have completely worn off, finally. And I called my boss and said I needed to take a leave of absence. I figured that would tell the killer that I've been scared into keeping my mouth shut. Thought that'd make it safer for you as well, until you can get in to the see the CEO."

"That's a very good idea."

"Richard suggested it."

"Suggested?" In the past, he would have ordered Carol to do it.

She chuckled. "Yes. He's come a long way. He also suggested we get out of town for a few days. He's taken the week off from work."

"Another good idea. I'm starting to like this new Richard."

Carol giggled. "Me too."

"Um, you might want to leave your cell phones home, and get some burner phones instead."

"Burner phones?"

"They're prepaid and preprogrammed with a random phone number. They can't be traced–"

"Kate, I know what burner phones are. I watch cop shows. I'm just kind of surprised that you'd think of that."

Kate let out a self-conscious laugh. "My husband's a P.I., remember? And he used to be a cop."

"Oh yeah, that's right. Okay, we'll stop at the mall on our way out of town. I thought I saw a kiosk there last week, advertising cheap prepaid phones."

They exchanged goodbyes, and Kate disconnected.

Despite her relief that Carol and Richard were taking measures to keep themselves safe, she felt a little off kilter inside. Her stomach was downright queasy.

Burner phones... The way we live, it's just not normal.

Her next thought was, *Do I want normal?*

She did, she really did. But when people were in trouble—good people like Carol and Wanda, could she really turn her back?

At three-thirty, Skip signed off on the last of the operatives' reports on his desk. He let out a contented sigh. Rarely was he able to clear that blasted in-box.

His cell phone rang. He didn't recognize the number, but he answered anyway. One never knew when it might be a potential new client.

"Mr. Canfield, this is Juanita Ramirez." She sounded somewhat frantic. "I should have let you in this morning and none of this would've happened, but now he's gone, and–"

"Slow down, ma'am. Tell me what happened."

The sound of air being sucked in. "Jimmy was here when you came around earlier. And then two police detectives came. I didn't let them in either. Jimmy had insisted. Said the police were, quote, 'part of the problem.' I went to school and when I came home–" She choked up. "He's gone, Mr. Canfield, and his room's a wreck."

"Sit tight. I'll be right there."

As he raced to Juanita Ramirez's house, Skip tried to figure out why he was resistant to calling Judith. That really should have been the first thing to do. Jimmy wasn't a fugitive, but at this point, he might be considered a material witness.

But still Skip drove on without making the call. Jimmy's comment that the police were part of the problem was bothering him. Yeah, the kid had been in trouble with the law when he was younger, and yeah, he was black, which would naturally make him wary of the police.

But Skip's gut was telling him there was something else going on here. What, he didn't know.

He swung his SUV to the curb in front of the professor's house, jumped out and took her six porch steps in two leaps.

She opened the door before he could knock. Her lips pinched together in a grim line, she gestured for him to follow her.

On the second floor of her large bungalow, she gestured toward a door. It led to a good-sized bedroom under the eaves. "My son's room, once upon a time."

It was turned upside down, drawers dumped on the floor, bedding stripped from the bed, clothes torn from the hangers in the closet.

The window sat open, curtains blowing in a slight breeze.

Skip walked over, stepping carefully around the things strewn on the floor. Wooden fire-escape stairs zig-zagged downward. This house must be older than he'd first thought, 1940s vintage maybe. He was pretty sure wood hadn't been used for fire escape construction since then.

"Anything missing?"

She shook her head and pointed to some clothes on the floor—a hoodie, two tee shirts and a track suit. "Jimmy bought those at a local thrift shop yesterday. The rest of this mess is stuff my boy left behind."

Skip scanned the room again. It hadn't been a thorough search. Either the searcher had found what they were looking for early on, or they'd mainly been looking for some indication of where the occupant might have gone.

Or they were interrupted.

He turned to Dr. Ramirez. "Did you hear anything up here when you got home?"

She shook her head again.

He grabbed two tissues from a box on the dresser, and keeping them between his fingers and the frame so he wouldn't leave prints, he closed the window. A tissue still covering his hand, he reached for the lock.

"Leave it open."

He turned to her. "Are you sure?"

"Yes," she choked out. "If he comes back, give him a way in."

Skip said, "He may not be the only one who comes back."

She stood perfectly still for a moment, her eyes shiny with unshed tears. "I'll go to my son and daughter-in-law's for a few days."

"Get your things. I'll follow you over there, make sure no one follows you."

Her eyes went wide, fear flashing for the briefest moment. Then she nodded.

He called Judith from his SUV.

"I'll send a couple of techs over to process the room," she said, when he'd finished filling her in.

———◆———

After dinner, Billy went to his room to play games on his computer, and Kate and Skip settled in the TV area to watch the evening news.

Kate noted how tame their evening had been without Edie, the drama queen. Yup, an empty nest might not be all that bad. But they had five more years before their daughter went off to college.

Kate swallowed a groan and a lump in her throat at the same time.

It was the third story on the local news. The governor's face appeared on the screen, announcing the task force's plan. Kate's chest warmed as he used the words *diligent* and *dedicated* to describe her and the task force.

The screen switched to a news anchor describing the basics of the plan, but this time she emphasized the additional de-escalation training the officers would receive.

Then the governor was on again. "Contrary to some portrayals of this plan, overly aggressive officers will get two chances to straighten themselves out, not three." He held up one finger. "They're identified and they go through counseling and additional training. If they screw up again, they're on probation." A second finger went up. "And then they're gone," he slashed the air with the two fingers, "if they don't straighten themselves out."

"Must be a slow news night," Skip said, "for them to give this so much air time."

"Darn good thing. It needs to be explained properly to the public."

Her cell phone rang, from her purse sitting on an end table in the living room.

She pushed out of her recliner and went to answer it, wondering if it might be Ben.

"Is that really what the task force recommended?" Wanda Brown's voice, sounding a little breathy.

"Yes."

Silence.

"Wanda, are you okay?"

The sound of a nose being blown. "I'm sure glad I let you into my living room that day, white girl." Now there was a slight chuckle in her voice.

"It's the plan we'd been working on anyway, but seeing what you've been going through, it's given me added motivation."

Another beat of silence. "I like it, but do you really think the police will go along with it?"

"That's the next big question," Kate said.

A half-formed idea solidified, one that had been percolating in the back of her mind for several days. "Hey, I had a thought. But feel free to say no if this doesn't work for you." This woman already had a lot on her plate. "When the dust settles some from all this, would you consider being on the team that goes around to talk to the police chiefs?"

A long pause. "Yes, I could do that." Her voice was more sober now. "If I can work it out with my work schedule. Might find some good in all this if we can keep some other mama from going through it."

"That is what's been driving me lately," Kate pushed past a sudden lump in her throat. "And we can take the police chiefs out to lunch or breakfast, or something, so you don't have to take time off."

"Then you're gonna be on this team too?"

"Yes, if the governor is okay with that. Truth be told, I had been looking for a way to get off the task force. But now..." She trailed off.

After a beat, Wanda said quietly, "But now maybe you can put your first husband truly to rest."

"Yes." She'd thought she had done that years ago.

Something shifted in her chest again. A warm, calm feeling spread through her.

"Yes," Kate's voice was stronger this time, "and create something good out of the senseless evil."

CHAPTER TWENTY-TWO

Once Billy was in bed, Skip settled onto the sofa next to his wife. He laid his arm across her shoulders.

Kate sighed. "It's been a long week, and it's only Wednesday."

"Yup." He slowly blew out air. "You know, I've been thinking about what you said the other night. I'm not that fond of paperwork, but these days I don't really get all that much of a thrill out of field work either. I do it because it's what I'm good at, what I've always done. It's how I make a living. I mean, I don't dislike it, but..."

He paused, gathered his thoughts. "You're probably right that I wouldn't be as tempted to get so personally involved in cases, if I were only supervising from the office. And with you easing out of your practice, moving toward just the teaching—maybe we can end up having a normal life. No more chasing killers, or, more importantly, being chased by them."

Kate had gone very still beside him. He turned his head and looked down at her.

"I've been thinking too," she said. "I agree that we shouldn't be courting trouble. But..."

She shifted in the circle of his arm and stared up at him, her blue eyes sparkling in the light from the lamp on the end table. "The expression on Wanda's face today, when I told her you'd found Jimmy, that he was alive-"

He grimaced. "About that..." He told her about the sequence of events at Dr. Ramirez's house.

"Damn!" she said when he'd finished.

"Yeah. I mean he's probably still alive and okay. We have no reason to believe whoever searched his room has caught up with him."

Kate sighed again. "Okay, so where does that leave us?"

"We keep looking for him." He hesitated, not sure if he should even bring up the other thing that was bothering him. It was probably nothing.

But then why hadn't she talked to him about it. They told each other everything.

He took a deep breath. "So, what is this important meeting tomorrow?"

Her shoulders tensed beneath his arm. She shook her head slightly. "I probably should tell you where I'm going, just in case."

Those words made his stomach knot up. "What do you mean?"

She turned a little more to face him. "Remember my former client who thinks there's a mercy killer at her hospital? I was trying really hard not to get too involved, just giving her a sounding board and some advice." She took a deep breath. "But then someone tried to kill her and set it up to look like a suicide."

Skip gasped despite himself.

"Tomorrow," his wife continued, "I'm going to see the CEO of the hospital and tell him what's going on."

His stomach clenched again. "Say what?" came out of his mouth, but he was thinking, *The hell you are!*

"I have to do this. My client won't be safe until others know what is going on."

His heart pounding, he glared at her.

"Look," she said, "remember the woman I told you about, the social worker at the hospital. She's been in on all this. How about I call her, and she escorts me to the CEO's office? Safety in numbers and all that."

He didn't respond.

"Skip, I have to do this," she said again, more emphatically. "Yes, there's some risk, but it's minimal. There's no reason to believe that anyone even knows I'm involved. I gave a bogus reason for requesting the meeting."

She paused again, took another deep breath. "And there's something else. This mercy killer may have killed Tyrell. There's a chance he might have recovered, but my client thinks he was never given that chance."

She gazed up at him, her eyes full of tears. "He was only eleven, Billy's age." Her voice broke.

His throat tightened. He gathered her up into his arms. "Okay, go with your plan to have this social worker accompany you."

And I'm gonna have Rose assign our best operative to shadow you.

Late Thursday morning, Skip was toying with the idea of going to the hospital himself to keep an eye on his wife, when his phone rang. This time, he recognized the number.

"Dr. Ramirez, what can I do for you?"

"He called, but I was in a meetink." Her accent, usually minimal, was thick from emotion. She sounded on the verge of tears. "It went to voice-mail. Listen!"

Rustling noises, then a male voice, young, black, and scared. "Dr. Ramirez, I'm so sorry I brought this down on you. Those men, they're the ones who are after me. I had to run. But I'm okay. I think I know what I need to do. Thank you for all your help."

More rustling and Juanita Ramirez said, "If I had only let you in." She started sobbing.

"Dr. Ramirez, Juanita, please calm down. At least we know he's okay. Are you still at the university?"

"*Sí.* Yes. In my office."

"Stay there. I'm on my way. I need to borrow your phone so the police can make a recording of the message." He paused. "We'll find him."

He knew he shouldn't make that promise. Yes, they'd probably find Jimmy Whitmore eventually. But they might not find him before "those men" did.

"Okay, I be here. Number 310 is my office, in the psychology building. It's—"

"I know the building. I'll be there in ten minutes."

He called Judith from his truck as he drove. Fortunately, Towson traffic was lighter than usual.

Theresa Barlow had called to suggest they meet for lunch, before Kate's meeting with the hospital's CEO.

But Kate had declined. She was too nervous to eat a big lunch and she wanted to spend some time with Billy.

She thanked Theresa for being willing to escort her through the hospital. "Skip's being paranoid, but I convinced him there's safety in numbers."

"I don't blame him. Not after what happened to Carol. See you at the hospital then at, say two-fifteen?"

Kate agreed and signed off.

She and Billy hung out in the TV room until it was time for her to get ready to go, watching *Big Hero 6* for probably the hundredth time. It was Billy's favorite movie.

When it was over, Billy said, "Okay if I go play in my room until Aunt Rose gets here?"

"Sure," Kate said, wishing that still meant playing with trucks or Legos instead of sitting at his computer killing aliens in some video game.

She ruffled his hair as he walked past her.

She dressed carefully in her best suit. Her nervousness wasn't so much about talking to the CEO—being on a governor's task force had given her plenty of exposure to supposedly important men—but she wasn't at all sure how he would take her news.

Would he believe her, or would he dismiss it or try to minimize what had happened?

If he doesn't believe me, I'll go to Judith with it, she thought, as she leaned toward the bathroom mirror to apply her lipstick.

Judith hadn't told Skip Canfield why she wanted to meet at his office rather than at the precinct.

Andy Russell opened the P.I. agency's outer door and stepped back for her to enter.

"Always such a gentleman," she teased as she walked past him.

He didn't rise to the bait as he would have in the past, with some comment like, "Well, even if you're not a lady, I still do what my mama taught me."

And she was pretty sure the lack of banter wasn't because she now outranked him. Despite the years and her more stellar climb up the ranks, their relationship had remained that of a senior partner to junior partner, with her in the latter position.

At least he looked slightly better than he had last night, when she'd stopped by his place to check on him. Today, he was clean-shaven and had on decent clothes. But his eyes were still bloodshot—she hoped from too little sleep and not from too much booze. His newly acquired paunch tested the limits of his shirt buttons.

He followed her into the foyer. She gave the receptionist a small nod.

"Hi, Lieutenant," the young woman said. "Skip's in the conference room."

The bullpen they walked through was nearly deserted, just one operative punching away at his keyboard, probably writing a report for his bosses.

The door to the glass-walled conference room was open. She stepped inside. "Hope you don't mind that I dragged someone along."

Skip turned from the white board and gave Andy a polite smile that didn't reach his eyes. "You're the client. How ya doin', Russell?"

Judith winced. She hadn't told Andy that she was footing the bill for the investigation.

He tilted his head slightly to one side, his eyes boring into hers. Then he looked away.

She knew his body language well. A rookie learns early on how to tell when his or her training officer is unhappy.

Andy took Skip's proffered hand. "I've been better, but I'm gettin' by."

Judith pointed to the white board, where *What We Know* and *What We Need to Find Out* headed two columns of items. "You all have been busy."

She expected Skip to go over what was on the board, but instead he said, "Kate's involved in something else today, that's probably unrelated to all this. But I want to fill you in on it real quick, just in case it goes south and I need your help. Better if you already know the background so I don't have to explain while we're running for our cars."

She gave him a quizzical look. It wasn't like him to be melodramatic.

Skip glanced at his watch. "She's on her way to meet with the CEO of Dulaney Valley Hospital, to inform him that he may have a mercy killer on the loose in his hospital. A clerk in the records office noticed a pattern, and she, um, happens to know Kate..."

Translation: she's one of Kate's clients, past or present.

"The clerk had an appointment with the CEO, but before she could meet with him, someone tried to kill her. They set it up to look like a suicide attempt."

"And I'm guessing none of this has been reported to us yet," Judith said.

"No, because all they have is a pattern of too many premature deaths in already very ill patients." He stopped, took a deep breath. "And Kate's conviction that this woman is telling the truth when she says she didn't try to kill herself."

Translation: she's attempted suicide in the past.

"And Kate's going to meet this guy by herself?" Judith asked, fighting the urge to shake her head. Kate was a brilliant psychologist, but she sure could be stupid sometimes.

"No, someone is with her, and we have Manny Ortiz discreetly shadowing them."

Judith nodded. Manny was a good man.

"I doubt anyone would even know that she's going there today," Skip continued, "but just in case, if I get a call and run for the door, please follow me. I may need your help."

Judith gave him a brief smile. "Sure."

Skip waved her and Andy to seats at the conference table. "Good. Now let me bring Detective Russell up to speed, and then I've got something interesting to show you."

"Call me Andy," he said as he settled his bulk into a chair. Judith sat beside him, where they could both readily see the board.

"Again, with the 'something interesting,'" Judith said. That's all Skip would tell her over the phone earlier. "Why so mysterious?"

"I'm probably being paranoid, but it occurred to me that there might be a bug in my truck." He pointed to number 8 on the board, under *What We Know*.

Listening devices planted in S and K's house.

Kate had allowed plenty of time, but at the hospital, she pulled up to the valet parking area out front. Today, she had no desire to walk through a deserted parking garage by herself.

She gave the young man her car key and started to turn away, then jerked back around. She'd spotted a familiar tan car in her peripheral vision, driving past the entrance loop in front of the hospital.

She gave a slight shake of her head, but she was smiling, more relieved than annoyed that Skip had sent a bodyguard.

She slowed her steps as she approached the hospital's sliding glass doors, giving Manny some time to catch up. The automatic doors whooshed open. Theresa stood on the other side waiting for her, even though she was a few minutes early.

"You look nice."

Kate gave her a faint smile. "Thanks for the confidence boost. I can use it."

"Seriously, that blouse matches your eyes perfectly."

Smiling a full-blown smile this time, Kate said, "Thanks. That's why it's my favorite." She nervously smoothed her black skirt and tugged on the bottom of her jacket. She thought of this outfit as her lucky power suit.

Theresa wore a pale blue pantsuit with a white blouse. She had pinned her flyaway coppery hair back on the sides with a couple of barrettes.

She and Kate had reached the elevators when the hospital doors whooshed again. Manny stepped through them.

Kate made eye contact with him across the lobby. He gave her a big smile.

He let me spot him on purpose.

Her insides relaxed considerably. She still had to face the CEO, but suddenly she felt that his response really didn't matter so much. She was giving him the courtesy of a heads up, before reporting the situation to the police.

Amazing what a little moral support from a friend can do, even from a distance.

Then she felt a tad guilty. Theresa thought they were friends, but somehow Kate just couldn't warm up to the woman.

The elevator finally dinged. They got on and went to the top floor.

Manny held back. She hoped he didn't try to hoof it all the way to the eighth floor. Most likely he'd take the next elevator.

She knew her mind was rambling, thinking about power clothes and how Manny would get to the executive floor of the hospital. Normally, she would be trying harder to focus on the task at hand. But right now, the thought of that task was making her too nervous. Distraction was better.

Theresa fell unwittingly into that plan. She pointed to the ladies' room down the hall. "We've still got a few minutes. I need to use the facilities."

Kate nodded. Wouldn't hurt to check her hair and makeup one last time.

A male nurse was coming the other way. He waved at Theresa. "I see they relieved you of porter duty, Ms. Barlow."

Theresa returned the wave without comment, her movements jerky. "They were short- handed the other day," she said to Kate. "I had to transport a patient."

I swear she's as nervous as I am.

Kate couldn't blame her. When the mercy killings came to light, as they inevitably would, the relatively new hospital might not survive the bad press. Theresa could end up without a job.

Kate led the way into the ladies' room, and Theresa entered a stall.

Kate leaned forward, staring into the mirror over the sinks. She finger-combed a few errant curls into place. There were a fair number of gray hairs scattered among her curls now. Maybe she should consider dying her hair.

It registered that strange noises were emanating from Theresa's stall, kind of a gasping sound. Was she having an asthma attack?

Kate was about to ask Theresa if she was okay, but the noises subsided just as her cell phone rang.

Edie, the screen informed her. Kate smiled and quickly glanced at her watch. Still nine minutes before her appointment time. She hit the accept-call icon. "Hey sweetie, what's up?"

Something was nagging at Judith's brain as Skip Canfield finished summarizing the *What We Know* List and moved on to the *What We Need To Find Out* one.

Andy interrupted him. "When did you decide I hadn't done it?" His tone was semi-belligerent, as if he wasn't sure Skip had totally come to that conclusion yet.

Skip pointed to number 8 again—*Listening devices planted in S and K's house.*

"Not when the fake cop and his buddy tried to run everybody off the road?" Andy asked.

"No. That seemed to be aimed at Wanda Brown and her son. My partner and my wife just happened to be there. And Rose doesn't think those guys expected a party." Skip paused, meeting Andy's gaze. "I figured there was a possibility they were buddies of yours. Although what they thought they'd accomplish with that stunt, I didn't know."

"But the bugs in your house," Judith said, "that was clearly aimed at you and Kate."

"Exactly. Why would Russell here, or his friends, be messing with us when we were trying to help him?"

"Okay, what's this mysterious new development?" Judith said.

Skip pulled a cell phone out of his pocket. He poked at its screen. "This phone belongs to a psychology professor over at Towson U, Jimmy Whitmore's teacher, Dr. Ramirez. He was staying with her until yesterday."

"He took off out the fire escape," Judith added for Andy's benefit, "before we could get over there. And then somebody trashed his room." To Skip, she said, "The techs found squat, by the way, except Whitmore's own prints, and Ramirez and her son's."

Skip nodded. "The new development is that Jimmy called her earlier today, but she was in a meeting." He poked the screen again and laid the phone in the middle of the table.

A male voice, young and most likely black, apologizing for getting Dr. Ramirez involved. Then, "those men, they're the ones who are after me. I had to run. But I'm okay..."

The nagging feeling was back, stronger. *Those men? What men?*

"Play it again," Andy said.

Skip did so.

Halfway through, Andy pointed to the phone. "I know that voice. He called me three times, a couple of months ago. Said he had some info, and could he become a C.I. for me. But he wanted me to somehow prove I was a good cop first. He was really hung up on that, making sure I wasn't a bad cop. I tried to trace the calls, but he must've been using burner phones."

Andy shook his head. "I remember thinking that maybe his info was about some dirty cops, and that's why he was so worried if I was one of the good ones–"

"Wait a minute!" Skip interrupted, staring at Judith. "What do you mean, before you could get over there? Juanita Ramirez said two detectives showed up, but she didn't let them in the house. And Jimmy bolted *after* that."

The pieces came together so fast and furious, Judith jolted a little in her chair. The unmarked car, the voice ID...

"What?" Andy was watching her, an eyebrow in the air. "I know that look."

"That *was* what the kid was talking about," she said, "dirty cops. And I know who one of them is. One of the unmarked cars BCPD has with 1 and 5 in their plate numbers, it was signed out to the same detective whose voice Kate identified as her mugger."

Both Andy and Skip were giving her confused looks, but she was staring at number 8. "Skip, what if these guys heard Kate making the arrangements for today's meeting? Before you all found the bugs." She jumped out of her chair. "Come on."

She bolted from the room.

Andy and Skip ran after her. "Who's the cop?" Andy huffed out.

"JJ Walker," Judith called back over her shoulder.

"Wha'?" Huff, huff. "Why?"

"Save your breath for running," she yelled.

CHAPTER TWENTY-THREE

Kate couldn't get a word in.

Edie was going on and on about how horrible her grandmother was being toward her. "I wanted this really cute purse we saw. It was patent leather with kind of a sparkly sheen to it–"

Trying to move the story along, Kate said, "And she wouldn't get it for you?"

"No, she got it, but she also bought me this really dumb looking purse. It was dark gray, with all these black, weird ovals on it. Grandmother said they were C's because the purse had come from a coach or something."

Holy crap, my mother-in-law bought my thirteen-year-old a Coach purse!

"She kept insisting I take the ugly gray purse to this dumb lunch thing we went to today, but I put the cute one down inside it, and when we were getting out of the car, I took it out and kind of hid it behind me until we were inside the restaurant. When Grandmother saw it, she grabbed my arm..." The girl was crying now.

Kate ground her teeth. *I'm gonna kill that manipulative, old bitch.*

"She was hissing at me, Mommy, about how I didn't 'preciate nice things and... You gotta come and get me. I can't stand it here another minute."

Kate's anger evaporated. After all, Edith Huntington had done exactly what she'd hoped for.

Hmm, looked like Billy was going to be spending part of the next few days raking leaves. She'd give him the ten bucks anyway though, if he truly did it without complaining.

"Edie, sweetie. I will come and get you, but I can't right now. I'm about to go into an important meeting."

"Damn it, Mother," Edie yelled in her ear. "You've always got some important something you've gotta do, and it's always more important than I am."

Anger flared again at the girl's disrespect, but the words also stung. Kate glanced at her watch. Two-twenty-seven.

Keeping more patients from being killed by a mercy killer was definitely more important than Edie having to stick around her grandparents' house for a couple of hours.

"I will pick you up at four. Be ready!"

Ignoring Edie's spluttering, Kate disconnected.

Manny stood at the corner of the hallway, peeking around it at the ladies' room door.

Come on! What were Kate and her friend doing in there anyway? But no one else had gone in, so he figured she was okay.

He checked his phone. Her meeting was supposed to start in three minutes.

And now someone was coming the other way, a tallish nurse in blue scrubs, with long black hair and very fair skin.

Bet she dyes that hair to get it that dark. She didn't look the least bit Latino or African-American.

He pulled his head back. *What nationality has hair that dark and skin that light?*

He shrugged, peeked around the corner again. She was almost parallel to the ladies' room.

Hands in pockets, Manny strolled nonchalantly away from the corner, waiting for the nurse to come around it and walk past him. She'd been moving pretty fast.

Nothing happened. No nurse.

He turned, trying to look casual about it, and walked back to the corner, peeked around.

The nurse had stopped near the ladies' room door and was staring at it.

Damn, she's gonna go in there. Now what?

He was supposed to stick close to Kate, keep her safe. But how was he gonna explain barging into a ladies' room?

The toilet flushed.

"We gotta hurry," Kate said. It's almost two-thirty."

Theresa opened the door of the stall. Her face was wet.

"What's the matter?"

The woman's hand was at her waist. It jerked.

Kate dropped her gaze. Theresa held a small silver pistol in her hand. Kate went hollow inside. Her mouth fell open. "What the–"

"I don't want to do this. I really don't." Theresa backed toward the ladies' room door, fresh tears streaming down her cheeks. She reached behind her and flipped a lever on the door, locking them in.

And locking Manny out! Kate's knees turned to jelly. She grabbed for the edge of a sink to steady herself.

"Don't scream or I'll shoot you."

"You're gonna shoot me anyway," Kate said, her tone calmer than she felt.

Theresa shook her head. "I don't want to, but when that Carol person said something about Tyrell Brown." Her voice broke for a second. "I didn't hurt him, but see, if I was accused of him too..." She was talking fast, almost to herself as much as to Kate.

She's losing it.

"The others, they'd never prove I did anything to them. They're long since buried, their blood replaced with whatever stuff funeral homes pump into people. Some of them were even cremated."

Theresa stopped, sniffed. Her nose was running. The gun shook a little in her right hand, as she scraped the back of her left across her face. "With the others, they'd probably just fire me, or even let me resign maybe." Again her words sped up. "They wouldn't be able to prove anything. But that boy. There'd be a big stink in the press. I'd go to jail, and if I ever got out, I'd never work again."

Kate's fists clenched. Adrenaline surged through her body. "You should've thought of that before you killed him!"

———◆———

Judith's car had been closer to the building's front door than his truck. Skip had piled into her backseat. Andy Russell was in front.

Skip called Kate. It went straight to voicemail. Had she turned it off before her meeting?

He punched Manny's speed-dial number.

Three rings and it went to voicemail.

Damn it, Manny! He punched the icon for text messages. But how the hell was he supposed to explain all this in a text?

Best he could come up with was, *Threat may come from tall black guy. Dirty cop.* He sent it, then thought to add, *Same fake cop from road chase.*

The guy was actually a real cop, but around the office they'd been calling him "the fake cop." Manny would know who he meant.

———◆———

The nurse had stopped at the ladies' room. She was leaning against the door, her back toward him. There was something off about her.

Manny's phone vibrated in his hand. He glanced down. *Skip*, his screen read.

He returned his gaze to the nurse, who hadn't moved.

Hmm, answer the boss's call? Which would require him to walk away so the nurse couldn't hear him.

Or keep an eye on this strange nurse?

He kept his eyes locked on her, still leaning against that door. Skip would understand.

His phone vibrated again.

He glanced down, quickly read the text.

Well, this nurse is on the tall side for a woman, but she's certainly not a black ma–

He looked up. The nurse was gone.

Theresa was crying even harder. "But I didn't kill him," she wailed. "He was young, not like the others."

"Look, Theres...Terry, you know you can't just shoot me. I'm a mother, with two kids who need me. Give me the gun." Her gaze on Theresa in front of the door, Kate took a step forward. Heart pounding, she held out a hand, palm out.

Her chin dropped. *What?* The door was opening.

Relief washed through her, made her knees wobble again. It had to be Manny.

She studiously kept her gaze on Theresa, as the opening behind the woman's head grew larger.

Then the door started to swing closed again.

Oh no! Where are you going?

Her stomach hollowed out. Maybe it wasn't Manny but some other hapless soul, come to use the restroom. Were they running away?

By the time they got help, it would be too late.

A cracking sound. A sharp ping echoed off the walls.

Heart spiking, Kate instinctively ducked, then looked up. Had a joist snapped somehow? Was the ceiling about to collapse?

Theresa yelped.

Kate's gaze shot back to her.

The woman's eyes had gone out of focus, and a hole had appeared on her shoulder, red spreading around it. In slow motion, she slumped to the floor, her pistol under her.

Behind her stood a nurse, fair-skinned, with freckles and long black hair. She grinned at Kate, as she reached back with one hand and flipped the door's lock again.

In the other hand, she held a large pistol, with a silencer on it.

Looks like Mac's Glock, Kate thought, her mind otherwise paralyzed.

"Finally we meet in person, Mrs. Huntington."

A deep voice, not female.

Her brain still stalled, Kate shook her head.

The hand not holding the gun yanked off the dark tresses.

A wig.

Under it was an expensively styled head of short, red hair.

CHAPTER TWENTY-FOUR

Was that a gunshot?

Manny ran to the door and shoved. Nothing happened. *Locked!*

Heart pounding, he put his shoulder against it and gave it all he had. The door didn't budged.

His phone buzzed again. Another text from Skip.

We're here. Where are you?

8th floor, Manny quickly texted back, while mumbling a prayer to *Santa Maria* that Kate was okay.

———◆———

"Who are you?" Kate managed to push out through her tight throat. Her whole body was starting to shake.

Was this guy in on it with Theresa, had he helped with the mercy killings?

"I'll tell you later." He yanked off the top of his blue scrubs. A padded bra was sown into it. Underneath was a silky, teal tee-shirt. It matched his blue-green eyes.

"Right now, we're walking out of this hospital. A loving man and wife."

He nudged off his shoes, drawing her gaze downward.

They were shiny loafers, expensive looking.

Her brain scrambled to understand. This wasn't the guy who mugged her. He wasn't tall enough, and she could have sworn that guy was black.

One-handed, he pushed down the scrub pants, revealing dark dress slacks. His gaze never leaving her face, he used the scrubs to rub his prints off the door lock, then bundled them up under his arm.

"If you don't do exactly as I say, your son will die. My partner is at your house right now, grabbing him and that Latino bitch."

The blood drained away from Kate's head. She felt dizzy.

This can't be happening.

The man nudged Theresa's inert form out of the way with his foot.

Then he waved the gun at Kate. "Come on, you go first. Unlock the door."

———◄O►———

Rose had decided to go old school. She'd brought a jigsaw puzzle to work with Billy.

He'd been resistant at first, until she showed him the picture on the front of the box, race cars whirling around a track.

It was a five-hundred piece puzzle, but they already had it half put together on the kitchen table.

A faint noise from the other room? Had she imagined it? Probably one of the animals getting into something.

"I'll be right back."

Billy didn't even look up as he fit another piece into the puzzle.

She stopped in the kitchen doorway, spotted Toby's golden tail where he lay on his bed in the TV area.

Her phone buzzed on the kitchen table, partially covering another noise—a rustling sound.

Where's the cat?

"It's Dad, texting you," Billy called out.

"Okay," Rose called back as she rounded the corner into the living room. "I'll check it in a–" She froze.

A big man, all in black, stood just inside the front door. He wore a ski mask.

"How the hell'd you get past my people?" came out before she had time to think.

The man laughed and raised a gun. "You should fire that stupid kid out front."

I'll do that, once I take care of you. She swooped down and yanked her pistol from its ankle holster. "Billy, stay in the ki–"

Air whooshed out of her lungs. She went over backwards. The guy had tackled her.

He was fast, despite his size.

And heavy. She couldn't get air in, not even to say, *Billy, stay in the kitchen,* much less yell it.

A dog barked.

Toby. He'd been roused by the vibration of people crashing to the floor.

Another bark. A flash of gold fur in the corner of her eye. But mostly she saw the guy's jacket mashed against her face. Her nose said it was real leather.

His weight lifted up some.

The sickening sound of a gun butt crunching against bone.

Toby yelped.

———◆———

Kate took a hesitant step toward the door.

The man moved aside, waved the gun at her again. "Like I said, loving couple, arm in arm. And I'll have the gun against your ribs the whole way."

"Why are you taking me with you?" Left unsaid, *why aren't you just shooting me here?* She didn't particularly want to promote that alternative.

But she was stalling for time. Where was Manny? Surely, she'd been in here long enough to have him worried.

"We need to know how much everybody knows."

"Not much. I have no idea who you are."

He gave her that nasty grin again. "All in due course, my love."

She shivered. Of course, he had no intention of letting her go, now that she'd seen his face.

She gritted her teeth. "What about Billy? If you hurt my son—"

"Sh, sh, it's okay," he soothed, like a lover with his mate.

She shuddered.

"My partner's wearing a ski mask. We'll let the boy go, once you tell us what we want to know." His face tensed. "Now get moving."

She raised her foot to take a step.

Two gunshots exploded in rapid succession.

CHAPTER TWENTY-FIVE

Kate jumped back, her hands flying to her ears. The horrendous noise echoed off ceramic walls and porcelain fixtures.

A red poppy blossomed against the teal of the man's silk tee. Eyes went wide. Mouth open, he crumpled forward.

She jumped farther back, her butt hitting a sink.

The door swung open. Manny hunched, ready to fight, his gun in his hand. A chunk of the door was missing, where the lock should've been.

Kate looked down. The man at her feet was still. Then he groaned.

Manny bent down and yanked the guy's wrists together. He pulled a plastic restraint from his back pocket.

Kate stepped around them and crouched down next to Theresa.

"Did I get him?" the woman whispered, barely making a sound.

Kate gently removed the small pistol from her limp hand. "Yes, you did."

Theresa coughed. Blood trickled from the corner of her mouth. "Good."

"Hang in there. You're gonna be okay. Heck, we don't even have to wait for an ambulance." She tried for a light tone, but she sounded semi-hysterical to her own ears. "We're already at a hospital."

Theresa stared up at her. Her eyes had gone dull. "Don't want to live," she choked out. "Don't want to go to jail."

Tears stung Kate's eyes. She blinked hard. "Damn it! Stay with me, Terry."

Theresa's eyes cleared for a moment. "Sorry. I'm so sorry." Then the light went out behind those eyes.

A sob broke loose from Kate's throat, even as her brain screamed, *Billy!*

A big hand wrapped around her forearm. She jerked and her head flew up.

Manny hovered over her. He shook his head.

She dropped her gaze again to the absent eyes. Terry Barlow was dead.

———◦◦◦———

The damn elevator had taken forever. But it was still faster than climbing eight sets of steps. Andy stood next to him in the confined space. "Breathe, brother," he whispered.

Skip wanted to punch him. Instead, his eyes teared up and his tight chest loosened a little.

Once a cop, always a cop. You were in the brotherhood forever.

Unless you turn dirty.

His chest tightened again. He clenched his fists.

The elevator doors opened, and Skip sprang forward. He quickly out-distanced Judith and Andy, racing down hallways, calling out, "Kate, Manny! Damn it, where are you?"

Nurses tried to hush him. A few doctors and orderlies stepped into his path. He shoved them unceremoniously aside and kept going.

"Kate! Manny!"

"Here, boss." Faint, from a distance.

He followed the sound. "Manny!"

"In the ladies' room."

He hesitated at the sight of a blasted away section of the door. *What the hell?* He shoved the door open.

His wife straightened from a crouch as he took two steps in and stumbled over a corpse. He veered around it and almost fell over another one. He looked down at the two bloody bodies on the floor, then reached out for her. "Thank God!"

She turned wide eyes toward him. "They've got Billy."

He grabbed her by the shoulders. "What?"

"The guy said his partner was going after Billy, to make me cooperate."

He let go and pivoted. "Stay with her," he ordered Manny over his shoulder.

The door opened. Judith and Andy both held guns in their hands. Andy looked down. "Crawley?"

Skip bolted past them. "They've gone after Billy."

"You go. I'll only slow you down," Andy said behind him. "I'll make the calls."

"You are hereby unsuspended." Judith's voice, yelling, as she raced to catch up with Skip.

Then she was next to him, both running full out.

———— ◄O► ————

Rose was having trouble sucking air into her lungs, but her arm muscles responded to her brain's commands. Her hand slithered down between her body and her assailant's. She found her objective and squeezed as hard as she could.

"Yowoww!" His body bucked into the air.

She rolled to the left, then twisted to the right, trying to flip them over, get on top of his back.

But despite the attack on his manhood, he still had some fight left. And he was bigger and stronger.

He wrestled her under him again, only now he was sitting on her pelvis. He frowned behind the ski mask. "You're gonna pay for that."

A small hand appeared next to the man's temple. It had *her* gun in it.

Rose's heart stopped beating for a second.

"Don't move, sucker." An exaggerated deep voice.

The man froze.

Rose's legs came up, knocking Billy's hand aside. She hooked her ankles around her assailant's shoulders and jerked downward, praying Billy didn't get smashed in the process.

The guy flipped over backwards. His head hit the floor with a satisfying thud. His gun skidded across the room.

Rose was on him. He was stunned, his eyes out of focus. She grabbed his wrists, yanked them together, then one-handed pulled loose her belt to wrap it around them. But her eyes were scanning Billy, who'd also been knocked to the floor.

He seemed a little dazed, and he still held her pistol.

She plucked it from his hand, amazed it hadn't gone off, and stuffed it in her waistband. Her eyes searched for Toby as she secured the man's wrists.

She spotted him, lying still, just beyond Billy. A lump formed in her throat.

Wait, had his tail twitched? Or had she imagined it?

The front door crashed open.

Instinctively her gun was suddenly in both hands, pointed at the intruder.

Skip froze in mid stride.

She lowered her gun.

Billy struggled up from the floor. "Daddy!" he yelled at the top of his lungs and ran to his father. "I helped Rose get the bad guy!"

Skip looked at her with the most desperate expression she'd ever seen. Then his face cleared, and he gave her a lopsided grin.

Judith screeched to a halt beside him. "You two all right?"

The dog staggered to his feet, let out a loud woof.

Now *you bark at strangers.*

Rose nodded, swallowing a bubble of semi-hysterical laughter. She reached out and stroked the dog's head. He quieted and licked her wrist.

"Y'all are a little late," she said, not completely able to keep a chuckle out of her voice.

Skip grinned full out, dropping to his knees and hugging Billy. In a Texas drawl, he said, "Yeah, well, we've pretty much been chasin' our tails for the last couple a hours."

"Daddy, I want to be a cop when I grow up."

Skip's grin faded and his face drained of blood. "Oh shit, Kate's gonna kill me."

CHAPTER TWENTY-SIX

Kate and Skip sat on poorly padded, metal chairs in an interview room in the Towson precinct. They were waiting for their statements to be typed up so they could sign them and go home.

Kate glanced at her watch. Nine-twenty. *Feels more like one-twenty in the morning.*

Rose had given her statement and had taken Billy home. She was going to swing by the elder Huntingtons and pick Edie up as well.

Kate was beyond caring what explanation Rose gave for why she was there to collect the girl. She just hoped that Edie wouldn't be too impolite to her grandparents.

She studied her husband. Even at forty-nine, he had a youthful face, but it was sagging some this evening. And his normally hazel eyes were a muddy brown—usually a sign that he was angry or worried or both, but tonight probably more from fatigue.

He leaned back, balancing his chair on its back legs, which always made her nervous. "Penny for your thoughts."

She wasn't about to tell him that she thought he looked tired, and older than usual.

"I'm a little worried about Billy. You sure he's okay?"

"Yeah." Skip put his hands behind his head in a casual gesture. "I suspect he thought the whole thing was a big adventure, like one of his video games."

Kate shook her head. "I don't want him thinking that violence is make-believe. Maybe we should restrict his game-playing more."

"I don't think he believes that." Skip's eyes shifted away from hers.

Kate's mom-sense tingled. "What aren't you telling me?"

Skip sighed. "It's more like he thinks it's exciting. He said he wants to be a cop when he grows up."

Her stomach knotting, Kate groaned.

She decided to push that worry away for now. It would be awhile before the boy was choosing a career. Hopefully he'd forget about the idea and decide on something else, like accounting maybe.

She smiled to herself. She'd always teased Eddie Huntington about being a boring accountant. Now she was wishing that life on her son, and found she didn't feel the least bit guilty. *May he and Edie both choose boring, safe vocations.*

Skip let his chair fall forward. Its feet clanked against the tile floor. "I've been thinking about what we talked about the other night."

"Oh?"

"We help people. That's who we are. Both our jobs are ultimately about that. Even teaching is about helping the students, right?"

Kate nodded, bracing herself. Was he going to backtrack about avoiding field work?

"I think we should make a pact." He turned his body toward her, holding out his fist, his little finger extended. "We won't go out of our way... indeed, we will strive to *avoid* other people's messes. But if someone needs our help, we'll do what we can, because that's who we are."

She processed that for a moment, a mild sense of relief washing over her. He was right. That was probably the best they could do.

"Sounds good," she said with a small smile. "Why are you holding your hand like that?"

"Pinky-swear."

Kate laughed. "What are you, ten?"

He let out a mock groan. "Right now, I feel more like a hundred and ten." But he poked his hand at her.

She hooked her little finger through his. He leaned forward, wrapped his other hand around her neck, and pulled her in for a kiss.

She let herself sink into the warm, tingling feelings. Muscles she hadn't realized were still tense slowly relaxed.

After a few moments, she broke away, laughing again. "A pinky swear sealed with a kiss. A double whammy of a promise."

He chuckled, scooted his chair over some, and wrapped his arm around her shoulders.

"It feels good to laugh," Kate said.

"Hey, you're off tomorrow, aren't you? We're having a meeting on the case at eleven, part debriefing, part where do we look next for Jimmy. Why don't you come? It'll save me from having to repeat everything to you tomorrow night."

"I'd planned to spend some time with the kids this week. That hasn't panned out so far."

"Take them to lunch and a movie afterwards."

"Good idea."

A light rap on the door. It opened partway. Someone clearing their throat, and then Judith stepped into the room.

Kate glanced at the mirror next to the door. No doubt it was a one-way. She felt her face flush.

Judith studiously avoided eye contact as she dropped some files on the table and settled into a chair. Her face was sagging as well, and her normally crisp white shirt and black slacks were a bit rumpled.

"Our culprits are two dirty cops," Judith said, "although we're not totally sure yet what they were up to. JJ Walker and Peter Crawley, both in the narcotics division. "

"Crawley," Kate said, "he's the freckle-faced guy who tried to kill me?"

Judith nodded. "He's in surgery as we speak, but the doctors are optimistic. Walker's in jail. He lawyered up. There's a chance he'll get bail, but the ADA's going to request house arrest and an ankle monitor."

She paused, took a deep breath. "I spoke to their captain. He had a bad feeling about them, but he thought they were just lazy. Took long breaks, weren't always where they were supposed to be. So when Andy transferred to their division, the cap reassigned Crawley to partner with him, and put Walker with another conscientious detective. He figured that would straighten them out."

"He didn't catch on to their expensive clothes?" Skip asked.

Judith shrugged. "They're both single. Crawley was married but is now divorced, no kids, no alimony. His ex makes more than he does. The captain figured they spent all their disposable income on clothes. We think they were running a protection racket with the drug dealers, taking a cut of their profits to let them continue to operate."

Kate opened her mouth to ask about Walker's clean record. Surely his captain had noted the laziness in his personnel file. Then she clamped her mouth shut again. They weren't supposed to know all that. Liz had found it by questionable means.

Either Walker or Crawley probably had good computer skills and had doctored their personnel records, as well as trying to erase the record of Jimmy as their C.I.

Judith was shuffling through the files in front of her, but she didn't open any of them. "I'm so sorry, Kate," she said, again not making eye contact. "I should have put two and two together sooner. One of the unmarked sedans in our fleet with 1 and 5 in its license plate was logged out to Walker. And the voice you identified was his..." She trailed off, cleared her throat. "He was one of the detectives I asked to make a recording as a foil for the voice line-up."

"You wouldn't have any reason to suspect a fellow police officer," Kate said.

She glanced Skip's way.

His jaw was tight. "Crawley knifed Dolph, didn't he? He was right there, just before it happened."

Judith shook her head. "We don't know. Probably. But unless we can flip one of them, we might not be able to prosecute them for that crime. We've got no evidence. We've got Crawley for Ms. Barlow's murder–"

"Which ironically saved me from being shot by her," Kate said. "And then *she* saved me by shooting Crawley."

Judith gave her a small smile. "We've got several assault and attempted murder charges we can prove, but we may not even be able to prosecute them for killing the Brown boy. Can his brother Jared testify?"

Kate shook her head. "He doesn't talk, except for a few words here and there, like *gurt* for *yogurt*."

Judith's face tightened. She shuffled the folders again and opened one of them. "The autopsy reports." She shuffled through some of the papers. "Looks like we do have two different killers at the hospital. Or two different methods at least."

"Autopsies?" Kate said. "That was fast."

And why plural? Only one person died today.

"These were done awhile ago, on some of the Dulaney Valley patients and on Tyrell Brown."

Duh! My brain is so tired.

Judith looked down at the file. "The boy had potassium chloride in his system. The M.E. didn't think anything of it at the time because it's a compound that naturally forms after death. But if a large dose of it is introduced intravenously, it can cause a heart attack."

She flipped to another file. "The mercy killer's victims, their autopsies found nothing that could have caused a heart attack, independent of their various injuries or terminal illnesses. The hospital still had blood samples from the more recent cases. They're now being re-examined via gas chromatography. The lab's looking for traces of aconite."

"What's that?" Skip asked.

Judith looked up. "Commonly known as Monk's hood or Wolfsbane. It's a purple flower that is highly toxic, mimics a heart attack, undetectable by standard autopsy methods. We found it growing in Theresa Barlow's garden."

Kate had trouble catching her breath as a vise squeezed around her chest. *Oh, Terry!*

"That's all we got so far," Judith said. "And we wouldn't have that much without you two." She said the latter with a touch of chagrin in her voice.

"Any idea what Crawley's and Walker's motives were for killing Tyrell?" Skip asked.

Judith shook her head. "And we may never know, unless we can get one of them to confess."

Something clicked in Kate's tired brain. "I think I know why they came after me."

"Oh yeah?" Skip's eyebrows arched.

"I've been going over in my mind what I said on the phone to Theresa and to the CEO's admin assistant, while the listening devices were still in the house." Kate took a deep breath. "What they heard me saying that day, it may have led them to think I was going to the CEO to report that someone had hastened Tyrell's death. I don't remember saying anything on my end of the phone about the other deaths."

Judith nodded. "Makes sense. I've got someone working on tracing the listening devices back to whoever bought them."

She blew out air. "Sorry for the wait, but I think your statements are about ready. I'll send a uniform in with them."

"Thanks, Judith," Kate said, "for sticking your neck out on this one. I know you did it for Andy, but..." Her throat tightened. She swallowed. "Anyway, thanks. And I'm sure Wanda Brown will be calling to thank you too."

Judith cleared her own throat, then gave her a small smile. "It was a good team effort."

The next morning, Kate left early for the debriefing meeting, allowing time for a couple of errands.

First, she dropped Toby off at the veterinarian to have him checked out after his close encounter with a gun butt. The vet was also going to run some hearing tests.

And she wanted to stop by Dolph's house for a visit. He'd been released from the rehab center yesterday. She wasn't sure what that meant.

Edie had still been asleep when Kate left, no doubt recuperating from the stress of dealing with her grandmother. Kate hadn't decided yet how to handle the way the girl had talked to her on the phone.

She couldn't let such disrespect slide, but that was what she was tempted to do. She was just relieved that everyone was safe, and that Edie had witnessed Edith Huntington's true nature.

At the Randolphs' house, Sue greeted her with a smile and a hug. "The doctors think Dolph will be able to walk again, with some physical therapy. But that hip was already bothering him—arthritis. He might need hip replacement surgery eventually."

Kate returned her smile. "That's great news. I mean not about the surgery, but that he's going to be okay."

Sue smiled even wider. "Hey, I need to run to the post office. Can you sit with him for a few minutes?"

Kate checked her watch. "Sure."

Sue grabbed up her purse and a jacket from a wooden bench in the foyer. "Down the hall and to the left. He's set up in the guest bedroom."

Relieved to see Sue in such a cheerful mood, Kate wandered through the house until she found the correct bedroom.

"Hey there, bossman's wife." Dolph grinned at her from the bed. He was on his side, his head propped with several pillows.

She chuckled. "You've been hanging around Manny too much."

She picked up a book from the seat of the armchair next to the bed, glancing at the cover. She recognized the name of an up-and-coming romantic suspense author, Jessica Dale.

Dolph gestured for her to put the book on his nightstand.

She did and sat down in the chair. "So Sue likes to get her excitement through reading about it."

"Yeah, she loves that stuff, tries to get me to read it, but I tell her it reminds me too much of what I did for a living all those years."

"The romance? What, you were a secret gigolo?"

He let out a bark of laughter. Then his face turned serious. "So you guys caught our perps, I hear."

She nodded.

"You mind walking me through it?"

She did mind—the memory was still pretty emotionally charged—but she figured if he wanted to live vicariously, she shouldn't deprive him.

His eyes closed somewhere along the way as she told the story. She thought he'd drifted off, but they opened again when she stopped talking.

"I just had a piece of memory come back," he said. "Defense attorney might shoot it down in court though. The power of suggestion, and all that."

"What did you remember?"

"Before it happened, a glimpse, out of my peripheral vision, of someone coming out of a stall. I think I saw a white hand on the stall door. And a flash of red hair."

"So Crawley hid in the stall until he could attack you."

Dolph nodded, the stubble on his chin rasping slightly against the pillowcase. "And then he probably went back in the stall and stood on the john, until there were other police in there, and he could blend in."

"Which may very well be how he and Walker got out of the alley without anyone suspecting them. They hid somewhere until the place was crawling with police and techs." Kate grinned a little to herself, imagining their displeasure that they had to crouch behind trash cans in their expensive clothes.

"And one of them managed to get that bullet out of the wall, during all the hubbub. Probably Crawley, since he had an excuse to be there. I don't think Walker was in the crime scene log."

"Why would they bother to remove the bullet?" Kate asked.

"Maybe they didn't want anyone wondering why it was that far away from the boy."

"They grabbed Andy's backup piece because he was lying on his holster..."

"Shot the boy with it," Dolph said, "and then put it in Andy's hand and shot at the wall, so he'd have residue on him."

He punched the mattress with his fist. "That bastard Crawley. He was a new detective when I retired. Pretty annoying. Spent more time kissing up to the brass than solving crimes. I dismissed him as bein' insecure 'cause he was green."

"I suspect the kissing-up was an act," Kate said, "so people would dismiss him."

Crawley was gutsy, she'd give him that—attacking Dolph right in the police station. Was he a psychopath who enjoyed taking risks and hurting people? The sick way he'd grinned at her yesterday, while holding her at gunpoint, definitely fit with that diagnosis—as did his willingness to kill the entire Brown family, just in case one of them had seen something in the alley that day. Such as his red hair that made him stand out.

The sound of the front door opening at the other end of the house. Kate pushed up out of the chair. "I need to get going. I've been invited to the debriefing meeting today."

A pained look crossed Dolph's face. Sue came into the room as he was saying, "I want in on that meeting."

His wife started to shake her head no.

But Dolph cut her off, his tone angry. "I got a right to hear why somebody stabbed me in the back."

Sue's face crumpled.

"Aww, I'm sorry, sweetheart." Dolph reached out a hand toward her. "I didn't mean to snap at you."

Sue sniffled and stepped toward him.

"Um, I'll have somebody call you and put you on speaker. See you two later." Kate backed out of the room and made a hasty retreat.

In the conference room at Canfield and Hernandez, Private Investigations, Kate was reporting on Dolph's progress to those already present, when Liz entered the room. Manny was right behind her.

Kate finished her update with, "He wants to be a part of this, but my phone battery's low."

"I'll call him," Mac said.

Liz held up her phone. "Rob wants in too, but he's currently driving to a bar association luncheon in Annapolis. I'm to put him on speaker once we get started."

Standing at the white board, marker in hand, Rose rolled her eyes.

Kate stifled a snicker. The meeting was threatening to turn into a bit of a circus.

On the white board, everything under *What We Need To Find Out* was marked through, except *Find older brother, Jimmy. What does he know?* And Rose had written at the bottom, in all caps, *WHY?*

That was definitely what Kate wanted to know, and not just for herself. Wanda Brown needed answers, so the woman could find some kind of closure and move on. Although Kate doubted one could ever really put losing a child behind them.

As they all settled into chairs, she said, "Ladies and gentlemen, man your cell phones."

Mac chuckled and punched his screen.

Liz laid her phone on the table. "Can you hear me, hon?"

"Loud and clear," Rob's voice boomed.

Mac laid his phone down as well. "Hey, everybody," Dolph said from it.

Kate had a momentary flashback to earlier times when they had brain-stormed around tables, big and small, and used this poor man's version of a conference call to include those missing from the room. Those memories were bittersweet. More often than not they were brainstorming because they were in danger.

But the strength of the bond between these people—she scanned the faces around her—it was forged through those bad times.

"Hey, Liz," Dolph was saying. "Thanks for pinch hitting with the computer research."

"No problem," Liz said.

Manny called out, "Glad we didn't lose you, man."

"Me, too." Dolph chuckled. "No way was I gonna have an obit that read, 'He was stabbed in a filthy men's room.'"

"Could we begin?" Rose pointed to the *WHY?* on the whiteboard. "Do we have any insight into the perps' motivation for killing Tyrell?"

"Their captain had reassigned them to new partners," Skip said. "My guess is that made them nervous and they started covering their tracks. Whatever they were into, somehow Tyrell knew about it. Maybe they'd used him to run errands."

Skip flashed Kate an apologetic look, which confused her.

"We had that erased record that Jimmy was Walker's C.I.," he continued, in a heavy tone she knew meant he was feeling guilty. "We should have suspected him, but when Liz couldn't find any more dirt on him—"

"And he told me he barely remembered the kid," Rose said.

Kate's confusion cleared. "So you never told Judith about that deleted record, because you didn't want to get Liz in trouble for hacking into the police department's computers."

"La, la, la, la," Rob sang off-key from Liz's phone.

Chuckles all around, but Skip's face remained grim as he turned to Kate next to him. "I'm so sorry, darlin'. If Judith had that piece sooner…"

She patted his arm. "There's no way you could have told her."

"Well damn it!" Liz said.

Every head jerked around toward her. Liz never cussed.

"It wouldn't have gotten me in trouble with her. I had her permission to go into the system. But I didn't tell her either because I assumed Skip had. I'm sorry, Kate. If–"

"Guys," Kate waved a hand in the air, "water under the bridge. But we should tell her now, about that connection between these two and Jimmy."

Rose shook her head. "I can't believe I didn't recognize Walker during that bogus traffic stop."

"A different context," Kate said. "But I think he recognized you. That's why he kept his hat pulled down and didn't get too close. Not just so we wouldn't be able to identify him later."

"Why'd the other guy take a shot at you two?" Manny asked.

"It had to be Crawley in that other car," Kate said. "I think that was an impulse, like attacking Dolph was. He didn't think either action through." And being impulsive would fit with her tentative diagnosis of him.

"It was pretty stupid," Dolph's voice from the center of the table.

Skip leaned forward. "He should've guessed that attacking one of us would just make us more determined to track down who did it."

"Yes," Rob said, "but we were supposed to believe it was somebody Dolph had busted in the past. That's why he used a shiv."

Kate started to shake her head, then changed her mind. "Well, yes, that was probably part of his thought process, but who carries around a shiv in their pocket, just in case they need to stab somebody? I think he has antisocial personality disorder."

Manny's eyes went wide. "As in, he's a psychopath."

"Yup."

"No wonder Jimmy took off after his brother was killed," Mac said. "He knew he was another loose end. And that's why they were watchin' the Browns' apartment, in case the kid came back there."

A lightbulb moment. Kate sat up straighter in her chair. "That day on I-70, how much you wanna bet they were planning on kidnapping Wanda and Jared, to get Jimmy to come out of hiding?"

Skip gave a slight shake of his head. "I'll take that bet. They went after them because they *did* know Jared had seen them. They could've requested to see the evidence in Dolph's assault case, to make sure they were in the clear for that, and they would've seen the boy's drawing."

"The two motives aren't mutually exclusive." Rose had moved over to a blank area of the white board. She raised her marker. "Okay, things we need to tell Judith." She wrote *Check evidence room logs*, then *Erased C.I. registration*. She turned back to the room. "Anything else?"

A throat cleared in the hallway beyond the conference room's open doorway.

"I heard you all were lookin' for me." A young male voice.

CHAPTER TWENTY-SEVEN

Kate whipped around in her chair. A young black man stood in the doorway—a stockier, male version of Clarissa, without the corn rows.

A collective gasp. Kate's heart rate doubled. "Jimmy?"

He looked at her in mild confusion. "Yes, ma'am."

"Your mother's worried sick."

He hung his head. "I know, but I–"

"We understand," Kate quickly said, gesturing him into the room. "You had to hide from them. What were they up to?"

The young man took one step toward them. "The way you all were talking... Are they really in jail?"

"Yes," Skip said.

"Are you Mr. Canfield? Dr. Ramirez described you, said I could trust you."

"Yes. Call me Skip." He reached a hand around behind Kate's chair. "Most of these folks work for me and my partner here, Rose Hernandez." He tilted his head toward Rose.

Jimmy nodded. But Kate could read hesitation in his eyes.

He took a step toward Skip and gave his hand a quick shake. Then he stepped back again.

"I'm Kate, Skip's wife. I've been working with your mom." She pulled out the empty chair next to her, on the other side from Skip, and made a sit-down gesture.

Jimmy remained standing. He scanned the room, his weight shifting from one foot to the other.

Keeping her voice gentle, she asked again, "What were those two up to?"

"I was their C.I. They paid me to tell them about drug deals goin' down in my 'hood. I knew the dealers from before." He stopped, swallowed hard. "I kinda went down the wrong path for a while, after my stepdad died. The money they paid me, I gave it to my mom, told her I'd earned it doing odd jobs. Then they wanted me to set up drug sales. They'd bust one dealer, skim some of the drugs they collected from him, then turn around and sell the stuff to another dealer. But I was always their middleman, so the dealers never knew who they were buying from, just that it was a policeman who could jam them up if they tried to cheat me."

He looked around the room, his eyes pleading. "I didn't want to do it. But they said with my juvie record, they could arrest me and tell the judge it was all me doing the dealing, and everyone would believe them, not me, a black kid with a record."

"We believe you," Kate said softly. She patted the empty chair. "Your brother Jared witnessed the shooting. He showed us what happened through his drawings."

The young man stared at her, his eyes filling with tears.

"Sit down, son," Skip said in a low voice.

Jimmy walked to the chair with jerky movements. He sat down and dropped his head into his hands.

Kate's throat closed. She took a chance and laid an arm across the boy's shoulders. They were shaking. "Shh, you're safe now. Your family is safe now. The bastards are locked up."

"You don't understand," he said without raising his head. "They went after Tyrell because I refused to help them anymore."

He turned his wet face toward her. "They told him they'd send me to jail, if he didn't help them set up the meets with the dealers. They needed a new middleman, and who'd suspect an eleven-year-old kid?" He shook his head hard. "He didn't know what to do. I told him to stay home from school that day, that I'd go to Dr. Ramirez and get her to go with me to the police. Then maybe they'd believe me, with her vouching for me. But he went to school anyway. He had a test that day."

Jimmy sobbed. "The stupid kid died because of a dumb English test."

"No!" Kate said fiercely. "He died because two corrupt cops killed him. He was trying to do the right thing. You were trying to do the right thing." Her heart squeezed in her chest.

He stared at her for a beat. Then he nodded slightly. "Who's this Judith you all were talking about?"

"Lieutenant Judith Anderson," Mac said. "Baltimore County Police Department."

Jimmy's expression turned wary again.

"She's a good cop," Skip added. "One of the best."

"She's definitely one of the good ones," Kate said, her hand now on the young man's arm. "And you're going to have to trust the police to handle this. They hate dirty cops more than anybody does."

She knew that was a tall order, to ask him to trust the police. As a black male, he would've had every reason to distrust them, even before those two s.o.b.s got their hooks into him.

Kate felt more than saw Skip nod in Manny's direction.

"This is Manny Ortiz," he said to Jimmy. "He works for me. He's gonna take you to see Judith, okay?"

Jimmy glanced at Manny.

Good choice, Kate thought. Manny had a knack for connecting with people, and his skin was only a shade lighter than the young man's.

Jimmy's gaze was back on her, his eyes shiny. "What's your name again?"

"Kate. I'm going to call your mom and tell her you'll be home in a little while. Okay?"

He nodded, then rose slowly from his chair and followed Manny out of the room.

Everyone was quiet for a moment, giving them time to get out of earshot. Then the collective sound of air rushing out of lungs.

Skip stood and headed for the hallway. "I'll call Judith and let her know he's coming–"

Kate called after him. "And get her to convince the prosecutor that those two should *not* get bail. Tell her that her consultant says at least one of them is a psychopath."

"She should be successful," Dolph's voice from the center of the table, "now that she has Jimmy's testimony. The quality of her case just went up quite a few notches."

"And now we know," Rob said, from his cell-phone berth next to Dolph's, "why Crawley went after you in that men's room, when you were asking Missing Persons about Jimmy."

Mac nodded. "They didn't want Dolph to find him before they did."

"So how do we think this went down in that alley?" Dolph said.

"Jimmy's refusing to help them anymore," Mac said. "His kid brother doesn't seem too happy to take his place, and their captain's switched them to other partners. I agree with Skip. They got nervous and started tying up loose ends."

"So they put out a BOLO to use the department to find the kid," Skip said, disgust in his voice. "Because their captain's right. They're lazy."

"But why put the BOLO out in Andy's name?" Kate asked.

Mac shrugged.

"They may have been looking to jam him up," Rose said. "Maybe they thought their cap might put them back together, if Andy was out of the way."

"And maybe they were hoping to be able to frame him for Tyrell's murder." Kate shuddered at the thought of how close they had come. "So how'd they get to the alley so fast?"

"They didn't have to get there all that fast," Dolph said. "At least one of them was probably hanging out near the boy's home, waiting for him or Jimmy to show up. They heard on the radio when the uniform who'd spotted the kid called it in. The officer said in his report that he lost the kid, didn't see which street or alley he'd ducked down. He searched for about twelve minutes and was heading back to his cruiser when he heard the shots. Then it took him a few minutes to locate their source."

"If they were in the area," Kate said, "and obviously knew where the kid lived, they could get to that alley pretty fast. We don't know how long Andy was unconscious."

"So he's out cold," Rose said, "and Crawley and Walker get there while the uniform's still looking around for the kid."

"They must've figured it was their lucky day," Mac growled, "when they saw Russell there on the ground."

Kate repeated the theory she and Dolph had come up with, about how the two got residue on Andy's hand and then must have hidden in the alley until they could pretend they'd shown up with the rest of the police.

"But they put the gun in Andy's right hand," Rob said from Liz's phone. "Crawley was his partner. Wouldn't he know he's left-handed?"

"They hadn't been partners long," Dolph said. "And they were in a hurry, once the first shot had been fired."

"And," Kate said, "Crawley's narcissistic enough to not really notice if a new partner is left or right-handed. Hey, does Jimmy need a lawyer? To make sure they don't prosecute him for the stuff those bozos made him do."

"Already thought of that," Rob said. "I've turned my car around, heading for the precinct now."

Kate grinned. "Since you're talking while driving, does that mean you've finally mastered your Bluetooth?"

Liz's low chuckle from across the table. "I think *mastered* is way too strong a word."

"Have we plugged all the holes?" Rose asked, picking up the white board's eraser.

A beat of silence as they all went over it again in their heads. Kate said, "Why did Tyrell stick around after Andy slipped and fell? Why didn't he keep running?"

Another beat of silence and a few shrugs. "We may never know that answer," Dolph said from Mac's phone.

Rose started erasing the white board, except for the items they needed to remember to tell Judith.

Kate called Wanda Brown, and the others silently listened to her end of the conversation.

"Kate, I was about to call you. Jared's teacher said he drew another picture that she thinks is–"

Kate cut her off. "Jimmy's surfaced. He's fine."

The woman was quiet for a second, then sobbed in Kate's ear. "Thank you, Jesus!"

"Amen!" Kate gave Wanda a brief summary of what Jimmy had told them and finished with, "He should be home for supper."

"I'm gonna take off early today and go shopping. That boy's getting all his favorites tonight."

Kate chuckled. "Hey, you were saying something about another picture?"

"Yes. She described it to me, said it looked like a boy standing over a man on the ground."

Kate's throat closed. That's why Tyrell was still there when the dirty cops showed up. He'd been worried about the strange man who'd fallen and maybe hurt himself. She imagined Tyrell standing over Andy saying, "Hey, mister. You okay?"

Her eyes stung.

"Kate, you still there?" Wanda said.

"Yeah." She cleared her throat. "Hang onto that drawing. The police may want to see it. And... give Jared a hug for me, if he's up for it." She stopped short of promising that he wouldn't be dragged into the legal case somehow. She couldn't be sure of that. The D.A.'s office might think of a way to get his drawings in as evidence.

"I will." A low chuckle. "And I'll give Clarissa one too, and say it's from you. That'll make her squirm."

Kate laughed out loud.

"Take care, Wanda. I'll call you soon." She sank back into her chair, relieved but also exhausted as the last of the adrenaline from the case drained away. *Dear Lord, let this be the last "case" I get involved in.*

She told the others about Jared's latest drawing.

"That answers why the boy stuck around." Liz's voice was subdued.

Kate looked around the table. "Thank you, all of you. We got Tyrell justice." The others' grim faces brightened some.

"And got Andy out of hot water," Dolph added from Mac's phone. Then he signed off, sounding way too cheerful for a man still confined to bed, with a long stretch of physical therapy ahead of him.

Kate wondered how long he would be able to stay away from the agency. He still got a natural high from solving cases.

She and Liz rose from their chairs. Mac followed them toward the door, as Rose finished erasing the white board.

Skip came back into the room. "Hang on a sec, Liz."

He nodded to Kate, then turned to Rose. "Partner, I'm gonna be staying at my desk more, only doing field work when you absolutely need me to."

Kate braced for questions, but they didn't come.

Rose turned from the board. "I'll need to hire even more operatives then, 'cause I'm gonna be cutting back my hours in the field as well. I'll be working from home some of the time, doing the paperwork and coordinating things from there during non-school hours."

Kate's mouth dropped open a little. "You're going back to school?"

"No." Rose stopped, visibly sucked in air. "Mac and I, we did something we'd been thinking about for a while. We applied to become foster parents, and we specified older kids, school-aged at least, who might–"

"Need some tough love," Kate finished for her, while studying Mac.

He nodded but didn't look as enthusiastic about the whole idea as his wife did.

Rose flashed her a smile. "Exactly. And after the conversation I had with Edie last night, I'm feeling more confident I can handle this."

"Oh?" Skip said.

"She was bitching about how her mom always had something 'important' to do." Rose made air quotes and did a good imitation of an Edie eye roll. "And I asked her if she thought a woman should be able to pursue whatever profession she wanted. She said yes, of course, with that *duh* expression of hers. Then I asked if she believed that professionals like doctors and detectives and lawyers did important things—I intentionally left therapist off the list."

Guessing where this was going, Kate smirked at her.

Rose smirked back. "Yes, of course, Edie said again. Then I asked if maybe it was reasonable that her mother, who is a professional, would sometimes have important things to do. Or would she prefer that you stay home and bake cookies and always be available at a moment's notice whenever she needed you?"

Rose's smirk turned into a grin. "Then Billy said from the backseat, 'No, please don't let Mom bake cookies. Then we'll have to eat them.'"

They all cracked up. Kate joined in. She was the first to admit she was a lousy cook.

"Edie and I laughed too, last night, and then she got real quiet. You might even get an apology out of her."

Kate threw her arms around Rose, startling her into dropping the eraser. "Thank you, thank you. That was brilliant, and so much better coming from you than from one of us."

"Much better than my plan," Skip said.

"Which was?" Liz asked.

"Grounding her for a year or two, until she developed some horse sense."

A low chuckle from Liz's phone startled Kate. "Hey, I'd forgotten you were there, Rob."

"Great. Good to know I make a strong impression."

"Hey," Skip said, "I'm glad you're still there, because I have a proposition for your wife."

"Say what?" Rob said with mock indignation.

Skip turned to Liz. "How would you feel about becoming our official computer geek, for pay, of course, and part-time, when you can work it around your day job?"

She broke into a grin. "I'd like that a lot, but I won't have too many scheduling problems, except when we're traveling. Can I tell them, hon?"

"Sure, go ahead," Rob said.

"We're both retiring in a few months, but Rob's going to keep teaching part-time at the law school. And we're going to spend our summers seeing the world."

Kate squealed and threw her arms around Liz.

"Hey, don't I get a hug?" Rob complained from the phone in his wife's hand.

"How'd you know I was hugging her?" Kate asked.

"Not that hard to deduce."

"It's a little tricky shoving a hug through a cell phone. How about a rain check?"

"Okay. Take care, sweetheart."

"You too," Kate said.

They had moved out into the hallway while talking. Liz waved and strolled away down the hall, chatting with her husband on the phone.

Maybe they're planning their first trip, Kate thought wistfully.

Then it dawned on her. *Duh!* With her practice closed and Skip doing less fieldwork, they could travel more too.

Rose sketched Kate a wave and headed off to her office.

Skip pecked her on the cheek. "See you tonight, darlin'."

Kate turned and gave Mac a hug. "You really okay with this?" meaning the foster child thing.

He nodded. "Just scared," he admitted in his gravelly voice.

She stepped back and looked him in the eye. "Good. That is the appropriate attitude to have toward parenting—willing but terrified. And we'll help, in whatever way we can."

His weathered face relaxed into a smile. "Thanks." He reached over and tugged on one of her curls.

"Take care, sweetpea."

AUTHOR'S NOTES

If you enjoyed this book, please take a moment to leave a short review on the ebook retailer(s) of your choice. Reviews help to sell books and sales help keep the stories coming! You can readily find the links to these retailers on my website (https://kassandralamb.com/books/police-prote ction/).

Police Protection is the last book in this series. But we haven't seen the last of Kate. She will be making appearances in many of the stories in my new series of police procedurals, The C.o.P. on the Scene Mysteries. The protagonist of this new series is Lieutenant Judith Anderson (from the Kate series), who takes a new job as Chief of Police of a small Florida city. See the excerpt from Book 1 below.

To get a heads up about new releases and to receive a free prequel novella to the Kate Huntington mystery series, *Sweet Sanctuary*, please sign up for my newsletter at https://kassandralamb.com. (Note: I only send out newsletters when I truly have news. You will also get a free prequel novel- ette of my Marcia Banks and Buddy cozies, *The Tell-Tale Bark.)*

This book was proofread many times by many sets of eyes, but proof- readers are human. If you found any errors, please e-mail me and let me know. Thanks!

Heck, e-mail me anyway, just to say hi. I love hearing from readers! My e-mail is kass@kassandralamb.com.

Let me spread around some much-deserved gratitude and then I will address some of the issues in this story and share some interesting tidbits.

First, the early readers from my street team—Pernette, Mary, Marilyn, and Dwayne, thank you so much for that early feedback that reassured me I was on the right path. (I hope I didn't forget anyone.)

And of course a huge thank you to my delightful daughter-in-law, romance writer, GG Andrew, who did her usual thorough critique, and to Kirsten Weiss at *misterio press* for her wonderful feedback.

And my editor gave me the compliment, regarding this book, that she was impressed with how much I had learned as a writer, and so fast. I may be a good student, Marcy, but you are an excellent teacher!

And of course I can never leave out my loving husband and proofreader *extraordinaire*—thank you for doing the final read-through, and for putting up with my weird hours and babbling about plots and characters.

There are several reasons why I chose to write this story. My parents were active in the Civil Rights Movement when it was in its infancy, and growing up, words like *racism, bigotry* and *discrimination* were frequently part of the conversation flying over my head at the dinner table. In college, they became more than words as I witnessed black friends experiencing prejudice. And for the last five decades, I've watched, and sometimes participated in, the halting progress being made to combat bigotry.

Three things came together a couple of years ago that led to the seed for this story. One, of course, was the sad frequency with which unarmed African-Americans were being hurt or killed by police officers. After one such incident, I read a blog post by a gentleman who is a police officer, and is also one of the most profound thinkers I've ever encountered. He mentioned in that post the technique I talk about in this story for identifying overly-aggressive officers.

Look at the number of "resisting arrest" charges they have added to other collars, he had said. Those with a higher than normal ratio are the officers who are, at best, not doing a very good job of de-escalating tense situations, and most likely they are escalating them.

Shortly after I read that blog post, I attended a conference called the Writers' Police Academy. It is presented by a group of people—former law enforcement officers turned writers and some current LEOs and trainers of LEOs—who want to give crime writers like myself a chance to learn what really goes down on the street, in the crime labs, and in the courtroom. It was the best conference I've ever attended, and I hope to go back again.

A few presenters at that conference hinted at, and one came right out and said, that many law enforcement agencies do not provide sufficient training. Not because they don't care or they're too cheap (although cost is a factor), but because they don't always realize that their training is inadequate. The biggest shortcoming was not enough simulated training and physical practice of things such as how to subdue a suspect without drawing one's weapon.

Another presenter at that conference talked about the understandably high incidence of PTSD in police officers and how this psychological disorder can result in excessive anger and bad decisions on the street.

All of these elements came together to give me the idea for the plan that Kate's task force presents to the governor in this story. But being a writer rather than a politician, I wrote about it.

Maybe I'll send a copy to Oprah and see if I can get the concept to "go viral."

I don't recall exactly when it occurred to me to add a character who is on the autism spectrum. But once that idea took root in my head, I made a couple of decisions. One, he would not be one of the high-functioning people we hear about and see portrayed on television and in movies. Not that there is anything wrong with portraying high-functioning folks. But 30% of kids on the spectrum never learn to talk beyond a few simple words or phrases.

My two grandsons fall into that group. Although they might learn to speak eventually, with each passing year, that becomes less likely. And yet they are obviously bright children.

Second, I wanted this character to play a role in solving the mystery. Having him draw to communicate what he had witnessed seemed like a plausible approach.

And now, a few other interesting tidbits of background.

Regarding women's biological clocks, the pressure to have a child "before it is too late," is probably mostly socialization. But there is some research that indicates the endocrine system makes an effort to stimulate the release of more estrogen in a woman's late thirties. Whether or not this results in more of a tendency to reproduce has not been established.

Psychologically, the issue is all wrapped up with aging issues in general. And even women who have never wanted kids of their own, like Rose, may find themselves obsessing about that choice, as the physical window to have kids starts to close.

As mentioned in the story, the plant Aconite, which is indigenous to the mountains of the Northern Hemisphere and produces a lovely purple flower, has several cool names, like Wolfsbane, Monk's Hood and Devil's Helmet. It can cause a heart attack by interfering with sodium channels in neural and cardiac cells, which in turn interferes with the heart's electrical signals. And it is relatively undetectable during an autopsy, unless unusual methods like gas chromatography are used.

Heaven help me if the FBI ever gets wind of the search history on my computer!

And in case anyone has noticed, Easter occurs ridiculously late in this story, which is set in 2018 (the year I started writing the first draft of it). But it's late date is not totally unrealistic and was necessary. Both the anniversary of Eddie Huntington's death in mid April and the kids' spring break (which in Maryland public schools is usually linked to Easter) were important to the story, so I exercised a little literary license and used the 2019 calendar, when Easter did fall on April 21st.

I also thought it a fitting symbol of rebirth that Kate and Skip are launching their crime-free lives at Easter time. Or should I say, relatively crime-free. You may have noticed I left the door open for some future Kate on Vacation mysteries, just in case we all get to missing these characters too much.

And again, we will get updates on Kate's life occasionally, as she and Judith Anderson keep in touch after Judith moves to Florida. She makes that move partly because of the events in *Police Protection*, and partly because she wants to be more hands-on again with cases, instead of stuck behind a desk all the time. Thus the title of the series, C.o.P. (for Chief of Police) on the Scene.

~~

Excerpt from *Lethal Assumptions, A C.o.P. on the Scene Mystery*:
CHAPTER ONE

Eight days on the new job, and here I was, at my first homicide scene.

I stared down at the young woman who had once been attractive, before someone had gone at her with the proverbial blunt instrument.

It was the middle of the night, of course. And it was raining. Spritzing really, drizzle with some umph behind it.

Swiping moisture from my face, I noted the position of her hands. Resting on her thighs, on top of a short tan skirt that was *not* shoved up. But there was blood on it. Odds were fifty/fifty whether she'd been sexually assaulted. "Any sign of a weapon?"

"No, ma'am," the uniform beside me said, shaking his head forlornly. Or maybe the shadows cast by a nearby lamp pole just made him look forlorn.

The uniform's name badge read *Collins*. The stripes on his sleeve put a sergeant in front of that name. Mid-thirties, medium height, thin, dark hair. I knew the name but not the face, until now. He'd been on vacation for the last week.

Helluva welcome back.

"What've we got?" I directed this to Lieutenant Nathan Jacobs, my second in command. He oversaw the other detectives, but the department was so small, he was also in the major crimes rotation. And he'd apparently caught this miserable case.

"No purse, no ID." Jacobs ran a hand over his blond buzz cut. "Could be a working girl. Blunt force trauma, but also ligature marks on the neck, so COD's a toss-up. The ME is on the way."

I'd tensed at *marks on the neck*. Hiding my reaction behind a neutral mask, I stared at him.

"No witnesses." He paused. "Yet. Uniforms will start canvassing shortly."

Yeah, good luck with that at two in the morning.

Said uniforms were currently walking a grid, scanning for evidence on the damp ground of the park, shining lights up into the palm trees. Between the rain and the humidity—outrageous even at night, and in *October*—the officers were a bit wilted.

Except for Jacobs. Fortyish, slender, and slightly below average height—he only had a couple of inches on my five-seven—he looked like he'd stepped out of a men's fashion magazine. Tailored pinstriped suit, crisp white dress shirt. He shot his cuffs, and gold cuff links glinted, catching the weak light.

I scanned the crime scene again—a small park that had seen friendlier days. Not much I could do to be useful, without getting in the way. "Keep me posted."

I turned away, then intentionally glanced back over my shoulder. "And don't be jumping to conclusions, gentlemen. For all we know she was a UNF sorority sister out with friends for a night on the town."

Both Jacobs and the sergeant bowed their heads. You would've thought I'd said the victim was a nun.

I chuckled internally.

As the new Chief of Police of Starling, Florida, population roughly eleven thousand souls, it wasn't absolutely necessary for me to go to crime scenes. But I'd told the dispatchers that I wanted to be called for all major crimes.

I needed to get a feel for the types of crimes my department encountered. While Starling is a small city—or medium-sized town, depending on your perspective—it's only a few miles from Jacksonville, which has all the big-city problems as my hometown of Baltimore.

Plus, one of the many reasons I'd taken this job was to get back into the field some. I'd considered it providence when I'd seen the recruitment ad for a new police chief of a town big enough to match my salary but small enough to allow me to be more hands-on.

Of course, that salary in Baltimore County had been for a homicide lieutenant, while here it was for the police chief. But the cost of living was lower, so it was still a step up.

I contemplated my feelings about providence—fate, or whatever—as I drove through Starling's minuscule red-light district.

Do I still believe in some sense of order and direction in the universe? I suppose I do.

The image of that young woman's battered face flared across my mind.

One thing for sure, I didn't want to think that I was in this battle against evil alone.

~~

ABOUT THE AUTHOR

Kassandra Lamb has never been able to decide which she loves more, psychology or writing. In college, she realized that writers need a day job in order to eat, so she studied psychology. After a career as a psychotherapist and college professor, she is now retired and can pursue her passion for writing.

She spends most of her time in an alternate universe with her characters. The portal to that universe, aka her computer, is located in Florida, where her husband and dog catch occasional glimpses of her.

Kass has completed ten full-length novels in the Kate Huntington Mystery series (set in her native Maryland), plus four Kate on Vacation novellas. She is also the author of the Marcia Banks and Buddy cozy mystery series, about a service dog trainer and her sidekick and mentor dog, Buddy. There are thirteen books in that series, which is set in central Florida. And Kass is currently working on Book 4 of her new police procedural series, the C.o.P. on the Scene Mysteries, starring Judith Anderson from the Kate series.

To read and see more about Kate Huntington and Kassandra's other books, you can go to https://kassandralamb.com. Be sure to sign up for the newsletter there to get a heads up about new releases, plus special offers and bonuses for subscribers. (And you get free stories!)

Kass's e-mail is kass@kassandralamb.com and she loves hearing from readers! She's also on Facebook, Goodreads, and Pinterest, and is trying to get used to Instagram. She blogs about psychological topics and other random things at https://misteriopress.com.

Kassandra also writes romantic suspense under the pen name of Jessica Dale.

~~

Please check out these other great *misterio press* series:

Karma's A Bitch: Pet Psychic Mysteries
by Shannon Esposito
Multiple Motives: Kate Huntington Mysteries
by Kassandra Lamb
The Metaphysical Detective: Riga Hayworth Paranormal Mysteries
by Kirsten Weiss
Dangerous and Unseemly: Concordia Wells Historical Mysteries
by K.B. Owen
Murder, Honey: Carol Sabala Mysteries
by Vinnie Hansen
Full Mortality: Nikki Latrelle Mysteries
by Sasscer Hill
ChainLinked: Moccasin Cove Mysteries
by Liz Boeger
To Kill A Labrador: Marcia Banks and Buddy Cozy Mysteries
by Kassandra Lamb
Steam and Sensibility: Sensibility Grey Steampunk Mysteries
by Kirsten Weiss
Never Sleep: Chronicles of a Lady Detective Historical Mysteries
by K.B. Owen
Bound: Witches of Doyle Cozy Mysteries
by Kirsten Weiss
At Wits' End Cozy Mysteries
by Kirsten Weiss
Payback: Unintended Consequences Romantic Suspense
by Jessica Dale
Steeped In Murder: Tea and Tarot Mysteries
by Kirsten Weiss

Travels of Quinn
by Sasscer Hill
Maui Widow Waltz: Islands of Aloha Mysteries
by JoAnn Bassett

Plus even more great mysteries/thrillers in the *misterio press* bookstore.

www.ingramcontent.com/pod-product-compliance
Lightning Source LLC
Chambersburg PA
CBHW030939260626
47169CB00002B/545